MW01680209

Power Split

W. Ron Drynan

Artairus

Certain research cited in this book is real, although dramatized for literary effect. Refer to the bibliography for factual references. The author's intent is to give due credit, and to provide interested readers with further lines of detailed inquiry.

The use of real government agency, company, and trademarked product names is for literary effect only and without permission.

This is a work of fiction. Names, characters, places, and incidents are products of the author's imagination or are used fictitiously and are not to be construed as real. Any resemblance to actual events, locales, organizations, or persons, living or dead, is entirely coincidental.

Neither the author nor the publisher has any affiliation with or control over third party internet sites listed herein.

ARTAIRUS

P.O. Box 19251
Sarasota, Florida, USA 34276
www.Artairus.com – www.WRonDrynan.com

ISBN: 978-0-9835039-0-3

Library of Congress Control Number (LCCN): 2011905515

First Artairus printing: May, 2011
Printed in the United States of America

This book is also available in eBook and audio book formats at most online retailers.

Cover design by Jera Publishing.

10 9 8 7 6 5 4 3 2 1

For Lisa:

The best friend and teammate I could ever imagine.

She is the Love of my Life.

Many thanks to Jim, Teri, Lauri, Jacqui, Mari, Greg, Tim, Marcus, Claudio, Bruce, Bob, Matt, Dave, and the dearly departed General Patton McFluffy.

The most savage controversies are those about matters as to which there is no good evidence either way.

—Bertrand Russell,

Unpopular Essays

PROLOGUE: JULY 13TH, 1977

"Well, did you do it?"

Jenny hesitated. She wanted to tell Emily everything, but wasn't sure she could be trusted. Not after she'd been caught plagiarizing last winter. Not when Emily was getting good enough to take over lead violin in pre-college at Julliard.

Jenny glanced at James packing up with the team in the dugout. The game had been a rout, nine to three, and he was well on track for senior varsity. His maturing physique would be even more delicious wrapped in a letter jacket.

"Not here," Jenny said. "Let's take a walk."

"You sure? It's getting dark."

"Yeah, just to the water."

They walked along the third-base line and continued into the woods. Sheltered in this quiet patch of oaks and maples, it was tough to imagine the bright lights and big city action just forty miles down the Hudson. They walked without talking, blending the crunch of twigs with the chorus of crickets. When they emerged at the water's edge, Emily grabbed Jenny's arm and turned to face her. "Come on, this is killing me."

"OK, OK." Jenny took a deep breath and sighed. Trusted or not, she had to tell someone. "We did it."

"Oh my God, oh my God." Emily squealed, bouncing in place.

"Hush. You can't tell anyone."

"Alright, I know." Emily spun down and curled a lock of hair behind her ear. "Tell me everything."

"Well, a week ago Tuesday my folks went to one of their fund-raisers in the city—"

"Hold on," Emily said. "After almost six months of going steady and three missed chances, you're telling me the big crescendo came a week and a half ago?" She took a step back, crossed her arms, and turned to stare at the sailboat silhouettes across the cove. "I'm just finding out now? Who else knows?"

"Don't worry, you're the first."

"Seriously?"

"You're still my best friend. Well, James too, but no-one else knows. Now, do you want to hear this or not?"

"Details, I want all the details."

"Before we get to that, let me tell you what's got me worried." Jenny took another deep breath and exhaled diminuendo. "The rubber broke."

"No it didn't." Emily whirled back to Jenny. "No way in Hell."

"Seriously. I don't know how, but when he took it off he said it broke and it was mostly empty."

"Ewww. I don't want those details."

"Focus here."

"Jeez, don't go all Conductor Wilkinson on me."

"The rubber broke and I don't know what the Hell I'm going to do about it."

"Are you sure you're . . . you know, um . . ."

"Pregnant? No, I'm not sure. But I know enough to know there's a pretty good chance. Remember Eileen 'One-Time' Duffy?"

"You have some money. We can get it taken care of." Emily put an arm around Jenny.

Jenny shook her off and cried, "No way. No way that's happening. I can't even think about that. Father Donato would never forgive me even if I Hail Married my way through college."

"So, what then? You can't have a baby. Can't bring it to rehearsals. Can't play the Met with a diaper bag and a stroller."

~~~

"Where the hell is Connor?" Adams asked the intercom.

"I don't know," the intercom squawked. "Something about the containment grid. He's checking it."

"Jesus H. Christ on a popsicle stick. Get over there and confirm the levels yourself." Adams stubbed out the most recent of a dozen cigarettes in the past hour. "If this thing blows we're all cooked," he shouted into the box and at everyone scattered throughout the lab.

"Problems?" William Daxton knew that in certain situations, when dealing with certain subordinates, addressing panic with panic would not carve a path toward resolution. Daxton had plenty of panic in reserve, but he was positive this experiment would solidify his place next to Goddard, Von Braun, and Fermi. He was not about to waste the bulk of his considerable fortune on trivial mechanical failures.

"No sir." Adams snapped to attention. "Just confirming levels."

"Fine, fine. Let's get to it then." Daxton turned to address everyone in the large room. "Gentlemen, you'll be telling your grandkids about this place, on this night, when the first practical
~~~

and fully contained antimatter propulsion test was conducted. Of course, you'll have to wait fifty years for the patents to expire so you can tell them how we did it. I trust that none of you will be sharing details before then."

Nervous chuckles circled the lab.

"In just a few minutes, we'll begin the countdown." Daxton was walking slowly around the lab. "I want to thank you all for your dedication and team spirit. Countless sequestered man-hours and admittedly unconscionable deadlines have led us to this crucial moment. Tonight, we will prove to all the skeptics that interstellar travel will indeed be possible in our lifetimes. Well, that's true for most of us anyway, Gunter." He shot a quick wink toward the octogenarian chemical engineer.

"NASA will be begging us to tag along on our commercial starships, and they'll pay dearly," he nudged the comm engineer, "if we let them. They drank Tang on the Moon eight years ago, but soon that will just be a jumping off point for distances and destinations they can only dream about."

He heard the muted cheers and saw the congratulatory pats on the back, but didn't feel any real exuberance. That would come after the test, assuming they were still part of the known universe.

"I realize we've had slightly unorthodox working conditions here in Unit 1, but when Con Ed shut down this reactor, I knew it would be the perfect facility for our research. Believe me when I tell you how difficult it was to *obtain* the permits and take over this tower.

"Many of you have expressed concerns about performing a test of this magnitude so close to the active Units 2 and 3, in such an affluent and heavily populated region." Daxton completed his circle and was back at Adams' control desk.

"I believe we've addressed those concerns fully with the new containment grid. I see by your continued presence here that you either share my belief, or are comfortable with our remuneration package.

"If only the general public could understand such an obvious risk-reward proposition, we'd have Cronkite here to cover this properly."

"Excuse me, sir. All systems go," Adams said to Daxton's ear.

"Excellent. I've just been informed that we are ready to proceed."

"The current time on my mark will be exactly 8:36 p.m. Commence the sixty second countdown in three . . . two . . . one . . . mark."

~~~

"What was that?" Jenny asked. She spun on her heel to face the Hudson directly.

"Just lightning. No problem, it's still down river a ways," Emily said.

"That wasn't lightning, it was different. That was weird. Did you see how it was all green and lit up the trees?"

"Now you focus." Emily said. "I'm not going to let you do this. You've worked too hard for too long, and I'm not ready to be lead violin. Not yet."

Jenny ignored her and hustled up the path, craning to get a look around the corner.

"What's over there, some kind of factory?" she asked.

"No, goofy. It's Indian Point."

"The nuclear plant? You sure?"

"Sure I'm sure. My cousin got a job there after they started
~~~

up the other two reactors. He loves it."

"I think the flash came from there," Jenny said.

"No way. There'd be sirens wailing everywhere."

"Not right away," Jenny said. "Look at the marina, all the lights went out. It's getting creepy out here. Let's go."

~~~

The reporter ran up to the car and knocked on the window.

Daxton could split. His candy-apple 308 GTB had plenty of juice. Nah, let's have some fun with this hack. He waited until the window slid all the way down before taking off his sunglasses. "Sorry, son. I've already read this month's *Watchtower*."

"Mr. Daxton." The reporter paused to catch his breath. "Mr. Daxton, what can you tell me about the blackout?"[23]

"Randle would have struck out anyway. Mets were down 2-1, so it's just as well."

"I heard you ran some kind of test last night."

"It's brutally hot out there. Go write another Son of Sam piece. Can't let Breslin get all the scoops," Daxton said.

"Did you cause the blackout?"

"I have a plane to catch."

"JFK and LaGuardia are still backed up from the shutdown."

"I'll wait somewhere else."

"Mayor Beame is blaming ConEd. Said it wasn't an act of God, it was negligence."

"I'm not with ConEd. And yeah, they screwed up."

~~~

Two years later—Cape Canaveral, Florida

"Honey, I'm home," Sean said. He tossed his keys on the table by the front door.

"We're in here," replied Susan from the living room.

Where else? Before he brought Allison home this last time, he had a hospital bed set up in the living room so she could be more comfortable and watch TV. Susan probably had to wake her for *General Hospital*. Just one more round of chemo before wait-and-see again.

"Late lunch, or taking the afternoon off?" Allison asked.

"Susan, you can take the afternoon off too. Thanks," Sean said to the nurse. She was surprised, but very appreciative as she backed out of the room and went to collect her things.

"What's the matter? Is Mr. Engle being a pain in the neck again?" Allison asked.

"He's still a box of rocks, but no. Well, sort of." He pulled the stool next to her bed. "I need to talk to you about something."

"Uh oh."

"It's about the future," he said. "My future."

"We've been all through this, Honey. I want you to find a pretty girl, but not as pretty as me." She brushed a hand over the bandana covering her bald head. "Have some kids and live—"

"No, no. I mean my career."

Allison shifted her weight in the bed, and scooted up so she'd be closer to his eye level. Sean had her sit forward so he could adjust the back to a more upright position, wincing as she winced with the bending.

"I'm not getting any younger," he said. How hard must that be for her to hear? She let it go, as she had eventually learned to after the diagnosis. "I've been there almost five years now, and now three other guys have been named Assistant Flight Director before thirty."

"Really? They gave it to that brown-noser Donald Marshburn? Everyone knows he's only half the leader you are. Oh, Honey, I'm so sorry." She put her hand on his knee.

"Yeah, well, he earned it." There he goes, unintentionally wounding her again. He couldn't disagree more, but she believed that so much time taking care of her had set him back in management's eyes at Kennedy. He knew it was his constant questioning of their sloth-like progress and misguided priorities. "Anyway, I have another offer."

"Oh, wow. They're going to let you take charge of another Pioneer 2 probe? Your team ran rings around the others."

"No, this is outside. It's private enterprise."

"You can't quit NASA[22], that's your whole life." She coughed after the outburst and winced again.

"This will be even better," he said. He grabbed a Kleenex and wiped her mouth. "Besides, Nixon approved STS right after I started there, and they're still nowhere near launching it. It'll be another couple of years before they get one of those stupid shuttles off the ground. They're wasting their time on reusable Earth-based space ships."

"I know, I know," she said. "You've said it a thousand times, 'We need to launch from space.'"

"Right. This guy, a really rich guy, stopped me in the street and invited me to lunch last Tuesday. We sit down at El Adobe, and he tells me he's adding to his team. Says they're working on stuff Carter's buffoons won't even look at, much less approve."

"Like what?"

"Antimatter." His eyes were wider than before.

"But you said that was theoretical; that nobody was even sure how it worked and they couldn't produce it cost-effectively."

"Aha, so you do listen to my gibbering."

"Of course I do."

"Well, according to Mr. Daxton, they not only figured it out, they had a successful test two years ago."

"Are you telling me you met *the* William Daxton? The man who bought his first stock as a ten-year-old, then embezzled from his parents' crop sales to start a hedge fund at twenty-two?"

"He told me it was paid back ten-fold in five years. His father even forgave him on his death bed. Anyway, we both had a nice arroz con pollo, and . . . he invited me to join his team."

"Sean McKinley, I do believe you have some pride showing there."

"Sure, I'm flattered. But there's a catch."

"There's always a catch with guys like that."

"I suppose. And this one's for real." He ran his palms down his thighs.

"Well, what is it?"

"I need to disappear."

Allison waited for him to complctc the thought.

"No, seriously. He wants me to come work for him in New York now, then in this huge complex they're going to build in Palm Bay. He already proved that antimatter can work for propulsion. He's going to build a space telescope that will blow away the OAO NASA put up. In fact, it's way better than even LST will be, especially since they got their budget slashed to $36 million."

Sean was up and pacing the room. "He designed a space station that'll make Skylab look like an outhouse, we don't have to work with the Russians and it won't crash in Australia. I can even wear my bowling shirts to work instead of the same silly white shirt and black tie. He's going to take up space tourists—can you imagine that? Tourists in space?"

"Slow down, Honey, you don't have to sell it to me." When he stopped and focused on her, she said, "Why do you have to disappear, and what does that even mean?"

"Technically, I do have to sell it to you," he said. He sat down and took her hand.

"And why is that?"

"Because, I . . . well . . . I already took the position." What a relief to come clean.

"Oh . . . And when do you start?"

"It's more complicated than that," he said. "We need to live there, New York for now and . . . later in Palm Bay. And we can't discuss this with anyone."

"We?"

"Allie, listen to me carefully." He recalled his ninety-fifth rehearsal from the weekend. Yes, that was the one he liked best. "I'm so sorry to say this out loud, but I know we don't have much more time together, and I want to stay close to you." His eyes welled to match hers. "You know I'd do anything for you, I always have. You know I love you more than anything. I've never asked you for anything . . . until now."

She stared at him.

"I told Mr. Daxton you had to come with me or I wouldn't go. All I'm asking is that you move with me so I can start working right away. Mr. Daxton said you'd get the best care possible, that you'd be even more comfortable there than Susan and I can make you here."

He offered another Kleenex but she waved him off. "He's even offered us a week to say our good-byes and get our things in order, as long as we don't tell anyone what we're doing."

"How could you agree to all this without so much as asking me?"

"I'm so sorry, Allie. I thought of you first, but I got swept up in all the grandiose stuff he was talking about. And he wouldn't give me any details unless I agreed to sign on. Apparently, signing on with this guy is a one-way street."

"That should have been your first clue."

"No, no, this is a good deal. He'll cover all our expenses, handle the move, and help sell the house. I get twice what I'm making now, and best of all, I get to be part of something big. Mankind big. He's aiming high and wants me to help take him there."

She stared at him.

"Honey?"

"I see that spark in your eye."

"And?"

"I've been missing it. I know you can't keep slogging through all NASA's politics and mission delays."

"It's not that—"

"Let me finish." She took the Kleenex from him. "I want to die with dignity in my own home. Our home."

"We can—"

"Ah-ah." She put a finger to her lips. "Listen, Sean. You said it, and I know it. I guess in a selfish way I've adjusted to not needing long range plans anymore."

"But—"

"I'm not saying no. I'm just trying to wrap my head around it."

"Oh, thank God," he said.

"I'm still mad at Him, too."

Chapter 1: Present Day

The manatee bucked. Leon fell off.

Shy Guy was one of the biggest, roundest, brownest, most giant-baked-potato-looking manatee in the Sarasota Bay area. He threw the long skinny kayak and the tall muscular human in less than one of the eight seconds to which bull riders aspire. Leon was instantly upside-down and feeling the turbulent effects of a saltwater brainwashing as his ears and sinuses flooded. The brand new top-of-the-line Sony video camera in the even newer Bluefin underwater housing cut a nasty gash in his calf while banging around between his legs in the cockpit. Had the lashing come undone on his three-thousand dollar new toy?

Leon hung upside-down underwater for a moment. He couldn't literally catch his breath, but he did pause to collect his thoughts. Where did his paddle get off to? Had he really forgotten to leash it? And what a rookie-move letting it slip during the scuffle.

He had run his kayak aground on the manatee's back as if they bumped into each other while texting on the sidewalk. At least he was skirted into the boat so he didn't have to suffer the indignity of a wet exit and be seen flailing around trying to crawl back into a flooded cockpit.

The other good news was that all of his gear was still below deck. Banged around but probably still functional. It better be. He hated trashing new gear before its time.

Leon leaned back far enough to touch his head on the stern deck, then swung his right arm in a wide arc toward the sea bottom and followed through until it was fully extended sideways. As he broke the surface of the water, he continued the momentum of one fluid motion by flinging his left arm over sideways and flicking his hips to right the ship.

Now back in the sun, he took a deep breath and sheepishly hand-splashed along to retrieve his paddle. There were few people other than Bonnie in sight. But all it takes is some punk fisherkid posting an embarrassing YouTube video to give his agent another ulcer.

"Nice maneuver," Bonnie called out. She rounded the dredging barge and paddled toward Leon.

"You talkin' about *Coneheads* or *Apollo 13*?" He twirled his paddle once overhead to orient it properly.

"I'm talking about your yard-sale avalanche off Manatee Mountain."

"Must have been *Coneheads*. In *Apollo* it was 'no easy maneuver'," Leon said.

"How do you remember all that stuff?"

"C'mon, Bon. I was a teenage boy and those are classics."

"You OK?"

"Fine. Just a little out of whack today."

"You get whacked?"

"Nope, just missing a chunk of leg. Hope my boat doesn't flood with blood."

"Got first aid?"

"Yup."

"I'm gonna head for the mangrove tunnels in a few." Bonnie

pulled a Fruit Smoothie PowerBar from her pocket. "Wanna get some footage of the osprey having breakfast in Brushy Bayou."

"No prob. I'm gonna shoot Shy Guy." Leon popped the skirt on his kayak and bandaged his cut. Then he reached between his legs for the mask and snorkel. He affixed a one-inch-diameter hose to the end of the snorkel and threaded it under his life jacket, then through the waist band of the skirt, and into the cockpit.

"Why don't you just get out and swim right-side-up like a normal person?" Bonnie asked.

"No fun."

"You actually like the taste of musty plastic?"

"Reminds me of scuba."

"Yeah, why not that?" She took another bite of smoothie.

"Too clunky. And I hate the bubbles."

"Don't put any of your own bubbles in the boat."

"Not a problem," Leon said. "No Sheila-chili until tomorrow night."

"She's quite the little housewife."

"When the boys are older we'll all get back out there."

"Great." Bonnie hid her eye roll. "Why not a tube to the surface?"

"Tried that, too. Rogue wave flushed my lungs."

"Bummer."

"But hey, I ported the bulkheads so I can go fifteen minutes submerged now."

"Sheila OK with that?"

"I was born to be shot, so I'll never drown. Besides, she knows you'll bail me out if I sink."

"Maybe," Bonnie said. "Get me some Grivel Quantums for Valentine's and I'll think about it."

"That's some long range planning."

"A girl has to think ahead."

"Yeah, but next year? Don't you want the latest and greatest then?"

"You'll figure it out." She swept her paddle in a wide arc and spun her kayak toward the south tip of Lido Key. "I'm outta here."

"Later."

~~~

Shy Guy was going to earn his nickname now. The manatee knew Leon was still around, could hear the drip-drip-sploosh of his paddle as it drew him closer. He didn't care and didn't have to. It was the kayak-guy's challenge to find him, not the other way round.

A kayak is no worse than a handheld back-scratcher to an animal of such bulk, so his panic subsided quickly.

He wondered where the rest of his herd had gotten off to. No biggie, he'll meet up with them at the grass flats this afternoon. He just hoped they weren't getting their pictures taken by a tour group. Shy Guy liked being in pictures. He tried to wave once, but the nice Milwaukee lady in the rented kayak got very scared, so he just gave her the lips.

He would hang out for a while by the old rusted and mostly sunken dredging barge. Stupid pelicans and cormorants poop all over it, but the turtle grass on the bottom tastes the same. Yum.

~~~

Leon saw the behemoth poke his eyes and nose above the water for a breath. He was munching a big snoutful of grass, much of it hanging out and some floating away. Only God could design something so huge, smelly, and ugly that it's actually adorable.

"Hey Dude," Leon said. "My bad."

Leon halved the distance between them, then hit the hydraulic brakes by paddling backwards a few strokes. He strapped the paddle lengthwise along the boat and splashed one hand playfully in the warm water to coax the beast hither.

The lazy oaf was deciding whether to approach, go back to breakfast, or jettison another mana-turd. Leon spit-rinsed his mask, then put it on and bit down on the mouthpiece of the modified snorkel tube. Lack of oxygen does not cause hypercapnia or suffocation when breathing from an enclosed space; it's carbon dioxide poisoning that'll get you.

He sealed the skirt and rolled upside-down again, this time on purpose. Ah, that's better. It was nice that the mask also covered his nose. He quickly adjusted to the extra effort required for breathing through the hose, and double-checked the camera to ensure it was ready in all respects.

The early morning sun was higher now and turbidity was low, increasing visibility and making it easy to see Shy Guy saunter over with one flip of his giant beaver-like tail. Leon quickly calibrated for the light available with a Secchi disk reading of about eight feet, then brought the camera forward and started recording.

He specifically wanted mating scenes, but that wasn't going to happen unless Super-Sized Sally came along and they got funky. He'd learned this as a kid about photographing wildlife: They do what they do, not what you want them to do. Despite that, Leon always had an uncanny ability to get the best shots of the most fantastic action sequences.

This was going to be a nice frontal approach as Shy Guy drifted in. The manatee stopped short as his giant whiskered snout bumped lightly into the lens, as if to say "Oh, we're doing this again?"

Leon momentarily paused recording as the manatee rolled over for a belly rub. The Marine Mammal Protection Act of 1972 says, with professional exemptions he couldn't justifiably apply today, humans are not allowed to touch an endangered species. But Leon couldn't resist the temptation. When a cute and fuzzy dog willingly shows you their belly, you rub it. Unless you're a fundamentally evil person.

~~~

The silhouette of what looked like a large hammerhead, probably two-thirds as long as Leon's eighteen foot sea kayak, swam through his peripheral vision on the deep side of the shelf.

What's a hammerhead doing on the inter-coastal side of the island? Must be lost and looking for Midnight Pass back to the Gulf. Oops . . . more likely, blood from his leg was still on the camera housing when he put it in the water. That's two rookie-moves today—bad Leon, no biscuit. Even a trace amount could be enough to attract such an efficient predator through New Pass and around the corner in search of an easy meal.

Shy Guy had nothing to fear from the shark; a manatee is simply too big around to take a bite. On the other hand, Leon hanging upside-down skirted into his kayak wasn't quite so secure.

The manatee seemed to have lost interest in being
~~~

photogenic anyway, so when the shark started closing the loop, Leon figured he'd pack up and head for shore. He tethered the camera to the deck, and the big olive-green menace was still in sight off the starboard when Leon started to execute another kayak roll. He took one last breath of plasticky air from the boat, but stopped in mid-swing of his right arm.

Since when did he get queasy around sharks? Blood or no blood, the feeling coming on right now was different. It was a sudden, oncoming dizziness like the Doppler effect of an approaching siren. His eyes felt like the mounting pressure behind them would build until they popped into his mask and splattered on the Plexiglas. This was a distinctly unpleasant and unfamiliar feeling.

Tunnel vision started closing in. He could almost make out the fuzzy shape of the hammerhead, while someone was hammering railroad spikes inside his. There were staccato bursts at first, each metallic ping echoing into the next. The pace quickened, and rattled into the steady work of a jackhammer without respite. It came on so quickly that he barely had a chance to register twelve and a half minutes of good air left; but not to fully grasp that he was blacking out.

~~~

Leon came to with a violent shudder and almost spit out the snorkel mouthpiece as a reflex. He was still submerged upside down, and it was darker than he thought it should be. There was no sense of how long he'd been out, but according to his dive watch he was fifty-eight seconds beyond usable air in the hull. That meant hypercapnia was soon to follow, even with the presumably shallower breaths taken while unconscious. His
~~~

skin already felt flushed, and his limbs had started twitching big-time. Not good.

Shy Guy was parallel on the starboard side, casting an impressive shadow. Leon could see the turtle grass a few feet below his head was higher to the port, so the shore was not far away. He cursed himself for not practicing kayak rolls on both sides equally, but who could predict when you'd be upside down with a ginormous manatee crowding your dominant side? Either way, he'd better get topside in a hurry.

The left-handed roll wasn't graceful, but it was sufficient to flip him upright. While gulping air and sputtering, he glanced around. There was the dorsal fin, a hundred yards or so east, pointed the right way and showing no sign of returning.

"Thanks for running interference, big Guy."

Shy Guy didn't speak English, but Leon knew he could understand it. The beast gave what appeared to be a nod of his head, then submerged and drifted away leaving a trail of bubbles. As the bubbles popped at the surface, Leon got an olfactory reminder of why some people call the manatee a *sea cow*.

"Jerk."

~~~

The paddle back to the put-in wouldn't take long, less than twenty minutes. He crossed the dredged channel and headed for the grass flats. What on earth was that blackout all about? He got into a smoother rhythm and picked up the cadence.

He passed by two roseate spoonbills wandering the shallows close to the tangled archwork roots on a tiny mangrove island. A squadron of adolescent brown pelicans glided within twenty
~~~

yards of Leon. They were mere inches above the mirrored lagoon, as if they weren't rushing off to anywhere specific; they just thoroughly enjoyed coasting in formation.

As with any normal weekday in early June, there were a few motorboats zooming through the main channel way over by Bird Key, but the jet-ski renters and parasailers would still be sleeping off their Floribbean debauchery of the night before. Two Joes were out on their standup paddle boards. Those law partners plied these waters every other morning before heading to their office and suing another hapless homeowner.

A few minutes later, he recognized two wading fishermen as the Meyer brothers. He didn't like those guys, liked Brian even less than Steve, but they had more or less quit terrorizing locals and tourists, so the cops had laid off.

They were still crass and juvenile for their mid-twenties. Their tattoos were as ridiculous as most, plus they took more mullet and redfish than they should. Leon wondered if they were the ones who knocked over the ABC Liquor Store on Siesta Key last week.

Leon became queasy and heard the internal siren wail approaching. He wondered if this time his eyes would actually fly free since there was no mask to contain them. His throat seized up as he tried calling out to Steve. The cacophony is his head reached fever pitch. His kayak capsized and the momentum dragged his face through the water, then along the sandy bottom until he came to a stop. Upside-down . . . again.

~~~

"Whut's he up to?" Steve asked. "We're all real impressed with the flippy-floppy kayak thing, but now he's jes showin' off."
~~~

"Whaddya mean?" Brian asked.

"He's over there rollin' around like a pig on a spit, scarin' away all the mullet."

"Don't look like he's doin' much rollin', more like he rolled over and quit." Brian pulled in and started untangling his net.

"Yeah. Kinda does look like he run aground."

They stared for a moment until the complete lack of movement finally sparked some concern.

"Should we check him?" Steve asked.

"Whut fer? Looks like his fuckin' problem."

"Asshole."

"Ehh, whut the fuck." The older brother started stomp-wading over to the capsized kayak.

They both took a deep breath and bent over to check on Leon, saw his body hanging limp and decided to pull him up.

Straining from the effort, Steve hoisted Leon waist-high using the shoulder straps of his life jacket as handles. Brian was on the opposite side, and grabbed Leon's arm so together they could heave him upright. Leon was slumped forward, motionless, and they both had to steady the boat to keep it from rolling again.

"Nice camera," Brian said. "Think he'd think it fell off and sank?"

"Sure, but whut the hell would you do with it, dickweed? Benny ain't gonna fence nuthin' like that rig. Too weird."

"So, what do we do with him?"

"Well duh," Brian said. "Drag him ashore, call 9-fuckin'-1-1, and git the hell outta here."

~~~
~~~

"What the hell is wrong with him?" Daxton asked. He kept his wrinkled hand cupped over the microphone and stayed out of the camera shot.

"Could be jet lag," McKinley said. "He has, after all, just been to another planet." Then he barked over his shoulder, "Get the Flight Surgeon over here."

On screen they could see Ryder Pelse in his flight suit, still neatly strapped into the tiny capsule's only chair. Eyes shut, mouth slightly open, and head listing to his left. There was no sign of movement other than the rhythmic on-screen oscillations of the medical monitors on their end.

"Heart rate is 62; BP 100/60. All other vitals are in perfect range as well," Gajra said.

"Yeah, perfect range for a vegetable." Daxton slammed his fist on the console and moved to the next where he could review vitals for the ship itself. "Goddammit. The ship performed flawlessly, and as usual it's the wetware that's messed up."

"Oh no, Mr. Pelse is a very healthy man," Gajra said. "His vital signs are perfectly normal for a person of his exceptional fitness."

"I get it. He's in better shape than anyone in the fifty thousand years we've been making homo sapiens, ya-da, ya-da, ya-da. Can you wake him up or not?" Daxton's patience didn't typically last until T-minus two days, let alone T-plus thirty-three minutes when things weren't perfect.

"What about it Doc, time to hit the contingency?" McKinley asked.

"I am not certain what has caused him to lose consciousness," Gajra said. "I will administer the emergency dose of adrenalin remotely if you wish."

As if on cue, Ryder stirred. He rubbed his eyes with the heels of his hands, then shook his head and glanced around quickly. His glazed stare found the screen showing three very serious faces: one stern, two concerned. He appeared puzzled for an instant, then snapped his focus directly to them and cracked a smile.

"Hey guys, looks like I lived," Ryder said. "Unless the Pearly Gates are on Skype now."

"What happened? You get bored and nod off mid-flight?" Daxton asked.

"Kinda did, yeah."

"Well, you scared the shit out of us down here!" McKinley said.

Daxton leaned into the camera. "First manned mission to Mars orbit not interesting enough to hold your attention. That it?"

"Not exactly." Ryder hadn't determined how much was relevant to explain, especially with the attendance of the Curmudgeon, as he referred to Daxton behind his back. "Give me a second to clear out the cobwebs."

"Oh sure, take all the time you need." Daxton threw up his arms and spun away from the screen. "At $2 million a minute, go ahead and take another nap."

Ryder rubbed his eyes again, recalling how happy he was they were still in their sockets. He was flabbergasted by the in-flight blackouts. Didn't see that coming. Both had come on immediately after launch, and he awoke almost immediately after all stop. And what was with the hammering and clanging and sirens? That sounded like the Medellin cocaine-gang had started a street fight between his ears.

Ryder hadn't had so much as a headache before. All the training, preparations, what-if scenarios, disaster recovery procedures, and contingency plans . . . and they hadn't once talked about him blacking out. He bet NASA would have thought of it.

The capsule's inertial dampeners couldn't partially fail, they either worked or didn't. If they failed and there was a G-force induced loss-of-consciousness, that would happen milliseconds before he became a big red smear on the panels behind his seat. And that would happen nanoseconds before the whole capsule went from spherical to flat as a pancake to completely obliterated.

This baby had a full-blown antimatter propulsion fire-and-forget launch sequence. The horsepower and thrust numbers are off the charts. The ship goes from zero to just shy of light-speed, or near-c, faster than Daxton's Ferrari Aperta can break a hundred.

Ryder reviewed the mission as best he could. Launch sequence was fine, then the excruciating pain, noise, and tunnel vision. Then the blackout, and the next thing he knew he came to and looked out the window at Mars. Flight time at near-c[25], which in this case was 99.99935467 percent of c, was 13 minutes, 32.5164 seconds; exactly on schedule. His relative flight time in the capsule was just under three seconds plus four on each end for launch and stop.

He had shaken off the fog quickly, as he had only six minutes at the apex of the mission. That was as long as they could currently determine that no asteroids or other debris would wander into his path. The 'cow-catcher', as the team affectionately referred to the strained graphene magnetic carbon shield out front of the ship, could deflect minor space particles and debris up to about the size of a pinhead. Anything with more mass would be the last thing that went through Ryder's mind or body at that kind of speed.

He had taken the hi-res pictures, various readings, and collected high-orbit samples while the ship rotated 180 degrees and presented him its best guess for the trajectory home. He had confirmed the calculations just like he'd been taught. After a triple-check, he'd braced himself for the possibility of another painful blackout. He'd hesitated briefly but went ahead and punched the launch button. The noise and pain had seared through his brain exactly as before, and he promptly blacked out again.

He would now be forced to come up with some explanation for the Curmudgeon as to why his thoroughbred stallion couldn't keep his eyes open at speed.

~~~

Leon snapped out of it at water's edge, still sitting in his kayak but leaning on the arched mangrove roots at the put-in. An ibis stopped poking its beak in the shallows and looked at him. There was no twitching and convulsing, but it would take forever to get all the sand out of his ears and nose. The park was empty, no one around. The ibis went back to feeding. How did he get back to the put-in?

He sat grounded in his boat for several minutes, staring aimlessly. Was that a siren again? Jeez, can't a dude catch a break? There was no pressure or disjointed symphony building in his head. The ibis flew off and he cocked his head to hear the real siren of paramedics. The EMTs skidded to a stop and hurried down to the boat launch, medical boxes bouncing as they ran.

Leon held up a hand and said "I'm OK, never mind," but they
~~~

wouldn't have it. They walked him to a picnic table under the Australian pine and gave him a thorough examination.

"Vitals are all good, how do you feel?" the female paramedic asked.

"Well, aside from that gnarly slice in my leg, I'm cool. Your field dressing is way better than mine, by the way."

"You just blacked out?"

"Yup. The shutter slammed shut."

"Any history of this?"

"Nope."

She glanced at her partner and they both shrugged.

"Do you want to go in for testing?" she asked.

"No need, I'm over it. Probably just dehydrated." Leon hadn't told them about the first incident with Shy Guy because he didn't want them jumping to conclusions about recurrence and patterns and such. That had already crossed his mind, but he decided to sort it out later.

"That's fine, but you need to have someone to pick you up," she said.

"My friend Bonnie will be back soon," Leon said. "I'll have some Gatorade and a banana, then call her if she's not back. Thanks."

Telling Sheila about this would not be easy. She was as supportive of his expeditions as any man could ask his wife to be. But each time he came home with a new parasite, scar, or broken bone, that gnawing feeling of dread in the back of her mind became more intense.

~~~
~~~

"What's up?" Bonnie paddled up to the put-in, popped her cockpit skirt, and hustled over to Leon.

"Nothing."

"EMTs don't show for nothin'."

"I'm fine."

"C'mon Boss. You hired me to watch your back."

"When I need it." Leon walked to a trash can and tossed the banana peel. "Your real job is to shoot my front."

"You gonna tell Sheila 'bout the 'medics?"

"She's worried enough as it is."

"That's her job."

"She wasn't always a Mom."

"Really." Bonnie wriggled out of her skirt.

"Yeah. She was hard-core like the rest of us."

"What happened?"

"Got smart."

"Got boring."

Leon sat on top of the picnic table and let his legs dangle. "You should have seen her at Kaokaland in Namibia. We had separate Land Rovers with duplicate everything in case one broke down. Held her own just fine."

"How'd you get into Kaoka?"

"I interned with a couple of old fart biologists. They had an in with the local army guys."

"Aren't you the old fart now?"

"Long time 'til forty."

"She a shooter?" Bonnie asked.

"Not bad. Better with stills."

"Published?"

"Some of the shots in my first book were hers."

"*Untamed Glory in Glacier Park.*"

"Did your homework."

"Can't risk life and limb with a stranger."

"We will." Leon took another swig of Gatorade G2 Natural and offered the bottle to Bonnie.

"I'm set. How long has she been out?"

"We adopted the boys as babies. Uh, four years ago."

"Long time."

"She loves it. So do I."

"You still get to go play."

"Love that too." He winked.

"Me too. Sure we can't do Zambia?"

"I have a sort of unofficial deal for North America now."

"With the networks?"

"With Sheila."

"You're whipped."

"Better medical, harmless parasites, no radical dictators. Starting to sound better to me too."

"You gonna take the weekly?"

"Can't do it."

"Fans want it."

"Sheila wants it too. But it's tough enough keeping the blog updated on a mini-series shoot."

"I can handle the blog," Bonnie said.

"I can't handle being tied to a studio," Leon said.

"For sure. Heard anything on Flade?"

"The leg is toast, most of his left arm too."

"Shit no." Bonnie shook her head. "Great shot though."

"Great white hitting a seal in super slo-mo 3D. The Holy Grail."

"Paid the price," she said.

"Paid one price. Time in the wild is always better than money from a cubicle."

"The philosopher photographer."

"That's me."

"Hmm. Never shot a philosopher before. Might be fun."

"Only if they run. C'mon. I gotta roll." Leon hopped off the picnic table and helped Bonnie load her kayak into the roof rack.

He really didn't want to stress Sheila out yet again, but two significant blackouts more or less back to back was nothing to sneeze at. Better ask Bonnie to drive back.

~~~

"Feeling better now?" Daxton asked.

Ryder shut the conference room door behind him. He chose the chair next to Gajra and across from Daxton and McKinley, hoping the Flight Surgeon would join him in us-versus-them. "Never felt bad really, except at the onset of the blackouts."

"Yeah," Daxton said, "and aside from that, how was the play Mrs. Lincoln? You expect me to send you up there again when you won't even bother to stay awake?"

"Wasn't like I had a choice," Ryder said.

"And therein lies the problem," Daxton said. "I have more than a few billion dollars invested in this thing, and I'm not about to risk it all before we figure out what the hell is going on in your head."

McKinley took over. "It's bad enough we had to hide the telescope, and worse that we have to launch in secret from a space station full of tourists. If I have to explain to a medical examiner that our test-pilot's head exploded, it'll get tougher to stay off the radar."

"I've been off the radar for a long time," Ryder said.
~~~

"Give it a rest Fly-Boy, nobody's kicking you to the curb yet," Daxton said. "What's his status?"

"We have confirmed the absence of any lasting ill effects," Gajra said. "In fact, Mr. Pelse is still functioning at peak performance levels, despite the stress of such extreme acceleration and deceleration."

"Oh, I see," Daxton said. "It's because he can bench two-fifty and kick the ceiling that he came through this fine. No credit to the inertial dampeners we spent thirty years developing."

"I meant no disrespect, sir. I am merely indicating that he is completely fit for the next mission."

"And ready to go again," Ryder said.

"That's important." McKinley glanced at his notes. "Basset's feet started getting cold when I briefed him on the ultimate destination."

"Did he bail?" Ryder asked.

"He's still in, but he's not as fit as you are," McKinley said.

"Any idea why he blacked out?" Daxton asked.

Gajra got up to pace and began considering the options quietly out loud, but not directed at the men in the room.

After several discarded ideas, she said, "Perhaps we should send Captain Bassett on a short test flight to determine if he loses consciousness as well."

"Excuse me?" Daxton dropped his hand on the table. "Are you seriously proposing that we shoot another monkey into space, run him up to light speed, and watch him black out too?"

"The biological readings we have were steady throughout both the outward and inbound flights." Gajra sat down. "Mr. Pelse resembled a coma patient more than a man under stress during the flight. I believe this to be the only path to certainty with regard to the pilot's loss of consciousness."

Daxton smacked the arms of his chair as he jumped up and began pacing. It was his turn to mumble, but he was unable to do so quietly. “No way I’m going to hazard my ship just to knock Basset out on a one way trip to nowhere. It’s insane. Bad money after good. Even if he still wanted to go, he’d probably freak out and miss the return window. He’d run out of air in that golf ball while sending love notes back to his wife and kids, then shoot me a wish-you-were-here postcard as a final ‘fuck you’. Ain’t gonna happen, it’s just not worth the—”

“Gentlemen.” McKinley disregarded Gajra’s gender and took the calculated risk of interrupting Mr. Daxton. “We’re here to ascertain Ryder’s fitness for the next mission, and determine next steps.”

Daxton let the insolence pass and plopped into his chair. He looked like he was hoping none of his blood vessels would burst before McKinley got things back on track.

“In my opinion, Mr. Pelse remains the best qualified pilot, both physically and mentally,” Gajra said. “My suggestion is that we install an EEG in the capsule for recording in-flight. We can compare brain scans pre- and post-flight to determine if there are any irregularities.”

Ryder was relieved that sending Bassett was off the table, even if it was temporary. He liked being the top gun on this operation, especially with the ultimate stakes of the future mission being so astronomically high.

“Will that tell you why I blacked out, assuming it happens again?” Ryder asked.

“Not why, but it will give us at least enough information to select a direction of inquiry,” she said.

Ryder thought she always looked delicious with her hair pulled up. And her neatly pressed lab coat couldn’t fully conceal the curves beneath. She was from Mumbai, but in dim light she could pass for most of the mamasitas he'd hooked up with at El Refugio in Bogota.

Daxton picked up his coffee cup, saw that it was empty, and put it back down. "Sounds expensive and inconclusive. Why don't we just put some smelling salts in his headset?"

"Should I shave my head again?" Ryder asked.

"Why not? It's better than that jarhead 'doo you have now," McKinley said.

"It would be better for the electrode contacts, yes," Gajra said.

"Will you still lust after me?" Ryder asked.

"More importantly, will it affect the electrical load on the ship?" McKinley asked.

"Let's not turn this thing into a crock pot for boiling star-jockeys," Daxton said.

Gajra thought for a moment. "I will defer to Engineering on the details and specifications, but I do not believe the additional weight, electrical load, or increased ambient heat will be outside mission parameters. This is especially true in the continued absence of long-term life support systems on Flight 2. However, I cannot guarantee this will be the case on the subsequent longer flight."

"Fair enough. Make it happen," Daxton said. He rose and tilted his head to crack his neck.

Ryder wasn't sure, but it looked like the Curmudgeon shot a wink his way just before turning to leave the room.

CHAPTER 2

An ice climbing axe can be a deadly weapon.

When two people are wielding one in each hand and wearing crampons on each Raichle ski boot—with two thousand bucks of carbon and hot-forged steel extending their appendages—they are well prepared to do some damage.

Leon and his family were among the crowd of onlookers at this year's annual Ouray Ice Festival[28], when an argument between two climbers began to escalate.

"Fuck off, man. That was not cool," the guy in the red Gore-Tex jacket said. He shoved the guy wearing green once they were both down and off belay at the base of Shithouse Wall. A few minutes prior, they were climbing different sections of overhanging rock, and had both tried to traverse onto 'hoffdee', or the 'House of Flying Daggers', from opposite sides. From this section of huge icicles, some as big as telephone poles, a piece had let go and narrowly missed crushing a young woman in a yellow jacket.

"Back off, dude, I had the line," Green Jacket said.

"Shit no." Red Jacket gave another shove. "I was totally on first. What the fuck were you thinking?" The crowd moved in to create an impromptu ring, some spilling into the area at the base of the ice wall. This was normally occupied only by belayers and climbers waiting to ascend. Not a good place for anyone to stand without a helmet.

Leon asked Sheila to stay put with the kids, and he moved toward the front of the crowd.

"Dude, you almost gnarfed my belayer." Green returned a shove. "That fuckin' dagger you kicked loose was five-fucking-feet long, and not even a shout out."

"I called it, dickhead. Your bitch was a-fuckin'-sleep." He turned to his belayer and asked, "Wasn't she?"

As he turned back, Green's fist caught him in the face. He reeled, then charged and planted a shoulder in Green's chest. They both went down on the hard-pack snow, sliding against the wall in a jumble of nylon and sharp tools. By the time they had spun away and stood, Leon was between them.

"Hey guys," he said, "let's chill out here."

"Fuck off O.G., this ain't your gig." Red wiped a trickle of blood from the corner of his mouth and started around Leon to continue the fight.

Leon blocked his way and grabbed a handful of jacket on the shoulder. Without thinking, Red brought his left arm up and then down in a wide arc, intending to brush the hand away. Leon knew that when Red's arm came down on his, the twenty-inch ice axe with the six-inch hooked, serrated, and very pointy head would continue downward, most likely catching one of them in the gut or leg. Red's Grivel Matrix axe weighed two ounces more than the Quantums Leon bought for Bonnie. Even more swing weight . . . bummer.

In one fluid movement, Leon stepped under Red's swinging arm and circled around behind him. He spun Red in a three-sixty then ran him into the ice wall, willing to chance that Red's helmet would also protect his face. With Red's right arm now in a hammerlock, Leon said from behind, “I asked nicely.”

The blow to his kidney dissipated through multiple layers of cold weather clothing, but it still got his attention. It seems Green Jacket was a turncoat, now defending a fellow climber against a common enemy.

Leon stepped aside and let the next blow hit Red in the lower back, just above his harness. While maintaining his hold on Red, Leon pivoted, planted his right foot behind Green, and clotheslined him with a right arm across the chest. The three of them went down, but none got up because Leon had Red in a wristlock with his left hand, and Green’s left arm twisted backwards and locked up with his other hand. The young men groaned, but knew enough not to struggle.

“OK guys, three choices,” Leon said. “We can lie around here holding hands; you can chill out and get back to climbing; or I can break your wrists and go get some lunch. Your call.”

~~~

“Ay, you’re that TV dude. No way! It’s B-Man!”

Sheila was still dusting some of the snow off Leon’s back.

“Yeah,” he said. Not the best time for another star-sighting. “Leon Berger.” He shook the young man’s hand. With Leon’s full beard, Turtle Fur hat, and long hair cascading over the collar of a Patagonia ski jacket, he looked like just about everyone else at the festival; but apparently still recognizable.

“This is my wife, Shelia, and the twins, Nathan and Felix. The big galumph here is Ralph.” Leon had grown somewhat tired of these random encounters over the years, but he knew it was each fan’s first time meeting him, and they felt they were an old friend of his TV persona. He did his best to be pleasant even
~~~

on the rare occasions he'd rather not.

"G'day," Trevor said. He made the rounds of the family. "I'm just going to call you blokes 'Little Bees'—twins can be so confusin'." He started to bend over and said "Whoa," upon realizing he didn't have to. "That dog's enormous, no?"

"Weighs more than me," Sheila said. Leon had heard it a million times before but it was still funny.

"Oh right, I'm Trevor. Me mates call me Limit."

"Did you see Daddy kick those guys' butts?" Felix asked.

"He's a badass, ain't he?" Trevor said. "Who knew?"

"He was just trying to keep them from hurting each other," Sheila said to the twins.

"No biggie." Leon watched the little guys throwing punches in a reenactment. "C'mon dudes, knock it off."

"Ay man," Trevor said. "I saw that thing you did on NatGeo last year in the Crystal Cave at Naica. Blew me away, totally ace!"

"Thanks much," Leon said.

"No, seriously dude, that was so fuckin' incredible. I mean, shit, can you believe how big those goddamn gypsum crystals got? That was some rad caving, dude. Me mates are still on about it."

"Messed up place though, way too hot and hard to breathe. Opposite of here, even though they look sort of the same."

"That's right Daddy," Nathan said. "The cave has big white crystals that look like ice but it's hot in there. They have real ice all over here, and it's really really cold."

"You got it," Leon said. He gave the boy's head a shake and Nathan's ski cap slid over his eyes.

As he pulled it up he said, "Daddy . . . "

Not quite a Little Man yet, but working on it.

"Heard you almost died in that cave, no?" Trevor asked.

"Well, my agent likes to spice up the press releases; gives them a better chance of getting read." Leon gave a sideways and downward glance toward the boys.

"Oh, right. No worries."

"So, Trevor," Sheila said. "Are you competing?"

"Right, then. Topped out in fourteen-twenty last year, top five. The blokes here are the best tool swingers in class, even after the Europeans bailed. And you? Here to shoot the insane ice park and cover the races?"

"We came once way back when Jeff was still running it," Sheila said. "Kept hearing about all the great new runs over the years, and now the boys are five and finally old enough to give it a try."

"Right on." Trevor bent down to the boys' level. "You Little Bees look more than ready for your first frozen waterfall."

Nathan nodded emphatically. Felix just nodded.

"Ay," Trevor said. "You just know I have to get a shot with the awesome B-Man for me mates. Totally cool. I can swap for one of your crew, yeh?"

"Why not?" Sheila said. "How about we all stand over here by the gorge? See if you can get some of those climbers in the background over there."

After the obligatory photo shoot, Sheila took the gang to sign up for tomorrow's Kids Climbing College, and Leon pulled Trevor aside.

"Let me ask you," Leon said. They strolled along the midway among various vendor displays. "I need some solid climbers for a run up in Banff next month. Serious heads only, no adrenaline-junkies, posers, or armchair mountaineers. It's part science, part wildlife shoot. Both mean there'll be plenty of prep work and waiting around in the cold. There's a few days alpine at first with bivvies, then mixed, and the main route is vertical ice."

"Who's leadin'?"

"I have Healey and his team up front, but I need a few grunts to carry more gear and we're all out of Sherpas."

"You got Todd-fuckin'-Healey? He's a total badass, that's sick, right? I'd carry your nutsacks for a chance to send with the B-Man and Healey on rope, don't matter how tasty the wall. We can make a quid, yeh?"

"Absolutely. It's a top-shelf sponsor, very well-funded. Got anyone up for it?"

"Reckon!" Trevor said. "Lemme ask a couple o' the blokes. They'll be keen."

"Great. We're at the Lucerne. Our motor home is the one with the manatee montage. Can't miss it. If we're not there we'll be hangin' with the kids in the vapor cave hot springs out back."

~~~

"Are you getting settled in OK?" McKinley set two mugs of coffee on the conference table.

"Sort of, but why am I talking to you at six-goddamn-thirty? And I'm not thrilled about being cut off from my friends," Christine said.

"It's a necessary precaution." McKinley chose not to tell her about the unfortunate accident that befell the documentary filmmaker she was replacing. If only LaFleur had been able to see the bigger picture, he wouldn't have felt the need to go public too soon. McKinley tried to convince Daxton there would be no fallout, and that no one would believe LaFleur's wild-eyed
~~~

accusations. All Daxton would say was that they'd managed to head him off at the pass, so to speak.

"Yeah, but entirely cut off?" she asked. "I can't even change my Facebook status to 'shooting on location while imprisoned at my Dad's secret-and-none-more-secret headquarters?' I mean, I couldn't even get past the front desk before."

"Absolutely not. No outside contact whatsoever, is that clear?" He pointed his mouse at her. "You may be Mr. Daxton's daughter, but no one here, and especially not your father, will cut you any slack. He gave you four years to pretend you were earning a broadcast journalism degree at Columbia. He let you traipse all over Europe with your glitterati-pals. This is your chance to repay that debt."

She nodded along with a shrug of her shoulders. "Whatever. Do I at least get to know what we're shooting?"

"You won't be filming anything just yet."

"Not even intros and outros? The camera loves this face." She turned to show him the profile of her other good side.

"Maybe later. We have plenty of video feeds around the complex and in the control room. Your job will be to document and catalogue the footage as we progress through various milestones in the project. We need something for posterity, from the human interest side."

"Catalogue? Sounds like geek-speak for filing."

"In a word, yes. At this point we just need you to archive the mission video, add your own notes from a layman's perspective, and keep out of everyone's way."

"I'm sure you meant to say lay-*person*," Christine said.

"No, I didn't. This is not your touchy-feely college campus, and we're not concerned with people's feelings. While we're on the subject, you're not to get touchy-feely with anyone, I repeat—anyone, while you're here. Not even a well-hung janitor. Understood?"

"Well, you better keep me busy with the cataloguing then." She peered seductively over the lip of her coffee mug.

"How much has your father told you about the mission?"

"Not much. Just that he's way ahead in the space race, he's blazing trails into uncharted areas, blah, blah, blah."

"That's the prospectus version for the space tourists. Care to hear some details?" McKinley flipped on the tiny projector connected to his laptop.

"Sure, it's not like I have anything better to do now."

"Alright, pay attention. We have to head down to Flight Control shortly."

An image of outer space appeared on the wall screen, with the Sun in the center, our solar system's planets in their orbits around it, and a transparent sphere around the outermost orbit. Outside that was an elliptical bubble, with our solar system inside and toward the left. A large fiery area of turbulence was to the far left, giving the impression that our solar system is in a sort of elliptical boat sailing through space. Two satellite-looking spacecraft were shown, one at roughly eleven and one at seven o'clock of the inside sphere.

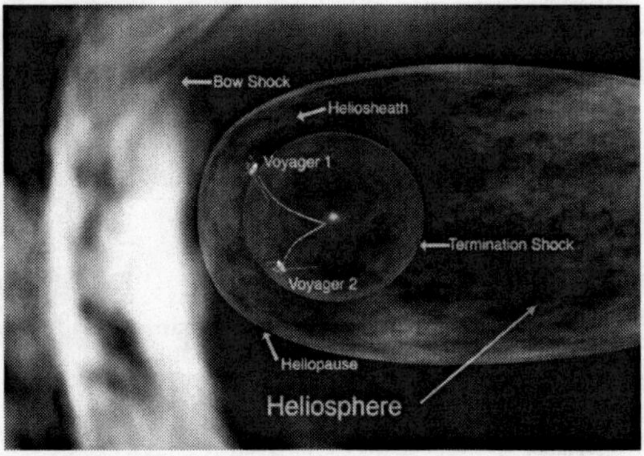

"I'll assume you understand the basics of what you're looking at,"[19] McKinley said. "NASA launched Voyagers 1 and 2 in the summer of 1977, the year before Ryder Pelse was born. He'll be the primary character in your documentary, and you'll meet him next month after Flight 2."

Christine appeared to be calculating Ryder's age and classifying him as a potential conquest. McKinley knew, in a purely empirical way, that Ryder was definitely as hot as any astronaut she'd seen in a movie.

"The craft have since traveled ten billion miles or so, and are still functioning properly after a few resets. Of course, they're using NASA's late '70s technology, some of which I helped develop. It took Voyager 2 twelve years to arrive at Neptune and to have transmitted five terabytes of data back to Earth. Ryder will be recording that much in each minute of the six minute apex on this mission."

"Terabytes?" Christine asked. "They had that kind of storage back then?"

"Of course not. They've been sending it back to Earth slower than most secretaries can type. But no matter how slow the transfer rate, year after year of streaming 24/7 piles up a lot of data." He paused while the screen refreshed. "OK, Astronomy 101: the Sun is traveling around the center of the Milky Way in an orbit similar Earth's around the Sun and the Moon's around the Earth."

"Really? I thought we were just on an arm of the Milky Way."

"We are, but almost everything out there is orbiting something else. It takes us 226 million years to complete one orbit, so the last time we were where we are now, it was all about the dinosaurs."

"Huh, didn't know that." Christine was revealing cracks in

her indifference.

"This outside elliptical bubble is called the heliosphere." He moved the mouse pointer around the perimeter of the outermost ring. "The Sun, and by extension our solar system, is toward the relative front of that bubble as we cruise through space. That's because of resistance from opposing interstellar winds. Understand?"

"Sure, it would be regular-shaped in a vacuum, but we're moving upwind so fast that it gets stretched out behind us." She was with him.

"Right. And the inside sphere is called the termination shock. It shows the point at which the solar wind slows down to subsonic speed with respect to the Sun."

"That would be a good name for the movie."

"No, it wouldn't. I have no intention of being shocked because no one is getting terminated. Moving on." He cast a glance to ensure she was focused, and continued even though she wasn't. "Voyager 1 crossed the termination shock late in 2004, and Voyager 2 crossed almost exactly thirty years after its launch. Ryder will cross it before the evening news after his launch this morning."

"What?" Her head spun and her eyes locked on him, but her hair kept going. "They can send a person way out there?"

"Not *they*. They still throw firecrackers at the Moon. *We* can send Ryder out there. In just under a day he'll travel farther than Voyager 1 has in his entire lifetime. In fact, last spring we sent him to Mars and back in about half an hour." McKinley was reminded how odd it felt to discuss the missions with someone new. He'd been working only with team regulars for so long, he almost forgot their accomplishments would shock a neophyte.

"Really. And how did you do that?" Christine asked. "Did he

top off the tank and grab a hot dog at the BP on Mars?"

"The ship uses four antimatter pulses per trip. We aim it at the target and Pulse One accelerates it to near-c. Just before reaching the destination, Pulse Two decelerates to all stop." He was painfully aware that this was so much easier said than done.

"Same thing on the way back?" she asked.

"Yep, that's pretty much it."

"And where is 'near-c'?"

"It's not a where, it's a what," he said. "With 'c' representing the constant speed of light in Einstein's $e=mc^2$, 'near-c' is as close to the cosmic speed limit as we can get. He travels about one mile-per-second slower than light itself."

"Why can't he go faster?"

"Bad things would happen."

"Cryptic." She continued staring at him for a moment. "How do you know he won't run into something out there? I don't suppose he can steer at that speed."

"No, the antimatter pulses are the only form of propulsion aside from the small repositioning thrusters that flip the ship at the apex. We have a large space-based telescope that looks down the clear-path to determine that nothing major will cross or collide during the mission. Oh, and there's a shield that protects him from very small space dust and debris. Beyond that, it's hit and hope."

"And this guy Pelse, he's willing to take that risk?"

"Thrilled. Not only is he literally going where no man has gone before, if all goes according to plan, he'll be the face of a mission that will radically change the course of human history."

"Huh," she said. Looked as if Ryder's stock just went up a few points.

McKinley checked his watch. "OK, we need to wrap this up.

The ultimate destination for Flight 2 is approximately 150 astronomical units, or AU, away from Earth. One AU is the distance between the Earth and the Sun; it just makes the bigger distances easier to deal with than miles or kilometers."

"Sure, like dollars and lira," she said.

"The flight plan involves stopping about halfway between the termination shock and the bow shock, which is out here." He indicated the fiery turbulence in front of and beyond the heliosphere, where the front of the elliptical bubble was labeled as the heliopause.

"We call it the bow shock because it looks and acts similar to the wake of a ship's bow while underway–a cruise ship or motorboat that is, not a space ship. It's formed for similar reasons, although through plasma instead of water. That's why it looks like fire instead of water. You with me?" He saw her looking out the conference room window. Captain Bassett had paused at one of the desks outside, and was looking through the drawers in a way that could easily distract a young woman.

"Uh, sure. Bow shock . . . it's where we're plowing through space and stirring it all up." She looked back at him briefly, then back to Bassett.

"Close enough." He decided not to press it. "The mission is to collect enough information about the prevailing solar winds to prove or disprove the existence of a hydrogen wall between the bow shock and the heliopause. The secondary mission is to prove that Dax Space Corp. can complete in two days what NASA's Voyager probes will take forty years to accomplish, assuming they ever do."

"Oh, Daddy will like that," she said. Bassett was reaching into an overhead bin now.

"We're done here." McKinley turned off the projector and

closed his laptop. "Let's finish your tour and get you checked into your quarters. I'm sure you're anxious to see what a fabulous complex your Dad has put together. You'll even get to see some of the top-secret areas."

~~~

"It's been three days without droppin' a pissicle," Trevor said. "Never thought I'd get sick of these views, but I'm ready for some righteous hot-tubbin'."

"No doubt, man. This is gettin' old fast," Freddie said. "My friggin' lungs are all iced up inside. At least we go vertical today."

"Right, then. If that climb is half as tasty as they said, it'll blow away Tupungato." Trevor shifted the weight of his overstuffed backpack to lessen the load on his down-slope shoulder. He continued plodding through knee-deep powder, using his alpine axe as a third leg.

"Just glad we got off-rope for a while." Freddie said. "Tying in with dickwad over there totally sucks. Dude can't walk a line."

"Seems a lazy bastid for this run, yeh? Can't believe he's still breathin' after draggin' gear plus twenty . . . Never quit though, Biggs is a battler."

"If he'd go Paleo he'd drop that twenty and feel twenty times better."

"Reckon," Trevor said. "But you're the only one got time enough for that shit. Get a job, yeh?"

"Got one." Freddie shook off the rebuke. "I drag your ass to all these rad places. You'd go nowhere without me."

"Fuck you then, right? I landed this gig on me own, you're just a fuckin' tag-along on this walkabout."

Trevor looked up at the mountain peak, then down to the
~~~

cliff edge and across the vast expanse. It was one layer cake sedimentary rock and white snow valley after another, all with a generous sprinkling of conifers. Not a house or man-made anything as far as the eye could see, just as it should be. The Canadian Rockies are a treasure trove of postcards waiting to happen. A shot of dawn on a clear day is the perfect card that tells Mom, 'I'm doin' just fine'.

"Wish we could be up front with Healey and B-Man, no?"

"Fuck that shit, those dudes are haulin' ass, man."

"Reckon." Trevor was getting winded. "Must be past that next crevasse, can't even see the lead party."

"They better wait for us before they send, man. I don't wanna miss that for nuthin'." Freddie's backpack was grinding too, especially with the tripod hanging down and catching him in the calf every once in a while. "Hey, man, check out the bald eagle."

Trevor looked up, stumbled once and caught footing, but it gave way before he could holler. He was in a sideways glissade, racing toward the cliff edge in a flurry of snow. Trained reflexes honed on countless practice runs had him roll onto his belly and bend his knees to keep his boots from sticking and sending him into cartwheels. He brought the alpine axe down toward his chest, thankful he always kept it in the preferred self arrest position—uphill hand, pointy end forward.

He continued sliding uncontrollably, gaining speed after he caught some air on cresting a steeper downslope. One shot to get this right. He twisted the axe head in his right hand, pulled up on the handle with the left, and tried to arch his back. If he could get his knees and the axe point to dig in, he'd slow his descent and stop. Unfortunately, the overloaded backpack was preventing a big enough arch. That and the loose powder were making it impossible to dig in.

There was time to holler, and even scream, after he slid past the edge of the cliff.

~~~

“Would be nice to have the rest of the bat tags,” Healey said. “Too bad Limit is just scree now.”

“Yeah, he sure found his limit.” Biggs sniggered.

“Hey, knock it off,” Leon said. “He was a good head, could happen to any of us.”

“I didn’t see any other teams off-rope, even on the lesser incline,” Patti said.

“He was just gone, man. Would’ve taken me with him if we were tied.” Freddie was still shaking as he tried to unwrap a grass-fed beef pemmican bar.

“Not likely.” Leon stared at the spot where Trevor’s tent would have been. “One of you would have dug in. Man, that just sucks for him. Did you call it in?”

Freddie held up his hands. “I can’t call his mom, dude. That’s fucked up.”

“Yeah, right. Better she hear it from some deputy at her door. What’s wrong with you, man?” Leon grabbed the sat phone. “I’ll handle it. And I’ll get a chopper up here to retrieve his body.” He walked away from the camp.

“We’re at ATES-3 here, avalanches for lunch and dinner,” Healey said. “Bright and sunny now, but weather’s comin’ in. We have to send now if it’s gonna be today. Make it quick, man.”

Leon threw back, “That’s cold, dude.”

~~~

"Healey is sending first, then Patti, and Biggs on belay," Freddie said. "Who's on your rope?"

"You can take it, Jeff will run middle," Leon said. He put a hand on Freddie's shoulder and looked him in the eye. "I know you won't mess up twice today."

"No fuckin' way, man." Freddie truly appreciated the second chance, especially from the legendary B-Man.

Everyone double and triple-checked their gear. The racks of ice screws and carabiners dangling from their waist harnesses provided a gentle clang-clang-ding-dong as they worked without talking. They gathered at the base of the wall, afternoon sun providing the perfect light.

"You rolling?" Leon asked Bonnie. She gave a thumbs-up without looking away from the viewfinder of the camera on its tripod.

"Excellent. OK, quiet everyone." Leon smiled at the camera and continued. "Welcome back. We're here on day three of our grueling expedition in the triangle of Banff, Hamber, and Jasper National Parks. They have two seasons here in Alberta: black flies and snow flies. As you can see, there are no black flies out today."

"You've seen the spectacular Weeping Wall, Terminator, and all the other audacious frozen waterfalls from the safety of driving along the Icefields Parkway. We're so far off road now that very few people have ever laid eyes on these sheets, let alone climbed them. Now you're going to see what it takes to ascend twelve hundred vertical feet of sheer ice. That's about as high as the Empire State Building. Parts of this climb are rated WI-16+, that's just sick!"

"We're not only here for the incomparable Todd Healey's three-thousandth worldwide ascent; we're looking for one particular cave behind the ice. It's rumored to be a winter hibernaculum for an as-yet unclassified cousin of the Hoary Bat. Ice climbers reported seeing these furry bats hibernating here three winters ago, but they weren't able to get close enough for good pictures."

"Hang on, cut." Leon waved his fingers across his throat and walked over to get Healey and the team in the background. "OK, picking up . . ."

"A team of ice climbers reported three winters ago that these furry bats were seen hibernating in a small cave on this cliff. If we find them, they'll be the highest altitude bats ever documented. The climbers also reported that the bats had white noses. Of course, that could just be their natural markings, but we're going to find out if the 'WNS', or 'White Nose Syndrome'[29] that's been plaguing bats all over the northeastern U.S. has somehow found its way here. WNS is so-named because it's a white fungus on the muzzles, and sometimes the wings of affected bats. It has killed hundreds of thousands of bats in just the past few years, and biologists working with the Department of Fish and Wildlife need to know its range." He waved his hand again and said, "Cut."

"Got it," Bonnie said, "That's good stuff. Let's pick it up with swingers on ice."

~~~

"Here we go folks, let's make this happen." McKinley clapped his hands once as they passed T-minus three minutes to launch.

"Nice to see you again, Dad," Christine said as Daxton walked past, en route to the main control desk.
~~~

“Sure. You look great, kid,” Daxton said. “I trust Sean has been kind to you.” He leaned down and gave her an obligatory peck on the cheek.

“He showed me around, yes. Impressive setup you built here.”

“Only the best. What my hedge fund buddies and the Cayman bankers don’t know won’t hurt ‘em, right?”

“Sure. It’s austere for my taste, but appears to be functional.” She got up to follow him.

McKinley had rattled through the pre-flight checks with all departments except the last. “Comm?” he said. Then “Comm?” with more urgency. Ryder’s image from the capsule in geostationary orbit filled the main screen, his clean shaven head covered with electrodes for the EEG. There was no indication he could hear McKinley.

“Comm!”

“What the fuck is wrong with his headset?” Daxton asked.

Ryder continued reviewing his control panel.

“He’s cute, it’s a shame he’s deaf and bald,” Christine said.

Just as McKinley made a move toward the Comm Engineer’s station, Ryder cleared his throat. “I’m just messing with you. No need to beat the shit out of poor old Smitty over there.”

McKinley came about and appeared ready to burst, but decided not to give Ryder the satisfaction. “Very well then.”

“Zip it fly-boy,” Daxton said. “You have a very important ride to take in my ship.”

“Indeed, sir, Mr. Daxton, sir. Looking forward to it, sir.” Ryder gave a mock salute. “Hugs and kicks to you, sir.”

“Gajra,” McKinley said, “are you getting the EEG readings?”

“Yes, sir. All instrumentation is functioning properly.” McKinley looked at the large mission timer just below the main screen. "Alright people, let's cut the chatter. We are now T-minus two minutes and counting."

~~~

Leon finished threading another ice screw, clipped a carabiner into the head, and clipped in his rope. "On belay!"

"Belay is on!" Freddie's enthusiastic reply echoed from two hundred feet below. Hearing him was easy, but it was important to wait for the echo to dissipate.

"Climbing!" Leon said.

"Climb on!" Freddie echoed back.

Leon continued his ascent, sticking the crampons on his boots into higher spots on the ice wall one at a time. Then removing and swinging his ice axes one at a time. It was slow going, but the ice was pristine and he could hang with the best of them. He loved being out here, further up and away than most people ever fantasize. After a few more moves, he paused.

"Oh, shit," he said.

"What's up?" Jeff asked from thirty feet below along the rope between Leon and Freddie. "You takin' a break?"

"I think it's happening again," he said. The queasiness was a tip off, but hearing sirens in the wilderness was a dead give-away. He remembered that cacophony and hammering in his head as if it was yesterday. If this was the same thing, he had just a few seconds to prepare. He frantically started chipping away by his right foot, trying to make a sturdy ice step. His bulging eyes teared from the searing pain, and the icicles in his beard pulled apart as he squinted and grimaced.

"What the fuck?" Jeff ducked as dinner plates and ice shrapnel cascaded over his helmet.
~~~

“Falling!” Leon said. That’s all he could manage to blurt out through the wail of the sirens between his ears.

“Oh shit, falling!” Jeff said. He held fast and braced for the impact. It was a screamer fall, twice as far as the last protection he put in. Leon fell past him another ten feet before the dynamic rope barely slowed then caught his fall with a sudden jerk. At the end of the rope, Leon and all his gear bounced then hit the ice wall like a bag of hammers.

“I got him,” Freddie said. He puffed with redemption even though he was just doing his job as belayer. The ‘ATC’, or ‘Air Traffic Controller’ flawlessly locked the rope under load. He was pulled off his feet by the force of the larger man’s fall, but he heard and saw it coming so he got his feet out front of him and braced properly when it was his turn to hit the wall.

“Why’s he fuckin’ around? Tell him to flip up.” Freddie kicked off the wall and swung out for a better look. “I ain’t gonna hang him all day.”

“Dunno,” Jeff said, “I think he’s out cold.”

CHAPTER 3

Well, they say that consistency is the key.

Ryder shook off the effects of his third nasty blackout. It went exactly as Gajra had predicted; the blackout occurred just as painfully and just as quickly after launch. The EEG electrodes were all still attached at various points around his skull, and the machine appeared to be recording uninterrupted. He wondered if his aching eyes were having trouble regaining focus, or if he really was in the middle of nowhere. There was nothing but faint starlight out the window, which was a good thing as long as he was where he should be.

Unfortunately, no plan survives contact with the enemy. The enemy at this point was a malfunctioning telemetry calculator. Ryder looked at the 1202 error message and aborted routines with disgust. Here he was, fourteen billion miles from home, and he had to pin his hopes on that British bitch from the Garmin GPS saying 'recalculating'. The Earth and Moon continued in their orbital paths while he was away, and the computer needed to update those among many other variables based on his current starting point toward home. Now, with less than six minutes to go before the clear-path was no longer confirmed clear, it was starting from scratch.

At this range, he couldn't afford to miss the window. Even though his relative flight-time on the ship was only about four and a half minutes, it was almost twenty-one hours at light-speed back to Earth. A half-duplex radio conversation with Flight Control would double that. He instinctively looked to his right. On the wall, nestled neatly among the other panels was a small enclosure labeled 'Rations'. He could get by on Power Bars and Mountain Dew for a couple of days, but waste disposal wasn't installed yet. He'd rather crap in the jungle than bag it in here.

Stay calm . . . don't play what-if games. If he wasn't aimed properly he could just as easily hit Jupiter dead-center as come to rest within recovery range of the space station. He realized that was another what-if game and he didn't want to play anymore.

He looked at the mission clock and decided there was probably time for a complete reboot. There better be time. It wasn't like he could do the calculations in his head.

After a full two minutes and forty-two painstaking seconds, a three dimensional image map of the bow shock, heliosphere, the Sun, Earth, Moon, and his ship materialized on the console. The computer went back to doing its calculations.

~~~

"Oh, Baby," Sheila said when she heard him shudder and realized he was awakening. She rushed from the window to his bedside and smothered him with kisses.

"Where am I? What happened? Where's the team?" Leon asked.

"You're in Banff Mineral Springs Hospital," she said.

"Thank God," he said. "Did everybody make it out?"

"I'm afraid not." Sheila pulled her face back from his. "Do
~~~

you remember about Trevor?"

"Yes." Leon looked up and counted ceiling tiles as he relived the anguished wail of the young man's mother over the sat phone. Moving his eyes was still painful.

"Um . . . are you sure you're up for this?" Sheila took a step toward the door. "Let me get the doctor to check you out."

"I'm fine Baby, all good. Tell me what happened."

"Really? That's it, you're just fine?"

"Well, I know I blacked out, and that came with a head-banging."

"Jeff said you might have blacked out before you fell."

"I did. I meant my head was pounding just before that."

"You broke your arm again. When you hit the wall."

"Oh, man." He groaned at the cast. "Not the left, that's three times now." He fingered the electrodes on his forehead with his free hand. "What's all this?"

"Yeah, I know," she said. "They have you hooked up to everything in this place. Trying to figure out what's going on."

"Anything else missing or broken?"

"Just my nerves. I've been freaking out and the boys are out of hand."

"Where are they now? What did you tell them?"

"They're in the motor home with Bonnie. She's been a godsend through all this."

"Yeah, she rocks. Do they know what happened?"

"Sort of." Sheila sat down on the bedside stool. "I wasn't going to bring them in until tomorrow. I was hoping you'd wake up first. I'd rather not give them the visual of you in a coma."

"I'm fine, Baby, seriously."

"We'll see what the doctors say. You had some minor frostnip. It's blistered, but your nose will be fine. First thing Alex asked about was your face."

"Of course he did, he knows where his bread's buttered."

"Second thing he asked about was footage of the bats."

"Nope. Never saw 'em."

"Shouldn't your agent come up here at a time like this?"

"Why, because I passed out?"

"Three people died, Leon. The storm is the only thing keeping national press from flooding the lobby."

"Three? Storm? How long was I out? What the hell happened?"

"It's been . . ." She looked at the clock. "Almost twenty-one hours and I haven't slept since the night before yesterday. They had to airlift you out with Bonnie. You're just lucky the Canadians take helicopter rescue so seriously, or they wouldn't have had another chopper available while the Hamber team was recovering Trevor's body." She put a hand to her mouth. "If you had to wait for a round trip the storm would have socked you in, and then what? They're still up there riding it out." She started to tear up again.

"Who else didn't make it? How?" He slumped back in the bed, overwhelmed with the onslaught.

"You rest, Baby. There'll be time."

"No, seriously, I feel fine. Tell me who didn't make it."

"Todd Healey and Patti Beaudouin."

"Oh, man, not Healey, he was the best—lived on the ice. And Patti was no slouch either."

"They were just about to top out when an avalanche came over the cliff. Serves them right, if they'd come down for you straight away, they'd have been off the fall line. Only Biggs made it, he had to cut the rope when they got swept."

"Jesus, I knew that wall was ATES-3, but the forecast was

stable."

"Late afternoon and helicopters have a way of disturbing snow and ice." He caught her Mom-glare.

"They were still climbing when the chopper got there?" Leon asked.

Sheila stood up and walked to the window. "You know he wanted the three-thousand milestone to be a first ascent. I'm sure they'll still name it after him. Bonnie said he was still hamming it up for the camera, thinking she'd be shooting long range from the base while you were laying in a stretcher with a splint on your arm."

"Man, Healey was a good head. That's a crying shame."

"The news will say he was doing what he loved. They always say that."

"Better that than a heart attack in an office." He didn't catch her sigh.

"I talked to Bonnie when they brought you in." She walked back to his bedside. "Jeff was running middle, he told Freddie everything was going fine and you just peeled off. But he told Bonnie you said, 'I think it's happening again.' Do you remember what you meant by that?"

"It's a long story, Baby," Leon said. "You better sit down."

She pulled up the stool again.

"Hold on, Baby... Oh, hell. I think I'm getting queasy again."

~~~

There, that should do it. Ryder confirmed the results for the telemetry. He was as confident in the calculations as any amateur looking at rocket science with a gun to his head could
~~~

be. He recalled the seven 'P's from the PJs indoctrination: Proper Prior Planning Prevents Painfully Poor Performance. Not so much on this run.

Ryder approved the updated coordinates and trajectory values in the flight computer, took a deep breath, and exhaled quickly as he slumped back in the flight chair.

He took a moment to ponder exactly where he was at the moment. Further away from Earth than any human or anything manmade has ever been. Outside the confines of our solar system. The first Earthly anything to travel beyond the influence of the Sun. Best view of the cosmos anyone has ever had with their own eyes.

Only then did it occur to him that in Daxton's eyes, recalculating the return path was one very small part of the six minute agenda. Ryder had used more than half of the six minutes just staring at the status bar trying to figure out if the calculations would finish in time. Daxton had essentially just paid sixty-six million dollars to shoot him out to an empty parking lot and have him return home with no groceries.

The idea of punching that excruciating blackout button was no picnic, but the window was closing fast and he needed to get home.

~~~

"Oh my God, doctor . . . get me the doctor!" Sheila dashed out of Leon's hospital room and flagged down a passing nurse. "Send Dr. Davies in right away!"

"Yes ma'am, he's on morning rounds. I'll find him."

"What's wrong Mommy?" Felix asked. "Daddy is waking up. Hi Daddy."
~~~

"Daddy's awake!" Nathan and his brother scampered to the bedside while Leon was shaking off the after-effects of the latest blackout, and starting to focus.

"Oh, Baby, what is going on?" Sheila was between the boys and holding his right hand. "Are you OK? How are you feeling? Talk to me."

Leon felt the pain in his eyes receding and was soon able to focus. "Hey Baby. Hey Guys. How are my main men doing?"

"Bonnie took us on a ride with dogs in a sled. Felix fell off but I didn't. It was cold. I got to wear my new goggles."

"Did not!" Felix said. "I jumped, Daddy. The dogs were running and running and I saw a deer and a big bird. I liked Horn-Dog best. He's big and fuzzy and licks a lot. He goes first 'cause he's the best. But they didn't stop and I jumped out." He jumped away from the bed and then back. "And I wanted to see the deer. But then they stopped. So I got back in because the deer ran away. And Bonnie said it was hard to keep the dogs from running all the time. She got us corn dogs."

"She said we could be mountain dudes like you," Nathan said. "We got to see a big frozen waterfall like before, in . . . in . . . Yooo-ray. There were lots of big birds there. But nobody was climbing on that one. It was just big and sparkly."

"The snow was coming down hard," Felix said. "Lots and lots of snow. I never seen so much snow. How come we don't have snow at home? I like snow. Can we stay here in the snow?"

"Bonnie is taking us skating today. She said we're in Canada and we're too old to learn and skate as good as the other kids. But she's gonna take us. We'll do good."

"Yeah. I think it's like when we skate at home. It's the same but it's cold here. Skiing is easy, just like Wii. But Bonnie showed us the lake where the kids skate and it's all flat."

"Excellent, way to go dudes." Leon glanced at Sheila.

"Come on guys, let's slow down for a minute. Daddy just woke up." She gave Leon a knowing look and a shrug. "Let's see if Bonnie is back with the coffee."

Sheila slid the glass door open and Bonnie entered with a cup tray holding two coffees, two orange juices, and a banana. "Hey Boss, welcome back to our world."

"Hey Bon, good to see you," Leon said. "I'd luv a banana, thanks."

"Gave us all a big scare there. You back for good this time?"

"Let's hope so. It's dark in there." He pointed to his head.

"Bonnie! Bonnie!" Nathan pulled on her shirt. "Can we get hockey sticks like the other kids at the lake? I want to play hockey too. I think it's fun."

"Yeah, it's like Wii." Felix slurped his juice. "Tommy said he played hockey when he was in Canada. He said it was just like when he plays hockey at home but it doesn't hurt so much when you fall down."

"Sure, why not?" Bonnie set the tray on the credenza.

"Good morning, I'm Doctor Davies." The doctor gave Bonnie a quick scan and liked what he saw, but it also looked like his days in her league were long since passed.

"Come on little dudes, we can go back to the motor home and watch *Sponge Bob* one more time before we go skating." Bonnie set Sheila's coffee on the credenza and took the tray with her. She nodded to Sheila who emphatically mouthed, "Thank you".

Sliding the door closed felt like shutting out a hurricane. The three of them were silent for a moment, each regrouping in their own way.

Dr. Davies walked to the bedside and asked Leon how he was

feeling, while using a penlight to check his pupils for dilation.

"Just fine, Doc. All good."

"Really? That's what Mrs. Berger said when you awoke in Banff. Seems odd, don't you think?"

"Nope, I'm in pretty good shape. Where am I now?"

"That's true. Aside from frostnip, a broken arm, plenty of scars, and who knows what other prior injuries, I'd say you take pretty good care of yourself. Your labs and vitals are all fine. Optimal in most cases."

"Great. So where am I, and when am I?"

"Oh, sorry. You're in hospital at the Foothills Medical Centre in Calgary. They brought you over from Banff by ambulance late last night after the roads were cleared. Brutal storm."

"Is the team still stuck at the ice wall?"

"Yes," Sheila said. "They seem to be doing OK. I talked to Freddie on the sat phone and they have enough provisions for three more days."

"So I haven't been out long. Since the last time."

"Weird." Sheila looked at the clock. "It was almost twenty-one hours when you woke up last time. You were awake for five minutes or so, and now it's been just about twenty-one hours again."

"Interesting." Dr. Davies was reviewing Leon's chart. "And how long have you been awake this time?"

Leon looked at Sheila, and she said, "About five minutes."

They all paused and looked at each other expectantly.

"Well, it's very good to see you awake Mr. Berger."

"Nice to be back. Where did I go?"

"We're still working on that. Some of the best neuropathologists, myself included, are studying your case. It's quite fascinating. Your EEG, PET, and fMRI readings are unique."

"Unique, but not good. Help me out with the alphabet soup," Leon said.

"Oh, sorry. 'EEG' is electroencephalograph, it's a measure of the brain's electrical activity in almost real-time. 'PET' is positron-emission tomography. It measures glucose metabolism, blood flow, and oxygen uptake as a proxy for the extent of neuronal activity. 'fMRI' is functional magnetic resonance imaging, which measures brain oxygenation for the same purpose."

"And that purpose is . . ."

"I haven't had a chance to review this in detail; in fact this is a premature discussion. However, I did cross-reference your EEG from Banff, and what I've seen so far is . . . unheard of."

"Again, unique, but not good."

"I'm sorry, I don't mean to upset you. It's just that we're in uncharted territory here."

"That's where I live," Leon said.

"No, this doesn't upset me at all," Sheila said.

"Before I go on, let me assure you that there are no signs of clots, tumours, tissue damage, or anything physically wrong. I'm broaching this subject only because Mr. Berger has awakened again with no apparent ill effects. Please, allow me to take two steps back before we move forward."

"Please do," they said.

"Thank you. Alright, Hans Berger . . . I'm assuming no relation . . . was the inventor of the EEG that's still in use today. In 1929, based on the never-ending electrical oscillations detected by the device when in use, he theorized that the brain is always in a state of considerable activity. His idea was that even during sleep, unconsciousness, anesthesia, and even coma, the brain is always busy doing something. Unless, of course, some sort of trauma has discontinued higher brain function."

"So, what, it's busy when we're asleep, then it gets busier when we're awake?" Sheila asked.

"Precisely. Until very recently, the general consensus was that the 'inactive busy-ness', if you will, was just white noise. Something akin to snow on an old TV not tuned to a particular channel. In fact, most neuroscientists would filter out that apparent inactivity from their scans, thinking it was just a distraction from the waking activities they were attempting to measure."

"And how is my husband unique?"

"He has no white noise."

~~~

"You missed Valentine's Day with your beau? That sucks." Ryder looked out the cockpit window of the space plane as they broke tether with the space station. The tiny one-man antimatter capsule was safely ensconced with its tugboat in the hangar of Section 6, an area of the station strictly off-limits to tourists. Now it was time to head home with the paying customers.

"Yeah, but he'll make it up to me. He always does." Captain Tammy Roarke had the helm from the pilot's seat.

As they drifted away from the station, Ryder was surveying the Earth from two hundred miles up. He didn't take this view for granted, and neither did Tammy; but they both forgot how awe-inspiring it must be for the first-timers in the back.

"Hey, isn't that Heide's toolbox?"

"No chance," Tammy said. "It burned up."[10]
~~~

"Well don't run into whatever it is."

"Yeah, between that and a twenty-odd thousand other pieces of space junk, it's starting to look like Fred Sanford's front yard out here."

"Who?"

"Ah, ya brat. Hey, the Curmudgeon put together a lovers' package. Helps with sales to the lookie-loos."

"Not on comm.. They record this stuff." Ryder waved his fingers across his throat as if he actually cared about offending anyone in Flight Control.

"Oh, right. Sorry Mr. Daxton, if you're listening. I meant no disrespect, sir." She grinned at Ryder. Tammy was quite possibly the only female on the flight teams that did not pique Ryder's libido, but she was still fun to hang with.

"Lookie-loos? Is that what we're calling them now?"

"It fits. They pay a couple hundred grand to hop a ride into space with us, we let them float around in the plane and stretch their legs in the space station. Then we take them home."

"Yeah, it fits. How many back there?" Ryder looked at the monitor showing several people enjoying weightlessness.

"Six. All the seats have asses in them."

"Nice. I bet Galactica is still flying half-capacity at cut-rate fares. The usual bunch today?"

"More women this time. A Saudi prince and one of his wives, some diamond mine guy and his 'niece', and a movie chick. I forget her screen name, but her real name is Jessica Miller. She's B-List, but she was in that one that came out at Christmas. Oh, what was the name of it?" She checked readings on the dash. "Oh, yeah, *Prognosis: Negative.* The best personality is the kid from Make-A-Wish."

"Really? They're sending them into space now?"

"Yeah, the little guy can't quit smiling. And he's a precocious little bugger. I guess one of the Silicon Valley gals had a soft spot. Makes a nice photo-op for us."

"Yeah, that and the sex videos." He watched for her reaction.

"Not any more. We had to ban in-flight coitus."

"What? No more weightless nooky?"

"Nope, the Australians figured out that stem cells can't develop properly in microgravity."

"So what? Doesn't anyone use the pill anymore?"

"Too risky. If anyone actually did become pregnant up here, the zygote wouldn't be able to divide properly. Turns out the same process that causes muscle atrophy during extended space stays also screws up cell division."

"No shit." Ryder adjusted his five-point harness. "I heard NASA banned sex on the ISS, but I thought they were just prudes."

"Seems like they had a valid reason this time."

"I wonder if the ban applies to sex when you're alone."

"You looking for a trap door in your flight suit?"

"Oh, not me," Ryder said. "I'm plenty busy back on Earth. I was thinking about poor Bassett. His wife is frigid."

"Damn shame. I don't get why chicks don't put out. It's so easy to get a guy to do anything you want, why wouldn't you take advantage of that?"

"Anyone ask about the delay?"

"No, they were happy to get a few extra minutes up there."

"Thanks for waiting, not that you had a choice." He pulled up the sleeves on his uniform. "It's a pain in the ass sneaking into the plane hangar from Section 6, but hey, we gotta maintain appearances, don't we?"

"Hang on." Tammy flipped a switch for the cabin P.A.

"Attention astronauts, this is Lieutenant Roarke speaking. I'm so glad you're all having the time of your lives; and from all of us at Dax Space Corp., thank you for choosing to orbit with us. However, our journey is coming to a close, so I need you all to drift back into your seats and buckle in. We'll be transitioning through the Kármán line shortly, and that can get a little bit bumpy."

"Excellent." Ryder grabbed the co-pilot controls. "Let's drive fast and take chances."

~~~

"OK, docs, let me get this straight." Leon addressed the four doctors in the hospital conference room. On the wall screen were various images showing Leon's brain scans from the PET and fMRI. Sheila was sitting next to him, and they were back at Foothills for an update on his condition. "You're telling me that no one has been in a coma quite like mine before."

"I wouldn't phrase it quite like that," Davies said. "We can't technically classify your condition as having been a coma, even though it meets the basic criteria. The pattern is very strange, and doesn't match any historical cases with which we're familiar."

"Fine, let's call them blackouts. I was paddling along and I blacked out. Woke up for a few minutes, and splash, out again. I was up for a very nice climb on the ice, then wham, broken arm. Woke up in Banff, wham again, I'm in Calgary. That about sum it up?" Leon took the last bite of his banana.

One of the other doctors whispered to her colleagues, "We should assume the DMN went quiet during the other episodes as well."
~~~

Another doctor agreed, "There's no indication to the contrary."

"Excuse me? 'DMN'?" Sheila asked.

"Oh, sorry," Davies said. "She's referring to the 'Default Mode Network'.[15] It's a phrase coined by Dr. Marcus Raichle's research group. He's at the Washington University School of Medicine in St. Louis, and—"

Sheila waved. "I don't mean to be rude, be we don't really care who came up with it. We want to know what it means."

"Yes, sorry," Davies said. "As we discussed when your husband awoke two days ago, there's typically a great deal of brain activity even when a patient is asleep or unconscious. What I referred to as 'white noise' is technically called the DMN." He pointed at various areas of the brain scan on the wall. "It's the network within your brain that controls sub-conscious activity, as well as coordinating external stimuli to be processed."

"And mine is broken." Leon finished spreading the peel out on the table.

"In a normal patient, the DMN is active at all times. We're talking about activity that's not fully understood, but always present."

"Not always," Sheila said.

"This is not the basal brain functions of the medulla oblongata where things like breathing, digestion, heart rate, and other autonomic functions are controlled. The DMN describes the other subconscious activity throughout all regions of the brain."

"So you guys are calling me Abby Normal now?" Leon asked.

"Well, in a way, yes." Davies ignored the reference and focused on the banana peel. He realized now that it had been carefully reshaped to represent an octopus. “Your EEG, PET, and fMRI scans all indicate that in your case, the DMN goes completely quiet during these episodes of unconsciousness. Well, at least the last episode, to be sure. We have no evidence to suggest that this was not the case in previous episodes.”

“What does it mean for Leon?” Sheila asked. “Is this going to keep happening? Is it going to get worse? He said the first blackouts were less than fifteen minutes, and the last two were over twenty hours each.”

“Unfortunately, we have yet to find any sign of physical trauma that could be considered causal. In fact, based on Mr. Berger’s accounts of the incidents, there is no apparent trigger.” Davies turned to address his colleagues. “Are you all familiar with Bruce Siddle’s research on the SNS?”[18]

“I’m not,” Leon and Sheila said while the doctors nodded.

“Oh, sorry,” Davies said. “He’s best known as an authority in the study of combat human factors, and as a counter-terrorism specialist.”

“I was ice climbing, Doc, not storming a castle,” Leon said.

“I understand that, but your symptoms bear some resemblance to an SNS-trigger.”

“Nobody uses piton guns in the Rockies,” Leon said.

“Nobody uses pitons anymore period,” Sheila said.

“I’m sorry,” Davies said. “Let me be more clear. The ‘SNS’ is your sympathetic nervous system. Most people call it your ‘fight or flight system’. You said you experienced tunnel vision at the onset of the blackouts.”

“Big-time,” Leon said.

“And many loud, siren-like sounds.”

“More like one big siren, right between my ears.”

“But you weren’t able to hear other sounds you should

have?"

"The first time I was underwater, and the second time I was in the middle of nowhere. There weren't a lot of other sounds to hear."

"Are you suggesting auditory exclusion?" asked one of the doctors.

"It's a stretch, I know," Davies said.

"Can you just tell us what you're getting at?" Sheila asked.

"Right, sorry," Davies said. "Mr. Siddle has been pioneering research into survival stress since the '80s. He focuses on military and law enforcement performance upon perception of an imminent deadly force threat."

"Did you feel threatened prior to your blackouts?" another doctor asked.

"Not at all," Leon said. "Jeff was mid-line and I knew Freddie wouldn't screw up the belay."

"But you mentioned a shark in the first episode," Davies said.

"Not to me you didn't," Sheila said.

"It was no biggie, Babe. Shy Guy had my back."

"Oh, that's a relief."

"The point is," Davies said, "that even highly trained combat specialists experience an extreme degradation of performance when their SNS is triggered. Depending on the degree of the perceived threat, that is."

"It makes them black out?" Sheila asked. "I never heard of that."

"No, no," Davies said. "Specific perceptual, analytical and physical skill processes are hijacked when the SNS is triggered. It's your body's way of reprioritizing things to deal with a threat. The hijacking inhibits higher brain functions centered in the pre-frontal cortex—"

"Stick with the basics, please," Sheila said.

"OK... let's say you're wading along in a clear lagoon and you suddenly see a shark. We're all hard-wired to instantaneously become better at stabbing, slashing, or running. And in those moments we're no longer good at problem solving or fine motor skills."

"It's like when Scotty has to redirect power to the shields," Leon said. "In our case, the ship's computer would quit working."

"Um... sort of." Davies turned to his colleagues again. "I could understand a normal person fainting under either of the circumstances described, but this patient is quite accustomed to such activities, and has no history of this whatsoever."

"I'm still right here," Leon said. "And the abnormal thing is starting to bug me."

"Yes, sorry. At any rate, you can rest assured that we will continue our research. We are collaborating with several centres here and in the States. You've caught the attention of the neuroscience crowd, to be sure. We'd like you to visit Sarasota Memorial when you get home. They have the equipment needed for additional tests once we've determined a line of further inquiry."

"Yeah, between you and the news crews I can't catch a minute with my family." Leon swept up the peel octopus and tossed it in the trash.

"So that's it? Just go back to business as usual and hope it doesn't happen again?" Sheila asked.

"In the absence of additional symptoms, I'm afraid that's all we can suggest for now."

~~~
~~~

"Your file is sketchy here. It says two years as a stunt pilot before you joined the Air Force." Christine continued flipping through his file.

"Sounds about right," Ryder said.

"Isn't it usually done the other way around?"

"Aerobatics means you can fly any way you want."

"And exactly how long were you in the Air Force?" she asked.

Ryder shifted his weight in his chair and leaned back. "Long enough to know what's what."

"Seriously, you need to sit up straight or I'm just going to keep re-shooting this."

"Fine by me. I don't go up again for another six months."

"You're a prick." She adjusted the camera for a full head shot.

"We could be shooting something more interesting, you know."

"Had that bullet chambered, didn't you? How about we just slog through this for now?"

"Your call. Just listing options."

"OK," she turned the page. "You want to tell me about the PJs?"

"Yours or mine?"

"Ha, ha. You know I'm asking about Pararescuemen."

"No."

"No, as in you don't recall dropping out of test pilot training school and trying out to be a PJ?"

"As in 'no', I don't want to tell you about it."

"C'mon." She turned off the camera. "Just between us."

"They wanted me to fly their way."

"So you decided to jump out of planes instead of test them?"

"Kinda goes hand-in-hand."

"Depends on how the testing goes," Christine said.

"Good point."

"You made it through the ten week indoctrination, and were even deployed, then dropped out. Why was that?"

"How is this relevant now?" he asked.

"The public will want to know where their hero came from."

"They'll want to know where I'm going."

"That too. Now spill it."

"Mmm . . . No."

"You were a lot more fun when you were pissing off my Dad, you know that?"

"He loves me." Ryder winked.

"No, he loves what you'll do for him. If he could get Joe Schmoe to fly that golf ball, he would. What's it like up there?"

"You want the standard answer from the brochures?"

"No, I want to know what it's like to push a button that could kill you."

"You used to start your car every morning before you got locked in this playhouse with the rest of us." He leaned on the table. "What did that feel like?"

"Can't imagine it's the same thing. Last time I looked, my car didn't have an antimatter propulsion system."

"So far, the stats on driving versus space flight say you were in far greater danger than I was."

"Are you always this evasive?" she asked.

"Only when I want to talk about something else."

"Fine. How long have you been with Dax Space Corp.?"

"Boring. Let's talk about us."

"Us? That's a bit presumptuous."

"Maybe." Ryder sat up straighter. "Sure, we just met, but I've heard all about your depraved exploits in Europe. I see you've read a few things about me."

"I think the word is *cocksure*. Yes, that's more descriptive for you, Mr. Pelse."

"Spot on. I'm *cocksure* we're going to hook up."

"Really? No flowers, no serenade? You're just going to announce me as conquest begging to be had. I'm disappointed." She checked that the camera was still ready.

"Not too many flowers here in the East Wing. And besides, I could die on the next mission if your theory about the launch button is right."

"We can only hope. Alright, play time is over. Let's get some of this bio footage behind us so we can focus on the good stuff."

~~~

It would normally take about forty-eight hours drive-time to cover the twenty-eight hundred miles between Calgary and Sarasota. With the remainder of the team safely out of harm's way, they'd all packed up and set off for warmer climes. Everyone else headed straight for their respective home towns, but the Bergers had been on thc road for two weeks now. They meandered along the freeways and back roads, slower than they normally would with two drivers. Leon was completely willing to drive, but Sheila wouldn't have it.

They stopped to ogle a forty-six foot steel and stucco buffalo in Jamestown, North Dakota. They eyeballed a twelve foot ball of twine in Cawker City, Kansas. They'd seen waterfalls, caves, hiking trails, and just about every other natural wonder along their way.

It was also a welcome relief from the newshounds. There had been a deluge at both hospitals, all wanting to get some kind of
~~~

scoop or different angle on the heartbreaking death of Todd Healey and two unknowns. Then the press vultures circled around waiting for the remaining trapped climbers to descend, or not. Leon despised society's general lack of respect for loss of life, but he knew death and drama sell well, especially when packaged with great scenery. He also knew that kind of voyeurism was partly the reason for his lucrative career. If that's what it takes to get out and about more often than not, he could live with that.

They reached I-75 at Chattanooga, which would eventually take them through the heart of Atlanta and carry on down to Sarasota. The huge dog slept between the small kids on the lower bunk in the back of the motor home. The parents listened to the soothing sounds of the snorchestra behind them. Leon pondered their short-term destination while Sheila tried to focus on driving, but was more concerned with his long-term prognosis.

They would take a left shortly after Dalton and head for Amicalola Falls State Park in Dawsonville, Georgia. Leon hadn't seen those falls since he was a kid. Sheila and the boys had never been.

Apparently, there were now stairs and a boardwalk that would lead down to the base of the falls, then connect to a hiking trail leading further into the woods. If they walked eight miles to Springer Mountain, they'd be at the head of the Appalachian Trail, on which one could hike all the way to Maine through the mountain woods, if one were so inclined.

"I don't want you to go," Sheila said.

"To the falls? Why not?" Leon's questions were muffled by a mouthful of banana.

"No, to Zambia. I have a bad feeling about it."

"Baby." Leon swallowed. "You know I love you more than life itself, but you gotta let this go."

"I can't let it go, it's stressing me out. I can't focus on anything. I haven't slept since Banff. I even caught myself snapping at Felix yesterday. I always worried while you were on expedition, but not like this. Not before you even went. It's driving me nuts."

"I know, I know. Sure it's a risk, but everything I've ever done was risky."

"I don't think that ever really hit home. You know, 'Denial ain't just a river in Egypt'. I always knew you'd be safe because you're so good at what you do and you're not a stupid a-junkie."

"That's right." Leon was crafting a banana peel giraffe on the dash.

"But this time we came so close to losing you. Three dead climbers, a chopper rescue, a blizzard, two days pacing around in hospital rooms waiting for you to wake up . . ." She choked back the tears. She was tougher than this. He knew she wanted to stay on the road and stay on point.

"Maybe you should come with me. You love Africa."

"Yeah, I'd love to hit Zambia again. But anyway, that was before the twins. We can't risk it anymore. And definitely not together."

"And what about the fishermen? Some of them are barely teenagers. Aren't they taking risks?"

"Like they've done for thousands of years. And they'll keep doing it as long as they need the fish. The point is, I don't want you on that run."

"Baby, it's set in stone. They need me on this one. The funding is in place, all the teams are committed. The network is behind it a hundred percent. It's a six part series and the research will save lives—lots of lives. Bonnie and I need to be there to document it and help keep everyone safe."

"Why? Why do they need you more than we do?" She glanced in the back to make sure the boys were still asleep.

"That hurts, Baby. You know it's not like that."

"Yeah, I know. I'm just not used to being such a friggin' worry-wart." Sheila changed lanes to pass a big rig.

"Epictetus said, 'I cannot escape death; am I not to escape the fear of it?'"

"Really? You're going to start quoting philosophy to me right now?"

"Too esoteric? OK, how about Hudson in *Aliens,* 'We're all gonna die, man!'" He waved his arms and feigned panic.

"Better, but still not what I want to hear."

"Listen Baby, I get it," Leon said. "I know we sort of agreed to keep things on this continent. But this is the big one. I feel like I've been prepping for a shoot like this my whole life. I was born to do this."

"You know I don't want to be the nagging wife, but we have bigger responsibilities now. We talked about this before the boys. It's not fair to make them worry like that either."

"They want to go too."

"They're five!" she said. "They'd swim with sharks just to be like you."

"I know. We did that in Hawaii, remember?"

"You know what I mean." She changed back to the far right lane but overshot it. When they ran on the rumble-strips, Leon's giraffe collapsed. "I just think maybe it's time to settle things down. At least until we understand this blackout thing."

"Tell you what." He grabbed the pile of peel off the dash. "It was just over six months between the blackouts, right? Well,

Zambia doesn't head out 'til September." He spread the banana peel on his face like an alien starfish. "If I don't have any more problems before then, can I go? Huh? Huh? Can I? Can I? Pleeeease?"

"You're such a goofball. I'm going to pull over and take Ralph for a quick walk."

CHAPTER 4

"Sorry I'm late." Christine tossed her purse in the corner of the cramped medical exam room.

"It is not a problem," Gajra said. "We were just finishing up. You may put your shirt on, Mr. Pelse."

Ryder stayed seated on the exam table, having no intention of putting his shirt on any sooner than necessary. He and Christine had coordinated some fantastic trysts over the past six months, but he hadn't made any progress with Gajra. Here was another chance to play with the tension between the ladies.

"Everything still in good shape for the launch?" Ryder asked.

"You have continued to maintain peak physical condition," Gajra said. "That is not in doubt, Mr. Pelse. We are still researching the odd EEG readings taken during the last mission, but what concerns me is whether you, or anyone for that matter, can be mentally prepared for the journey you are about to undertake."

"All systems go."

"Really?" Christine asked. "How can you be so sure? The last two missions were within communication range of Flight Control. Sure, it's no fun waiting a day for a response, but you would have survived. Now we're talking about eleven days there and back."

"Oh, so you're saying that jumping into an antimatter-powered golf ball and swinging the Great Big Bertha is significantly more dangerous this time than say, dropping by Mars or leaving the solar system."

"Don't mess with me, Pelse." He loved it when she got angry, especially when she was mothering him.

"Ms. Daxton is correct," Gajra said. "Assuming the previous pattern repeats, you will be unconscious only during the flight. There is no reason to believe you would lose consciousness at the apex."

"You'd go nuts in that ball," Christine said.

He wondered how they ended up on the same side all of a sudden, especially since that side was not his.

"Look . . . Chuck Yeager climbed aboard the X-1 with two broken ribs and broke Mach 1. He told only his wife and his best friend. Since neither of you are either, I'm not about to discuss any namby-pamby worries I may have about this flight, even if there were any."

"So you admit you're worried," Christine said.

"Jesus. How did you get from here to there? No, I'm not worried. Well, not more than I was on my first night jump. The point is, even if I was scared I'd do it anyway. That's just one more in the long list of reasons your Dad picked me for this gig."

"Oh, for Christ's sake." Christine threw up her hands. "What about the life support?" she asked Gajra.

"The closed ecological system is not yet fully functional. I am afraid the autotrophs are not producing at required levels. Perhaps we are not paying them sufficiently." Gajra's attempt at a joke was momentarily mistaken for fact, until he remembered she was talking about algae. "It is also true that we missed the deadline for installation of the regenerative carbon dioxide removal system, because your father's associate at NASA was unable to deliver the remaining components."

"You're kidding. You mean he's headed out to the middle of nowhere and he has to hold his breath," Christine said.

"As before," Gajra said, "engineers at the space station will slightly increase the oxygen level in the capsule prior to launch. We believe this will delay the onset of hypercapnia."

"Gets me high," Ryder said.

"Remember, Mr. Pelse's relative time elapsed in the ship is less than one half hour on each leg of the flight. If the overall flight is executed as planned, he will not need additional oxygen. However, we have installed a closed circuit rebreather in the capsule, to extend that period if needed."

"Oh, perfect," Christine said. "Keep him breathing long enough to starve to death. Nice."

"Ladies." Ryder held out his hands. "Can we talk about something fun?"

"No, sir. It is not within my duties as Flight Surgeon to participate in a ménage-a-trois with the two of you." Gajra's joke surprised him, but he bet it surprised Christine for very different reasons.

"Excellent idea," Ryder said. "But believe it or not, that's not what I had in mind. I was thinking more about the blackouts. They're certainly no fun, but they haven't killed me yet."

"Ah, yes. My team has conducted extensive analysis on your pre- and post-flight EEG readings. We have not reached a formal conclusion, but it does appear that you enter a coma-like state of reduced brain activity. Reduced even further than anticipated. As with the first mission, there were no signs of permanent damage, or even impairment shortly after you regained consciousness."

"But the pain. I'm really more interested in preventing the

pain."

"I am afraid that sedation would only make things worse," Gajra said.

"Well, yeah. But there has to be something to at least lessen it."

"What's the matter?" Christine asked. "Is the big strong pilot afraid of a little headache?"

"They're not little. That pain comes from a place I don't know how deep."

"If you had approached me sooner, perhaps we would have had time for sufficient testing on various pain relievers." Gajra glanced at his chart. "With less than two weeks before launch, I cannot recommend modifying any of the mission parameters. I wish there were something I could do to help."

He thought about the three-way she'd mentioned, and how that would at least give him something good to focus on as his head was attacked from within. Unfortunately, pushing it would jeopardize he and Christine's friends-with-benefits arrangement. Not a worthwhile risk when they both had R&R coming up.

Christine must have noticed his mind wandering. She said, "Suck it up, big boy. You're not worried, right?"

~~~

Gajra did not like crowds very much. As a little girl she would accompany her mother through the crowded markets in downtown Bombay, as it was called then. Inside Gurpreet's store they would sell her fine saris and ornate wedding garb while Gajra would do her best to stay out of the way.

She did not like being out in public anymore. There was a
~~~

certain comfort in being able to do her medical research without interruptions other than Mr. Pelse's periodic flights and treating the relatively infrequent maladies of Dax Space Corp.'s on-site personnel. However, there was still a certain longing for true family, so when she heard one of her grandfather's paintings was coming to the Orlando Art Museum; she had requested a day pass to attend. If she could no longer talk to her mother or sister, she could at least make some small connection by standing next to a painting she knew they had viewed at one time. Mr. Daxton had been kind enough to grant the pass, even with only twelve days before the launch of Flight 3.

Gajra wandered the museum galleries slowly but with purpose, and had almost made her way to the room where Balpreet's painting was on display.

"It is a nice piece, don't you think?"

"Excuse me?" Gajra was unaccustomed to being approached by strangers.

The short man had a neatly trimmed silver goatee with matching hair and glasses. He motioned toward the sculpture on a pedestal next to her. "This one. It has a peaceful air about it, don't you think?"

"It does." She nodded and made her way toward a painting. He wore the standard green suit coat and nametag of a museum volunteer, but she was not in the mood to discuss art. She merely wished to look at it. The two men following maintained a discreet distance, but the volunteer followed her closely and tried again at the next stop.

"Now this work, by Santhosh, is what I would consider to be disturbing. You see how the artist has made the image resemble a photographic negative imbued with garish neon green, yellow, and red. The security guards are pouring out of a truck as bombs are going off in Mumbai. Awful incident, that."

"Yes, it was." Gajra continued into the next room, as did he.

"Ah, now this is one of my favorites." They approached another painting. "It is disconcerting that the Mughal Emperor Jahangir is taking such pleasure in watching this poor soul's execution by elephant, but of course, he did order it. Fascinating how Ranayan was able to depict such horrific scenes in such playful colors."

"You know this artist?"

"But of course. Balpreet Ranayan was a classic in the mid-twentieth century. It's a shame we don't have more of his work in this exhibit."

"Indeed." She looked closely at the painting and felt the warm security blanket of family wrap around her.

"Do you know anyone who's been in a coma recently?"

Gajra's blanket was torn off. "Pardon me?"

"Please listen, Dr. Ranayan, we do not have a great deal of time. Just keep looking at the painting and pretend we're talking about it, would you please?"

Gajra looked over her shoulder through the open archway at the two men who were following her. They were in her eye line, but out of earshot.

"No, no," the volunteer said. "Please focus on the painting. We need them to think this is just a casual art conversation."

"You have me at a loss."

"Yes, my apologies. It's just that you people at Dax have proven very difficult to approach."

"How do you know me? What is this about?"

"It is a long story. May I proceed to the matter at hand?"

"Not until you tell me why those men have not wrestled you to the ground. They can hear everything we are saying, you know."

"Very well, let us discuss cloak and dagger first. I understand that you are always monitored and that you have a security detail shadowing you. Suffice it to say I have temporarily dealt with that issue, and I would like to discuss your recent findings on a coma patient."

"I am afraid that is not sufficient for me. Why can they not hear us?"

"Yes, but please at least allow me to be succinct. Those men are currently listening to a pre-recorded conversation wherein you and I discuss this painting in great detail. They will be none the wiser if you would be so kind as to play along."

"When was this conversation recorded?" she asked.

"Three weeks ago in a Burbank sound studio patched to my recording booth. I hired a Bollywood voiceover actress to imitate your voice based on YouTube videos of your previous speaking engagements. You were quite prolific prior to your disappearance."

"And my security detail believes we are discussing my grandfather's painting. Tell me why."

"Because, as you so aptly indicated, they would attempt to restrain me should our discussion turn to other topics."

"Fine. You determined I might come to see this painting, but how could you possibly know anything about my current position or a coma patient?"

"Doctor." He smiled. "As proud as I am of my little charades, I'd really rather discuss neurology."

"Humor me."

"If you insist. You see, every person has a sort of signature way of writing. A style, if you will. We were busy researching a coma patient of Dr. Davies in Calgary, and the algorithm we use to track missing people of note came up with your name." He pointed to the painted toenails of the elephant on the canvas.

"We understood that segment of the work to be published under a pseudonym, with no official ties whatsoever to Mr. Daxton. But the pattern was unmistakable; it simply had to be you. It is somewhat easier to discern in technical writings, despite the common technical jargon."

"Who is we?"

"You may call me Hanlon. I am certain you have heard of me."

"The conspiracy nut?" She had blurted without thinking.

"The same." He did not seem to care for the label, but he did accept it.

"Oh, my. Mr. Daxton would be very upset to know I was speaking with you."

"Yes, I agree that he would. Without further adieu, may we discuss the matter at hand?"

"What do you know?"

"I know that you have been discussing with Dr. Davies a patient of yours who presents very similar symptoms to one of his. There have been multiple idiopathic incidents of lost consciousness, with one unique presentation . . . a quieting of the DMN."

"He said it was a silencing of the DMN." She instantly regretted the give-away.

"True statement. Silencing is a more accurate description."

"Why are you interested?"

"Under normal circumstances, this type of thing would be classified as 'awaiting further developments', but since it concerns a member of the Daxton organization, I felt compelled to investigate personally."

"One of our gardeners fainted and you feel justified in this elaborate ruse?"

"A valiant effort, Doctor. However, we both know the patient in question is critical to Mr. Daxton's ongoing efforts at interstellar travel."

"A valiant effort on your part as well, Mr. Hanlon. However, I have no intention of revealing anything with regard to Dax Space Corp. or its personnel."

"He does manage to recruit truly loyal associates, does he not?" Hanlon saw the two men of Gajra's security detail approaching from the adjacent room. He gave an odd sort of sideways wave as he turned on his heel and headed quickly for the exit door marked 'Stairs'.

Hanlon was through the door when the security detail hurried past Gajra. They arrived at the door just as a young man and woman were crossing in front of it. The security men paused for a second, waiting for the couple to pass, but got stuck in the awkward square-dance of trying to go around each other.

They were about to shove the couple aside when both men abruptly fell to the floor and began convulsing. Gajra gasped as the young couple darted through the door to the stairway and it drifted ever so slowly to a close behind them.

She was alone. In public. For the first time in three years she was not under the watchful eye, nor the protective blanket of Mr. Daxton's organization. Could she walk on heels in this jittery condition? It was important to leave that wing of the exhibit quickly, before the inevitable screams of museum patrons alerted the authorities to the presence of two unconscious men.

She walked as steadily as she could and distracted herself with thoughts of calling Dr. Davies from an untapped phone line. She would dearly love to discuss Ryder's condition directly with the other doctor, without having to guard her statements so carefully. However, Mr. Daxton would be very upset at the incapacitation of a security detail. She could only hope they did not know she continued speaking to Mr. Hanlon even after discovering his identity.

There would be no time for Dr. Davies. Her first priority was to leave the exhibit room without being questioned. Then she would call to advise that they'd be delayed in returning to the complex.

~~~

"Have a seat, Sean. Oh, grab yourself a scotch on the way, and another one for me too." Daxton was strewn on the overstuffed leather armchair, puffing lazily on a cigar. He looked awful.

McKinley looked through the one-way glass and over the lighted perimeter of palms and dense Floridian vegetation covering the marsh outside Daxton's fourth floor office. He tossed ice cubes into one, and poured scotch into two low-ball glasses. "Thought you quit drinking late at night."

"Quitters never win."

"Gajra is better now, she finally went for some sleep," McKinley said.

"Still swears she didn't know the guy?"

"Yes. Said she'd never seen him before."

"Bullshit. She may not have recognized him, but I'll bet dollars to donuts it was that sonofabitch Hanlon."

"He's done it before. Slippery bastard."

"Well, now he's drawn first blood," Daxton said. He actually
~~~

seemed pleased that the kid gloves were finally off. "Did Aiken get the security tapes from the museum?"

"It went down like she said. His cover audio prevented us from hearing their conversation."

"Slippery and tricky." Daxton held his glass up to the light and swirled the scotch.

McKinley's segue was awkward, but he felt it important. "Speaking of security issues, I'm concerned about Christine."

"Not to worry, my boy. That's been handled."

"I understand she breached by contacting one of her friends on the outside."

"The detail was all over it. They'd have shut her down if needed. She didn't discuss anything but what the friend was up to. Chrissy couldn't get a word in edgewise." He snickered.

"Um . . . that incident wasn't my only concern."

"You bothered by Pelse bangin' her? Non-issue. Better he get his rocks off in here than out there."

McKinley had some suspicions about the trysts, but had no idea Daxton had both confirmed and dismissed them.

"Aren't you worried about . . . longer term complications?"

"What, like having that prick for a son-in-law? No chance. She's as heartless as I am. She won't fall for him, it's just fucking. I've seen the tapes."

"Women have a way of turning it into more than that."

"How would you know? Last time you got laid you tripped on your bell-bottoms."

"Thanks for the painful reminder, sir." McKinley could have tried sarcasm, but he knew his boundaries. "I'm just worried that when she finds out the parameters of Flight 4, she could become a problem."

"Got it covered. What else is on your mind?"

"Aardvark Aerospace finally got their first tourists up. I just saw the bulletin tonight."

"About damn time." Daxton puffed his cigar. "Paweltsy called his Aardvark so he'd be first in the phone book, but he's always last to the party. At least none of those wannabees will figure out antimatter any time soon. What's the word on the CO_2 filters?"

"No news. I think Einhearst went dark at NASA after he almost got caught."

"Jesus. Everybody posts everything on the web like there are no secrets at all anymore. The internet has taken all the fun out of scientific espionage. But just try to save a few bucks by stealing hardware instead of research and they all freak out. Anything else? I'm wiped."

"Life support had a breakthrough, but it still won't be ready for Flight 3."

"Figures. No big deal, we won't need it until Flight 4. And as long as fly-boy goes coma every time, we won't need to keep him entertained."

"I suppose that's looking on the bright side." McKinley sipped his scotch.

"It's perfect. Here I was all worried about keeping some level of sanity in that yahoo over a longer flight, and he hands me the perfect out clause."

"I wouldn't call it perfect. We still don't know why he blacks out, or why it's painful."

"Doesn't matter. Long as he wakes up at the apex."

"What if longer flights make it worse?"

"We'll know soon enough. What are we at?" Daxton glanced at the countdown clock on the wall. "T-minus eleven days now."

~~~
~~~

"I'm going to see Tommy. I'll show him my new Stomp Rocket!"

"It's mine too!"

"Hey guys, I need you to straighten up your room before you go to Tommy's." Sheila turned the corner to their cul-de-sac.

"Did you hire a different lawn service?" Leon asked.

"No, why?"

"Because Lawnscapes is cutting our grass for us."

"That's weird, Curt just did it Monday."

"Hey guys, stay in the car for a minute." Leon got out in the driveway. Ralph was pacing the bay window in the living room, his deep bark resonating off the glass. A short man in a Lawnscapes uniform stepped out of the company van at the curb and approached the family. It was difficult to hear what he said over the large riding mower and two weed-whackers doing their thing.

"What?" Leon cupped his hand by his ear.

"I apologize for the noise, but it is for our protection," he said. "Would you please ask your wife to join us?"

"No. Who are you?"

"Please Mr. Berger, in the interest of saving time I would appreciate being allowed to address you both."

Leon appraised the man and decided he posed no immediate threat. He knocked on the car window and beckoned Sheila to join them.

"Thank you kindly," the man said. "Please, call me Hanlon." He shook their hands and handed them each his business card as they looked at him.

"Again, my apologies for the noise my associates are making. Now, please allow me to provide you with some unsolicited advice. I would strongly suggest that you not depart for Africa in the morning, Mr. Berger."

"What? Who the hell are you?" Sheila asked.

Hanlon paused and shuddered, then said, "I am merely an interested party who has become very curious about Mr. Berger's condition." He turned to Leon. "It would be greatly inconvenient for me if you were to make that trip."

"Why?"

"Because I believe you will have another loss-of-consciousness episode eleven days from now. If you were to end up mauled by a hippo on the Luangwa River, you would be unable to fulfill your purpose."

~~~

"That's fly shit in a pepper shaker, Pelse." Daxton leaned forward with his hands on the conference table. "Doesn't matter that the computer puked last time. Won't happen again."

"Why?" Ryder asked. "Because Connor says his team fixed it? That guy still uses a slide rule."

"Zip it. He's a good egg," Daxton said. "Been with me since the start."

"Maybe that's the problem. I finally got one of the old farts to 'fess up about your little snafu at Indian Point. Sounds like Connor's containment grid didn't quite contain everything, did it?"

"Ancient history." Daxton gave a dismissive wave.

"Could have made Fukushima look like a Boy Scout campfire."

"There was no chance of a meltdown."

"Easy to say that now." Ryder leaned back in his chair. "But if you pulled a stunt like that today they'd have to evacuate more
~~~

than twenty million people."

"Turned out nicely though," Daxton said. "If the Feds hadn't been all over us the guys would have taken five more years to get the deployment plane through the thermosphere. And it would have taken ten more years to get the space station up. Excellent motivator, hiding from the law."

Daxton's smugness was palpable. He added, "And it's a helluva lot easier hiding in plain sight with our tourists."

"Speaking of hiding," McKinley said, "I don't know how the hell they got wind of it, but the UFO conspiracy whackos are squawking about our telescope."

"No way they found it, it's behind the goddamn Sun," Daxton said.

"It's still listed as 'Unconfirmed' on Hanlon's web-site, but we have to consider the possibility of another leak. I know no one has jurisdiction in space, but we've been off the Feds' ground radar for a while, and I'd like to keep it that way."

"I'll have it taken care of," Daxton said. "What else is on the agenda?"

"Let's see." McKinley checked his notes. "Commercial tourism is booked solid for the next eighteen months—I guess we should be charging more, but that's your department. Oh, and we have the final report from the automated hydrogen test on Flight 2. I'll have Shepherd get it into the journals through the usual back channels."

"Still pisses me off that we can't take credit yet," Ryder said.

"You just focus on Flight 3." Daxton stared at the man he knew was defiling his daughter. "You screwed up once, there is no third chance."

"That horse is glue . . . sir," Ryder said. "You need to let that go, because I brought back your pretty little space ball in one piece and no worse for the wear. I was a little pressed for time thanks to the Fisher-Price computer, so yeah, I didn't have a chance to run all the tests. You'll still get your glory after Flight 4, but I'll be the only one of us who gets to bask in it."

"Let it go, guys." McKinley cut in to head off the escalation. "Let's go over next week's launch again."

"Hey Sean," Christine said. "Go through the details, will you? I want to get this all in one shot." She readied the camera and started recording.

"OK, fine." McKinley sighed and punched a few keys. A three-dimensional hologram of the solar system appeared over the conference table.

"In addition to confirming the correction of certain system failures in Flight 2," McKinley nodded to Ryder, "the mission of Flight 3 is to more positively confirm the clear-path for Flight 4."

He switched to his professor persona for posterity, and smiled at the camera. "Primary credit for this mission concept goes to Dr. Claudio Maccone of the SETI Permanent Study Group in Italy. He and his team suggest that the theory of the gravitational lens of the Sun rests on the mathematical foundation of the Schwarzschild solution to the Einstein field equations."[9]

McKinley waved his hands to zoom in on the Sun and continued, "Because light rays, that is, electromagnetic waves, can't pass through the Sun's interior, but gravitational waves and neutrinos can, there exists a focusing effect at a certain point opposite the Sun from where you want to observe."

Ryder yawned silently off-camera while McKinley stuck both hands into the hologram and spread them apart to the length of his arms. The image of the Sun in the center grew much smaller, the planets and their orbital paths shrank accordingly, and the

Oort Cloud appeared to surround the entire solar system at a great distance.

McKinley found a small green dot about thirty inches from the Sun, grabbed it and waved his hand in a circle. The image scaled to show the solar system at one end of the table by Daxton, and the green dot at the other end by Ryder and Christine.

"The plan for Flight 3 is to send the ship 978 AU away from the Sun, in the exact opposite direction of the intended Flight 4 path. This will place the instruments on the ship at the FOCAL point of the Sun's gravitational lens with regard to his ultimate destination."[7]

"Excuse me," Christine said. "Focal point?"

"That's right," McKinley said. "FOCAL can be regarded as an acronym for 'Fast Outgoing Cyclopean Astronomical Lens'. From that point, the ship will be able to confirm certain things in a way that our space-based telescope can't."

~~~

The boys were playing on the trampoline out back with Ralph looking on. Sheila was dicing celery and carrots for the lasagna. "You can still catch up with the expedition. I checked their blog and they haven't left Chilumba yet."

"Yeah, did you see the dailies they shot outside that village? Way cool stuff." Leon scooped a small spoonful of simmering sauce and had a taste. "Oh, Baby, you're goooood."

Leon put the spoon down, hugged her from behind and said, "I've been thinking a lot about it, and I think we made the right decision. That Hanlon guy was just too freaky. He knew way too much about us." Leon stepped back and leaned on the counter
~~~

to watch her cook. He loved her lasagna.

"I know, but you're driving me crazy staring at me all the time."

"Oh, so now you want me to go somewhere, just not Africa? How about Jersey, you OK with that? Take in a little smog and urban sprawl?" He tried the knife-fight dance from *Beat It*, but it came off more like Weird Al's version.

"As long as you agree it was your decision not to go, I'm good with that. We're thrilled you're still here, it's just that I don't want that kind of decision hanging over me."

"I know, Baby. Listen, I was this close to going, really I was. But there was a nagging voice in the back of my head that said I shouldn't." He chuckled then continued, "It was almost drown out by Alex tearin' me a new one. He said the best gig he can get me now is poop-scooper at Jungle Gardens."

"What tipped it for you?"

"Uh, I guess it was just an overall gut feeling. I knew I'd be safe and we'd get lots of great work done. And I want to spend as much time with you and the boys as I can. In the end, I guess Hanlon got under my skin."

"Yeah, he spooked me too. No way I'd get on a plane if that guy told me not to."

~~~

Approximately four and one half seconds after Ryder punched the launch button for Flight 3, he blacked out.

At precisely that same moment, while watching *Shark Week* reruns in his living room on Earth in Sarasota, Florida . . . Leon also blacked out.
~~~

CHAPTER 5

The call was picked up by machine, and Sheila said "Shit," as the outgoing message began in a digitized voice.

"Hello, this is not an answering machine. It is a question machine. It is about to ask you the two most important questions of your entire existence . . . Who are you? . . . And what do you want?"

After the beep, Sheila said "Um, Hi. Uh, I need to speak to Mr. Hanlon. Please call me back."

Sheila's phone rang a moment later.

"Hello? Oh, OK. Could I speak to Mr. Hanlon please?"

"Please, you may simply address me as Hanlon, Mrs. Berger."

"I'm sorry to call so late, but—"

"On the contrary. I'm surprised you've waited two days to contact me. How is Mr. Berger? Is he still in ICU at Sarasota Memorial?"

Sheila hesitated. "Um, yes. Well, he was in ICU but they moved him to the regular ward after twenty-four hours. He's stable, but he's been out longer this time than before. The doctors are stumped and I'm losing my mind."

"I understand. I believe he will come through this intact, Mrs. Berger. May I pay you a visit to discuss this in person?"

"I . . . guess so."

"Very good. Please call me immediately if Mr. Berger regains consciousness overnight. I will see you tomorrow morning. Say 8:30?"

~~~

Hanlon arrived in the Lawnscapes van and uniform, and stepped into the driveway. His associates unloaded lawn gear from the trailer behind their crew cab pickup truck and went to work on the lawn.

Sheila was sitting on the front porch with Ralph on his leash. She stood up to restrain him as Ralph started to bark at Hanlon's approach.

"May we step inside?" Hanlon asked over the din of the lawnmower, weed-whackers, and the very large dog.

"OK." Sheila herded Ralph through the door.

"He's a very majestic creature." They were in the foyer and Hanlon held out his hand to greet the dog. "Is he not a—"

"Yup, he's a Leo." Sheila kept a tight grip on the leash. "We get that a lot. Ralph . . . sit."

"I am certain. I understand they are prone to polyneuropathy."

"Yes, but we had him tested. Only one copy of the mutation, so he should be fine. Thanks for the free lawn mowing. I should have waited until we needed it."

"You are very welcome. I would like to come straight to the point, if I may."

"Absolutely. I'm dying to know what no neuroscientist in the country can figure out."

"Are you familiar with Dax Space Corp.?" he asked.

"One of the space tourist outfits. Sure, I've heard of them."
~~~

"They are doing things far more significant than tourism, I can assure you."

"Leon didn't mention them." She kept her eye on Hanlon while petting Ralph.

"He is not involved with them, at least not so far as I can determine. Not directly, anyhow. Let me suggest that he is being affected by them."

"What?"

"More specifically, he is affected by the launch of one of their ships."

"How?"

"It is very complicated. Please allow me to confirm some facts with you first."

"Yes." Sheila sighed. "He blacked out twice before, and each time he woke up halfway through for about five minutes. I've been through this with the doctors."

"I understand, but the timing is critical, and I have not been able to discover the exact date of Mr. Berger's first episode. Was it by any chance the morning of June ninth, almost sixteen months ago?"

"I don't remember the date, but yes, it was a year ago spring."

"Please try to be exact. It is very important that we confirm the date."

"Fine," Sheila tugged the leash. "Let me check my old calendar. Ralph . . . heel."

Sheila and Ralph walked to the kitchen with Hanlon following. She rummaged through a drawer and came up with the calendar in question. She scanned June but didn't find what she was looking for.

"I don't know for sure, because Leon goes kayaking at dawn

every chance he gets. I can tell you he was between shoots that week, and we didn't have anything major scheduled. I guess it could have been the ninth. Why does it matter?"

"I see. For sake of discussion, let us suppose it was the ninth, at 7:13 a.m. The total duration of the episode was thirty-three minutes, and he regained consciousness for exactly six minutes midway."

"I'm sorry, you've obviously spent a lot more time thinking about the timing than anyone else has. What the hell are you talking about?"

Hanlon stiffened and Ralph came to attention. Her curse word slapped Hanlon as surely as if it were the back of Peter's hand. "I would kindly ask you to refrain from the use of profanity. I find it very . . . disturbing."

"Oh. Um, why is that?" Sheila asked.

"I feel it reveals an inability on the speaker's part to effectively convey their meaning."

"That's a bunch of bull—. Oh, sorry. Yeah, I'm sorry, uh, what were you talking about?"

Hanlon released his tension slowly, then took a deep breath and said, "Your husband has lost consciousness each time Dax Space Corp. launched their antimatter-powered vessel."

"What the . . . Uh, what is an antimatter-powered vessel? There's no such thing, is there?"

"Thank you," Hanlon said. "There most certainly is, and Mr. Daxton has been sending it to very far off places. It is currently on its furthest mission to date, but I have not yet been able to determine the destination."

"What does this have to do with Leon?"

"It is my considered opinion that his soul enters another dimension with each antimatter pulse from the Dax vessel."

Sheila looked at her watch and said, "Oh my, look at the time. Yeah, I really have to go pick up the boys—"

"Mrs. Berger, I understand your resistance to this concept. Please, bear with me for just a moment longer."

It was Sheila's turn to stiffen. "Listen, Hanlon. My husband is lying in the hospital in a coma and I have no idea when he'll come out of it. The top neurologists on this continent are caring for him, and if you don't mind, I need to get back to the hospital."

"Yes, Dr. Davies is indeed very well respected. Good of him to travel all the way from Calgary."

"That's enough. You've obviously been spying on us and I want you to leave." Sheila and Ralph started walking toward the front door.

"Again, I beg your indulgence," Hanlon was keeping up. "What is of the utmost importance now is that you tell me when Mr. Berger regains consciousness. It will be brief, just six minutes again, but I would like to know the exact time that occurs. Will you do that for me?"

She turned to face him. "No. But I will sic my dog on you if you don't get the hell out of here."

~~~

The man had been in this hospital bed for almost three days now, and he was more than ready to get out. There was constant badgering by nurses to roll over, give blood, pee in the bottle, eat this Jell-O, take that pill, and so on.

He was thankful the man in the other bed was in a coma. At least he didn't have to muster the inane chit-chat that is sometimes required between patients sharing a room.
~~~

He passed the time pondering Hanlon's quest for The Answer. A man can't spend his entire life querying an either-or proposition without believing both options have merit. The unwashed herd may have doubts, but not we the faithful.

Still, everyone in The Cluster served Hanlon unfailingly. So when a man such as he says proof is required, then proof they would provide.

Now 4:43 a.m.; all quiet without coma-guy's wife and kids swarming the room like seagulls. After sixty-four and a half hours with nothing but cat-naps he was very fuzzy, but still very committed.

It was critical to stay alert, be ready at a moment's notice. He must not—would not—disappoint Hanlon. There would be only one chance for this and he couldn't allow himself to sleep through it.

Focus on the clock. Focus on the clock. That was his mantra.

When coma-guy stirred, it was like a blessing from God. He heard the moans through the curtain and knew the moment had finally come.

He made a mental note of the exact time, then quickly reached under the mattress. It wouldn't be long before the nurses arrived.

He was frustrated waiting for the cell phone to power on, but he dared not take the chance of a dead battery. He entered the time of coma-guy's first sign of consciousness into a text message and sent it. He replaced the cell phone under the mattress, then called out "Nurse!"

Once the commotion over coma-guy settled down, and hopefully before Mrs. Coma-Guy and the Wee Ones arrived, he could check himself out of the hospital and return to The Cluster. Hanlon would be pleased.

FOR IMMEDIATE RELEASE
Contact: Hanlon
E-Mail: Inquiry@IAskOfLife.com

DAX SPACE SHIP INDUCES COMA ON EARTH
Famed Explorer Leon Berger Still in a Coma

Dax Space Corp. has been secretly developing an antimatter pulse driven space ship for several decades. The ship is code-named the *Golf Ball* partly because of its appearance, and partly because, as Mr. Daxton is quoted as saying, "If you hit it right, it flies straight for a very long time".

Dax has completed two successful test flights in the past sixteen months, both of which have caused Leon Berger, the famed wildlife expert and explorer from Sarasota, Florida to enter a completely unresponsive state of unconsciousness, not unlike a coma. An unidentified member of the Dax flight team has also been rendered unconscious by the antimatter blasts. Both patients regained consciousness briefly at the midway point of the flights, and entirely after the return. Dax Space Corp. did not return calls of inquiry prior to this release.

The Dax ship is currently in flight toward Earth, and is scheduled to return five days from now, at approximately 8:49 p.m. Eastern Daylight Time. At that time, Mr. Berger will awaken having no recollection whatsoever about the prior eleven days, aside from a brief awakening this morning at Sarasota Memorial Hospital.

~~~
~~~

"Chrissy, I need that promo piped downstairs by eight tonight." Daxton led them briskly down the hall.

"Not until you tell me exactly which one of the positively-final-and-we're-not-changing-it-any-more versions you want," Christine said.

"Holy shit little lady, how many goddamn times do we have to go over this? The two-minute segment you did covering Allison, the space station with Section 6, the tugboat and the golf ball; that's the one."

"Really? You're going to show them the ship? When did we decide that?"

"I agree, sir," McKinley said. "I don't like that idea either."

"Just the quick exterior shot. The one where it's docked in Section 6 but the bay doors are open. Make sure the whole thing is holographic in the atrium, but send the 2D feed over the wire."

"I can't put a still picture into a holographic, it'll look horrible."

"Do what you have to do. Come on Chrissy, Hanlon only bumped our announcement up by a day; you should be ready for this. And make sure you use the updated 3D logos." He punched the elevator button, and gave McKinley a slap on the back. "After all these years, Sean, we finally get to go public."

"Very exciting."

"You sure you don't want to come say a few words?"

"I'm sure. Not much for the outside anymore, and I especially don't like the press."

"I just wish you'd bask in the glory with me. You earned it."

"That's plenty for me. I'll get it done, you tell people about it . . . and pay for it."

~~~
~~~

Daxton walked to the podium and tested the mic. There was continued murmuring for a few more seconds, then all went quiet. His Armani suit fit perfectly, and the sheen was a nice effect under these lights.

"Ladies and gentlemen of planet Earth." He was addressing a crowd of about thirty reporters in the atrium lobby of his headquarters, but knew this was broadcast to countless millions around the world via TV and internet. "I am now prepared to make an announcement that will shake the very foundation of how we view ourselves and our place in the universe.

"Exactly four days," he glanced at the countdown timer, "four minutes, and twenty-two seconds from now, at precisely 8:37 p.m. and thirty-seven seconds Eastern Daylight Time, you will all witness the return of a manned spacecraft from further out in space than any of you currently think is possible."

The crowd murmured again, then went quiet.

"At that time, Dax Space Corp. will complete the third successful antimatter propulsion-powered flight at near-c, which for our ship is roughly 99.999 percent the speed of light."

The crowd erupted, mostly into laughter. A few started packing as if getting ready to leave. Daxton gave everyone a minute to settle down.

"Do I have your attention now?" he asked. The crowd quieted. "I realize you are all accustomed to our competitors announcing things far sooner than they should. Kennedy announced the lunar landing almost seven years before Armstrong pushed Aldrin aside and jumped into the moondust. Some would argue we wouldn't have made it to the Moon without that bold announcement from the President.

"Long before NASA finally mothballed the space shuttles, you heard whispers that commercial space tourism[21] would be available within the next ten years. Quietly at first. Just in the journals and scientific papers. Then it was five, then down to two, then for a while they were absolutely sure it would be next year. Of course, it finally did happen, and we here at Dax Space Corp. have been thrilled to be a part of it. But add it all up and it's been a crazy roller-coaster waiting for people to actually do what they say they're going to do.

"I don't know how many of you noticed along the way, but no one at Dax, from myself to any of our PR people, in our entire history spanning back to the '70s, has ever announced anything of any significance until after it was done. I've always felt that was of the utmost importance; not only to do what you set out to do, but to shut up and do it. In a letter to her husband John, long before he was president, Abigail Adams said, 'We have too many high sounding words, and too few actions that correspond with them.' I believe she was right.

"Tonight I will deviate from that rule, but only slightly. As I said, we have already had two successful near-c flights, and the antimatter propulsion drive is an unmitigated success. These were not mere test flights; those missions are done, completed, and in our history books. We'll be sharing some details with you over the next few days. For now, let me just say that our astronaut took some fabulous close-up pictures of Mars when he was there." The laughter came again, but was muted. More like titters. He had the attention of the skeptics, but hadn't won them over yet.

"I'm well aware that there will be those who don't believe what I'm saying. Hell, there are still people who don't believe Hanlon had JVT assassinated." It was his turn to laugh, and some of the crowd joined in. "As you know, Dax has been first, and dare I say best, in many aspects of commercial space tourism. At this time, I'd like to play a brief montage showing our space vehicles and the space station you already know, then give you a glimpse of the ship that has already crossed another milestone in man's evolution of exploration."

He played the two-minute promo and most of the reporters were barely paying attention toward the end, as they'd seen so much of it before. When the bay doors on Section 6 opened to reveal the capsule, everyone was instantly focused. Uh oh . . . she managed to animate the still picture and get it into 3D, but the tech geeks on the web will shred that fakery in a heartbeat. They'll try to make hay with that, but they still can't dispute the facts of Ryder's return.

The promo ended and the room was buzzing with discussion of the ship. "Ladies and gentlemen, please." Daxton raised his hands to quiet the crowd. "Please, give me your attention for just a while longer, and I'll take questions afterward.

"I want to be very clear here, because the proof is in the observation. The first part is directed to our friends in charge of the various space-based telescopes out there. I'm talking about LEGRI, Fermi, INTEGRAL, Swift, JWST, and everyone else with a big eye in the sky. I will provide the exact coordinates they should be set to observe, and I expect they will temporarily retask their telescopes accordingly. Trust me, this is better than Kitty Hawk, or more specifically Kill Devil Hills in 1903. This time everyone gets to watch it happen as it happens.

"The second part is for everyone in the Eastern Time zone of the U.S. of A. I apologize to the rest of our friends all around the globe, but when you want to be on Broadway, you have to go to New York. Alright? So here's the task for everyone on the right coast of the States. Look up. That's it, just look up. You'll see a bright green flash in the night sky, and you'll be witnessing history. Aside from the Big Apple itself, it should be bright enough to see from the ground where it's not cloudy. It'll be about an hour and a half after sunset, so you won't even have to keep the kids up past their bed-times."

~~~

"OK, next question." Daxton pointed to the woman in the blue and white blazer.

"Thank you. Julie Melroy, CBN. Could you please restate the timeline. I'm sure we'd all like to confirm the details."

"Oh, Jesus." Daxton was losing patience as this continued to draw out. "All the details will be on our web site within the hour. You can cut-and-paste if you want."

"Please, I just want to get it straight for the immediate broadcast."

"You mean for when your talking head 'experts' sit around repeating what I just said and trying to sound more intelligent. OK, I'll go slow. He launched eight days ago, hit the apex at five and a half days, launched on return after six minutes there, and he'll be back in four days from now. 8:37 p.m. and thirty-seven seconds, make sure you get that right."

"And the telescopes will see the light from the antimatter pulses three seconds before everyone on the ground sees them, correct?"

"Three seconds before the last antimatter pulse stops his ship near the space station. Back near Earth. You only need a telescope to see the pulses from the apex."

"I'm sorry, but if he started the return flight almost six days ago, why do we see the flashes just three seconds apart?"

"Could someone please smack her in the forehead for me?
~~~

Come on Julie, keep up. He was far far away when he hit the button to come home. He's traveling just barely slower than light does, so the light from his return pulse will get here just three seconds before he does. Does anyone have a question not related to the flight parameters we'll be posting shortly?"

"Is it true the ship is called the *Golf Ball*?" an unseen woman asked.

"Sure." Daxton shrugged. "Why not?" Then he added, "And the repositioning ship is named *Tugboat Willie* after me."

"What about the space plane?"

"That's 'Allison' . . . And don't ask, it's personal."

"And the space station?"

"Come on, guys." Daxton's patience was razor thin. "We call it 'The Space Station'. Make something better up if you want. Can I get a serious question?"

"What's the astronaut's name?" a man in the crowd asked.

"Ah, there we go. Can't believe I got this far without mentioning Mr. Ryder Pelse. He's a good man, you'll meet him when he gets back."

"Is that Rider with an 'i'?"

"No, it's Ryder with an r-Y-d-e-r, and Pelse with a p-e-l-s-e. You're on your own with mister. Who's next? Over there, in the back."

"Hello. Sergei Tyurin, Wolfe News. What can you tell us about the astronaut?"

"Nothing at the moment. I'll let him speak for himself when he returns. We'll pipe the feed from the capsule shortly after he comes to all stop, and you'll be able to watch as the tugboat brings the capsule back to dock with the space station."

"Hi. Katy Pogue for *Aviators Monthly*. Since everyone thinks an antimatter pulse drive is still theoretical, can you tell us how you obtained permits for its operation?"

"You may need a permit to barbecue in your back yard, but I don't need one in space."

"How do you know it's safe? Where's the oversight and monitoring? Why hasn't the EPA or NASA been involved?"

"Let me be blunt. First of all, an antimatter pulse is not nuclear. I repeat—*not* nuclear. The byproduct energy is in the X-ray and gamma ray spectrum. We take every precaution to ensure that the vast majority of the rays are always directed away from Earth, so no one turns into the Incredible Hulk.

"As for the oversight and monitoring—those are only here on Earth, and everybody is still whining about the loss of a few space tourists three years ago. Tragic as that was, it should not have set space tourism back as far as it did. They bought their tickets, they knew what they were getting into.

"And for the record, nothing like that has ever happened on one of our flights. Dax Space Corp. maintains a one hundred percent flawless safety record."

"Good evening. Edward Linnehan. *Nation's Inquiry*."

"How the hell did you get in here?" Daxton asked. The crowd had a good laugh, but Edward didn't seem fazed.

"Mr. Daxton, do you deny the allegations in Hanlon's press release with regard to Leon Berger's comas being induced by the launch of your ship?"

"Hanlon is an idiot. Our sympathies go out to Mr. Berger and his family, but I can assure that his condition has absolutely nothing to do with our program. I can't be more clear than that."

"Which member of your team has also been in a coma?"

"Let's have a serious question here. Sergei, you got anything else?"

"How have you been able to maintain secrecy about the

development and execution of such a monumental program?"

"I'm good at what I do."

"And how has Hanlon managed to scoop everyone on this?"

"He's marginally good at what he does. But let's be clear, he didn't get everything right."

~~~

FOR IMMEDIATE RELEASE
Contact: Hanlon
E-Mail: Inquiry@IAskOfLife.com

DAX ASTRONAUT AND WILDLIFE EXPLORER ARE TWINS

Ryder Pelse and Leon Berger
Adopted Separately

The Dax Space Corp. astronaut will be returning home tomorrow evening to a twin brother he doesn't know he has. Ryder Pelse and Leon Berger were born in New York on Easter Sunday, April 10th, 1978. Both were adopted as part of a secret research project in the '60s and '70s that separated identical twins as infants and followed them in a one-of-a-kind experiment to assess the influence of nature versus nurture in child development.

The study[17] was headed up by Dr. Peter Neubauer, a child psychiatrist, and Viola Bernard, a child psychologist and consultant to the Louise Wise Agency. The study ended in 1980, and a year later, the state of New York began requiring adoption agencies to
~~~

keep siblings together.

However, by that time the two children were already established with their adoptive families, who were never notified of their child's twin.

The attached publicity photo shows Berger with his current long hair, beard, and two facial scars. The only photo currently available of Pelse is from his Air Force service record, taken when he was twenty-two years of age. However, a close inspection reveals that they are indeed identical twins, not paternal.

Berger's exploits in wildlife expeditions and television series are well known, but the condition by which he is rendered unconscious when Pelse departs in his near light-speed ship is not fully understood. Berger remains in a coma-like state in Sarasota Memorial Hospital, and is expected to regain consciousness immediately upon Pelse's return tomorrow evening at exactly 8:37 p.m. and 37 seconds Eastern Daylight Time.

Ryder Pelse was an accomplished aerobatic stunt pilot in his late teens, noted for his extensive and thrilling high-G chicane maneuvers. He then joined the Air Force and qualified for the Pararescuemen but received a BCD (Bad Conduct Discharge) and went to Colombia where he flew charter tours.

He was later named as the sole survivor of a kidnapping for ransom incident when he made a forced landing in the jungle outside Medellin, Colombia almost five years ago.

Peggy and Leland Weatherbee, tourists from Dallas, Texas were flying with Pelse at the time, and were also taken hostage by leftist guerrillas from the ELN. All three were tortured for seventeen days before the Weatherbees were killed and Pelse escaped. He refused to comment on the incident and has not been seen publicly since.

It's not clear how long he's been training and flying with Dax Space Corp.

~~~

"That Hanlon guy is killing me." Sheila paced around Dr. Davies' borrowed office at the hospital. "How the hell did he dig all that stuff up about this astronaut being Leon's twin? Can it be for real?"

"We don't have official confirmation yet." Davies was seated behind the desk. "But based on the photos and the records Hanlon presented, it certainly seems plausible."

"But Leon grew up in Florida. His parents didn't go to New York. Always said they hated it."

"We have to assume they were in New York at least for the adoption."

"Really? We have to take this crackpot seriously? He makes my skin crawl."

"I understand, Sheila. But what's important now is that the media are making it nearly impossible to provide proper care for Leon. They're relentless and the hospital administration is at their wit's end trying to deal with this juggernaut."

"I know. I thought we were done with them after Calgary, but they're like gnats buzzing in your ears and nose."

"I realize you've had only a short time to consider Mr. Daxton's proposal, but I personally think it would be best for
~~~

Leon."

"You don't think he just wants more publicity?" she asked.

"I'm sure he does. However, if we move Leon to the Dax complex there'll be far better security."

"Yeah, and those media assholes won't have to split time on both sides of the state."

"Mr. Daxton assures me they have all the necessary monitoring equipment and medical facilities on site."

"What if he wakes up on the way?"

"The pattern has been predictable so far, and Leon has had no lasting ill effects upon regaining consciousness." Davies stood up, then sat on the edge of the desk. "I think it's an acceptable risk. It would also be far easier for me to collaborate with Dr. Ranayan if both patients were collocated."

"Did she tell you what's going on with the other patient?"

"Not yet. She's only told me that the symptoms are virtually identical to Leon's. A complete quieting of the DMN during the episodes."

"Do you think that space ship has anything to do with it?"

"I can't imagine how," he said. "But just as with Leon's condition, we're in uncharted territory."

"How would this work? I mean the transfer."

"Mr. Daxton has agreed to provide a security detail and several vehicles for support. He will not announce the transfer until after it's complete."

"And what about me and the boys?"

"He said you're also welcome there," Davies put a hand on her shoulder. "They have complete child care facilities in the complex, and they'll assign private quarters for the three of you as well as Leon, assuming he awakens as predicted. Unfortunately, they can't accommodate dogs."

"I understand. Ralph can go to our friends' house. We cross-sit for their Labs all the time. You really think this is a good idea?"

Davies sat down in the chair again. "I think it's the worst case possible, except for the alternatives."

Chapter 6

"OK, cue the announcer in three . . . two . . ."

The announcer's voice boomed over the show's newsy theme music. "This is the *Every Day Show* with Jason Collins." The studio audience cheered and whooped.

"Ladies and gentlemen, welcome to the *Every Day Show*. My name is Jason Collins." The cheering continued as he scribbled wildly on his orange note pages and then reshuffled them.

"Thank you." He smirked at one of the audience members. "Thank you. Thank you ladies and gentlemen. Tonight!" He paused to straighten his tie as the cheering started to subside. "Tonight we have twins in the headlines.

"Of course you've all heard of Romulus and Remus, Ann Landers and Abigail Van Buren, Mary-Kate and Ashley. So sad. But tonight we find out about a set of twins well before they discover each other. That's right, apparently one of them is a guerrilla and one takes pictures of gorillas, but they haven't met. Hmm . . . I wonder how that could be?" A picture flashed on the monitor showing a chimpanzee bashfully shying away from a tourist with a camera.

"Oh, no. I kid. But this is a serious matter, because it seems they're going to meet for the first time night-after-tomorrow . . . wait a minute, when are we taping this?" Cue the laughs.

"Anyway, it's true that we all get to watch when one comes home from a long journey." He showed a picture of Charlton Heston meeting the apes. "And the other is in a coma." Up flashed a picture of Al Gore in a tuxedo, nodding off at a banquet table.

"Earlier today, we received photos of the twins. This headshot for Leon Berger, the extreme explorer extraordinaire; and this Air Force photo of Ryder Pelse." The audience laughed at the two dissimilar images.

"So, it seems to me that there may be other twins roaming among us. Unknown twins . . ." His sinister voice had the music to back it up.

"Let's take a look at some other folks who may be twins and not know it. How about Mike Tyson, and . . . wait for it . . . yes! That's right, President Obama had a twin waiting for him when he got back from India. Unfortunately, it turns out Tyson only wanted to chew the President's ear for a while.

"Now, as we all know, the word 'twin' comes from the Anglo-Saxon 'getwinn', meaning 'that which is divided'. Of course, the word originally referred to," up flashed the picture, "the United States Congress."

~~~

"That's all for me, I'm Kelly Kavandi and you're now in good hands with Bruce Phillips."

"Thanks Kelly. The news begins anew on the Wolfe Report—right now. Our top story has two separate components . . . space travel and twins.

"We've been following the story of Dax Space Corp.'s antimatter space vessel closely, and in just over twenty-four hours we'll know the truth about that. But tonight there are new
~~~

developments with regard to the alleged twins, Leon Berger and Ryder Pelse. First reported by the reclusive conspiracy theorist known only as Hanlon, and later confirmed by the New York Times, the two men are said to be twins who've never met and don't know of each other's existence. I guess we'll take care of that tomorrow evening as well.

"Tracing backward from their birth date in April of 1978, the twins' conception was probably early July of the prior year. And now an unnamed source has come forward to the Times and reported that the teen mother who gave the twins up for adoption lived in Buchanan, New York at the time. It's alleged that she was at or near the Indian Point nuclear reactors on the night of July 13th, 1977. That's the evening of the accident that was later found to have caused the New York City Blackout.

"The identity of the birth mother is being withheld, so she can't be reached for comment. Managing Editor for Wolfe News Health Central, Dr. Sunita Guttierez joins us for more information on how the nuclear accident may have affected the twins in utero. Dr. Suni, thanks for joining us."

~~~

"Mrs. Berger, how are you and the boys doing?" McKinley asked.

"You can call me Sheila. We're doing as well as can be expected. The boys were having a blast in that huge playroom, it's quite a facility you have here."

"Did they like swimming with the dolphins?" Davies asked.

"Oh, sure. Nathan does it a lot at home, but they hadn't done it in a tank before."

"How about the spaceflight simulator?" McKinley asked.
~~~

"Well, Felix loved it of course, he's the video game fanatic, but it wasn't really Nathan's bag. He wanted to go swim in the Atlantic because, as he said 'I know all about the Gulf'." The three of them shared a laugh.

"OK everyone, have a seat. Let's get this thing started." Daxton came in and motioned to the group of three standing by the table, as well as Gajra and Christine over by the coffee dispenser. Everyone took their seats while closing out their separate conversations.

Daxton, seated at the head of the table, addressed the group. "First off, let me formally welcome Mrs. Berger and Dr. Davies to our humble abode. You're the first non-Dax personnel we've had here in quite some time. I just wish it was under better circumstances. Did the boys go to sleep OK?"

"They were exhausted. Quite a day for the little guys."

"Quite a day for anyone," McKinley said.

"Very good. OK folks, we need to go over the plan for tomorrow night. But first, let's get an update from the doctors."

"Yes," Gajra said. "We have stabilized Mr. Berger in room three of ward two, and we feel that the cross-state drive did not negatively affect him. Of course, he will be quite surprised to regain consciousness in a different hospital setting."

"He's used to it," Sheila said. "Are they twins?"

"Yes. The twin DNA zygosity test returned a positive match," Gajra said.

"Oh, my God . . . that'll stun him."

"Indeed," Davies said. "As we've discussed, he regained consciousness with no lasting ill effects after previous episodes. However, I strongly recommend that we do not reveal this information too soon after he awakens."

"Why not?" Daxton asked.

"I'm very concerned about overwhelming him in a room full of people and a TV camera, then springing the news that he has a twin brother in front of the whole world."

"Come on, this guy wrestles alligators in the wild. What's the problem?" Daxton asked.

"Mr. Daxton," Sheila said. "I appreciate you inviting us here and the additional security and all that. I only agreed to it because Dr. Davies said it would be best for Leon. But if you're going to put my husband on *Jerry Springer*, we're out of here."

"I just don't understand why we can't make hay while the sun is shining."

"Because we're talking about my husband here, and I don't want him paraded in front of the media in some kind of freak show."

"I heard what happened in Banff; I think that ship has sailed."

"We need to consider the risks to Ryder as well," Christine said. "This is going to shock him too."

"No good. I have an iron-clad contract with fly-boy, and I fully intend to broadcast his return to the entire planet. Live." Daxton's demeanor indicated this was not open for debate.

"Listen Dad, that's just not right. After everything Ryder has done for you, all the risks he's taken, you're still going to treat him like a show-pony?"

"He is what he is. Now you listen to me. I've been working for this my whole life. Every day since I was a kid I've wanted to go interstellar, to see what's up there with my own eyes. I'm too old to get beyond the space station personally, but I'll be damned if I'm going to have some stupid family reunion steal my thunder."

"Can we at least delay the feed from Ryder in the capsule for a few minutes so he can shake off the blackout and get himself oriented?" Christine was as close to pleading with her father as she'd been since grade school.

"Hanlon and his cronies would have a field day with that." Daxton slapped the table. "I can see the headline now, 'Dax Blows the Timing'. They'll say the pulse had nothing to with the ship returning and we faked the whole thing."

"I'm sorry Mr. Daxton, but with all due respect, they could say that anyway," Davies said.

"No they can't."

"It seems to me that everyone will see a flash in the sky, then they'll see Mr. Pelse on TV from the capsule. How can you prove the correlation?"

"The boys at NASA will take care of that. They'll have space and ground telescopes monitor the return, and they'll triangulate the signal feed from the ship to the satellite. It's about time they made themselves useful."

"I have no problem delaying the feed for thirty seconds or even a minute," McKinley said. "We should at least let him snap out of it before putting him on camera. The media are already speculating that Ryder is the other one blacking out, there's no point in confirming it."

"Speaking of that, what have you two figured out?" Daxton asked the doctors.

"What we know for certain is that the DMN goes completely quiet for both men during the episodes," Davies said.

"Refresh my memory," Daxton said. "DMN?"

"Oh, sorry," Davies said. "DMN is the Default Mode Network. It describes subconscious activity throughout all regions of the brain, but is thought to be the overall controller of conscious activity as well."

"So what?"

"A complete silencing of the DMN has never been observed in any patient, not even one in an actual coma or persistent vegetative state," Gajra said. "Only patients experiencing complete brain death have a silent DMN. But of course, they cannot recover."

"Oh, Christ. Why didn't you tell me this was unique?"

"I tried several times, sir. I am afraid you may have been otherwise occupied."

"Maybe I just don't give a shit about wetware. OK, I'm paying attention now. What's the plan when we get the two guinea pigs together?"

"We are having an additional fMRI scanner installed to complement the EEGs. This way we can monitor both men simultaneously during a series of side-by-side tests."

"Who's paying for that?"

"Um . . . I suppose those expenditures will come out of my departmental budget," Gajra said.

"How much?"

"The initial estimate is not yet binding, but due to the accelerated timeline the vendor has quoted approximately $3 million."

"Not a fucking chance." Daxton's voice reverberated. "I agreed to bring the monkey-boy here to meet the fly-boy, but I'm not about to foot the bill for hardware I don't need."

Sheila got up to leave.

"Hold on everybody," McKinley said. "He's a nasty bastard but his bark is worse than his bite."

Daxton slumped back in his chair and sighed. He asked Gajra, "Exactly why do you need another MRI?"

"We have confirmed as best we can that both men lose consciousness as soon as the ship reaches near-c, and regain consciousness at all stop. No one has advanced a plausible theory as to why someone on Earth, and presumably only one person on Earth, would be affected in this way by either an antimatter pulse or near-c travel elsewhere. It seems there must be a connection between the twins, but what that might be remains unknown."

"What do you expect to learn by sticking him in a $3 million box?"

"If I may," Davies said. "An EEG is biased towards the cortical surface, and although it has a higher temporal resolution, the spatial resolution is insufficient. An fMRI does have a multi-second delay, but it will reveal activation localized to specific regions of the brain, in three dimensions."

"Ya-da, ya-da, ya-da, I'm not buyin' it. You're telling me you can't read them one at a time, and you can't send Berger somewhere else and patch in the boxes?"

Gajra looked at nothing in particular. "We could . . . do the initial studies via EEG and fMRI concurrently on each individual. With a series of control tests repeated over multiple iterations to determine causality."

"We could also take them both to my facility in Calgary, or any number of closer facilities," Davies said.

"Hang on." Daxton leaned over to whisper back and forth with McKinley. After their deliberation, he asked, "When would this box be ready for use?"

"Within a week. We gave the vendor notice immediately upon learning the men were twins," Gajra said.

"And this is ground-breaking research you'll be doing? Lots of upside potential?"

"Very much so." Davies nodded.

"Fair enough. Make it happen."

~~~

"Here we go folks, let's watch this happen." McKinley clapped his hands once as they passed T-minus three minutes to return.

On a bank of huge flat panel monitors were the various news broadcasts, all chattering about the upcoming slice of human history. Each had their screens split four ways: top left showing the feed from the Tugboat awaiting Ryder's return, top right with Flight Control currently showing McKinley barking orders; bottom left with Leon lying unconscious in the hospital bed; and bottom right showing either a reporter or anchor's talking head. They all had some sort of countdown timer clicking away to 8:37 p.m. and thirty-seven seconds.

"Chrissy," Daxton whispered, "you set to switch to the capsule feed?"

"All good."

The Wolfe Report swapped the anchor's feed for one of a large gathering set to watch for the antimatter pulse at Atlantic Beach. They were just a few miles south of JFK Airport and there was no air traffic because the TSA had grounded all flights on the eastern seaboard in case of unforeseen problems. Never mind that the previous two flights hadn't affected planes at all, they were simply avoiding liability.

The on-location reporter was describing how odd it was that so few people around the east appeared to be out watching for the pulse, but the anchor reminded him that indoor viewing parties were all the rage tonight. Public or private, solo or group, TV or internet, it seemed just about everyone from everywhere was watching some kind of coverage at this moment.

Daxton felt the same electricity he remembered from
~~~

watching the lunar landing in '69, and hoped everyone out there was feeling a similar connection to this event. He whispered to Christine, "Weird, wild stuff. You think?"

"Yeah, I get it Dad."

"What's the matter with you?"

"I'm still pissed at you for piping this live. It's not too late to pull the plug, you know."

"No chance, little lady. This is the big one."

"You're a dick."

"I'll be an immortal dick after tonight."

~~~

"Looks like it's getting close." Sheila glanced at the muted TV on the table. She had them turn it away from Leon's hospital bed so he couldn't see the live coverage. She wanted the first thing he saw to be her.

"Sure is ma'am. Just two minutes to go," the cameraman said.

"You mind getting me another coffee?" she asked.

The cameraman looked to the security guard for approval, and got it. They both stood up and the guard held the door for him. Sheila threw all her weight into her shoulder as it hit the guard between both of his. He was propelled through the open door and crashed into the opposite wall. Before he could collect himself, he heard the door latch shut, and the sound of Sheila smashing the electronic locking mechanism from the inside.

~~~

“What the fuck are you blathering about?” Daxton said into his cell phone as angrily as he could in a quiet tone. He paused for the reply. “Oh Jesus Christ. That ungrateful bitch!” His voice was louder than intended, and Christine hushed him.

“Fuck it. Too late to do anything now, they’d hear you over the feed if you broke in. Let’s just hope she doesn’t do anything stupid on camera.” He disconnected the call and turned to Christine. “I can’t believe she fucking locked us out of our own goddamn ward room.” His rasp was still too loud.

“You know how many mics are in this room.” That hushed him.

“You just get ready to cut that feed if she goes nuts. What are we at? T-minus thirty seconds.”

He heard McKinley tell everyone on the outside feeds that he was cutting audio from Flight Control until after the return. The news feeds still showed black space, McKinley, Leon, an anchor, and a countdown timer. A hush seemed to fall over the entire planet as some looked up, some looked on, some wondered, and Sheila hoped.

~~~

“Excellent folks, we have just a few seconds left before the big return,” Bruce Phillips said on the Wolfe Report. “Just to review, you should see a bright green flash in the top left panel of your screen. That’s the flash that most of you under clear skies in the east would see up above. It will be followed by the capsule as seen from outside the tugboat.

“Now, the tugboat will be a good distance away from the return stop, so the ship will appear very small even with the high-powered lens, especially since the capsule where Mr. Pelse
~~~

sits is spherical—that's why they call it the *Golf Ball*—and it's no bigger than a mini-van."

"Once the ship's successful return has been confirmed, we'll immediately switch to a live feed from inside the capsule. Then you'll see Mr. Pelse in that corner of your screen, and you should see Leon Berger awaken in the lower left."

~~~

All eyes in Flight Control were on one screen or another, watching intently as the countdown continued past ten seconds, then five, then two, then one . . . FLASH.

"Right on time!" Daxton and McKinley shouted in unison as the room erupted in cheers.

The image of Ryder appeared on the main screen in the room, but the news programs still showed the exterior of the ship.

"Ryder. Ryder come in. Please respond," McKinley said.

Daxton grabbed the mic. "Come on Fly-Boy, wake the fuck up."

Ryder remained motionless in the chair, head listing to one side. Everyone stared.

"Vitals are good," Gajra said. "He should awaken shortly if the pattern repeats." She heard a collective sigh of relief.

Daxton glanced at the news feed to confirm they still had the view from the tugboat, and noticed that Leon's face had been replaced with a black screen. Somewhat problematic, but he could live with it. Better that everyone watch the main attraction.

Ryder began stirring and rubbed his eyes with the heels of his hands. He groaned.
~~~

"Welcome back, now snap to," Daxton said.

Ryder groaned again. "Nice to see you, too."

"Let's go Fly-Boy. Get those silly patches off your head, you have a broadcast to do. Just like we rehearsed. Chop chop."

Ryder started removing the EEG patches, and asked, "All eyes on us?"

"Yes, soon," McKinley said. "But we've had a few developments while you were away."

"Oh yeah? Like what?"

"We'll tell you later. Now straighten up," Daxton said. "We're switching to broadcast."

"Oh goody." Ryder shook his head again, trying to get everything to click into place.

"Uh oh," McKinley said. "Where the hell is Christine?"

Daxton spun and surveyed the room. She was nowhere to be found. "Who else knows how to switch the goddamn feed?"

~~~

"This is a nice surprise." Leon groggily looked up and down Sheila standing by his bedside wearing only her bra from the waist up. She looked fantastic as always. He had chosen wisely.

She kissed him and kissed him and kissed him.

Then Sheila straightened up and put a finger over her mouth to indicate that he should not talk. He looked at her with a 'What's up?' expression.

She pulled the stack of large cue cards she'd gotten from Christine out from under his bed and took a step back. Leon could now see the TV camera behind her, and he wondered why it was wearing her shirt over the lens.

Sheila showed him the cards one after the other.
~~~

I love you. The boys love you. We missed you.

It was the same as the last two times.

You should be fine, they found no brain damage.

You're not in Sarasota. You're in Palm Bay.

This is not a hospital. It's Dax Space Corp. HQ.

Dr. Davies from Calgary is here.

You have been out for eleven days total.

The camera is a live feed to the news media.

You're part of a big news story.

Do you want to say hello to the world right now?

Leon considered what he had read. It seemed like relatively good news, but he wondered how an outfit like Dax Space Corp. could possibly figure in. He thought about the odd steps Sheila had taken to bring him up to date. Movement past her and the camera caught his eye. He could see a security guard peering through the small window in the door. He shook his head and mouthed the word 'No'.

Sheila put down the cards, walked to the camera, and shut it off. She waved to the security guard as she put her shirt back on.

~~~

"That's what I'm trying to tell you." Christine was alone in the dimly lit computer center. "It's only a matter of time before they figure out how to switch the feed and you go live to the world. Keep your hand over your mouth so they can't read your lips."

"You told me it was redirected," Ryder said.

"I'm in the server room and I can only tell that I still have the audio. Video is a wildcard, could be split."

"OK, OK. I got it," Ryder said through his fingers. "Why can't
~~~

I get this broadcast over with and get out of this tiny bubble?"

"Shut up a second and listen. I have some big, big news, and I need to know if you want to hear it now."

"Kinda busy here, Babe. Just got back from a rough couple days in outer space."

"You're impossible."

"No, I'm sexy. You said so yourself. Even when I'm bald."

"One more chance. If you want to hear this now, fine. If not, I have no idea how you'll hear it or who will tell you. You pick."

~~~

"OK folks, I have to say this has certainly been a bizarre presentation from Dax Space Corp. so far tonight," Bruce Phillips said on the Wolfe Report. "We're not quite sure what to make of all this. We have reports from our affiliates up and down the east coast confirming the bright green flash in the night sky.

"However, Gordon on location at NASA's Kennedy Space Center is still indicating no official confirmation for any of their space based observations. We're told a spokesman will issue a statement shortly, but we all know what that means.

"Here at Wolfe News, our engineers have enhanced the audio we got from Leon Berger's hospital room, and we can't say for certain, but it sounds like someone, presumably Berger but that's not confirmed, actually said 'This is a nice surprise' after that video went black. For continuing analysis as events continue to unfold, let's go back to our panel of experts. Dr. Suni, you had something you wanted to add?"

"Yes Bruce, thank you. What I'd like to point out is a few slightly reddish and very faint circular marks on Pelse's
~~~

forehead. You can also see what looks to be a small semicircular glue mark not unlike the residue an adhesive bandage would leave after you remove it. It might also be residue from conductive gel."

"Thank goodness for HDTV," Bruce said.

"You think he was wearing some kind of helmet during the flight?" one of the panelists asked.

"No, this would seem to suggest the presence of EEG electrode patches on Pelse's head during the flight. There was quite a gap between the return of the ship and when we finally started receiving video. He would have had plenty of time to remove them."

"And what do you think that might indicate?" Bruce asked.

"Well, this is just speculation, but it seems to me they may have been monitoring him for symptoms such as those exhibited by Berger."

"Bruce, let me jump in here," one of the other panelists said. "As you know, but I want to remind our viewers that I was a soldier in Vietnam and retired as a colonel. What I'm concerned about is NASA's corroboration. Now, I don't want to cast any aspersions on NASA, they've certainly been a solid government agency over the years. But let's not forget Dax Space Corp. has some pretty shady things going on, and they still haven't come clean as to how they've done it."

"Wow, we certainly have a lot to digest here folks." Bruce turned back into the camera. "But for the moment it seems the action has hit a lull, so we're going to take a quick commercial break before we check back with Gordon covering Cape Canaveral."

~~~
~~~

FOR IMMEDIATE RELEASE
Contact: Hanlon
E-Mail: Inquiry@IAskOfLife.com

DAX ASTRONAUT IS THE COMA PATIENT
NASA Confirms Antimatter Pulses from Ship

Unnamed sources have confirmed that Ryder Pelse, the astronaut who returned from outer space tonight is in fact the Dax Space Corp. team member who has been experiencing loss of consciousness during the ship's missions. In all three flights, Pelse's symptoms exactly matched those of Leon Berger, the wildlife expert who has been positively identified as Pelse's identical twin.

Other unnamed sources at NASA have confirmed observations made with both the JWST and Swift space-based telescopes. Both devices observed gamma rays consistent with an antimatter pulse and originating at 978 AU (Astronomical Units) away from Earth. The rays arrived as predicted by Dax Space Corp. earlier this week: 3.14 seconds before Pelse's ship returned, and having originated in precisely the predicted region of deep space.

It should also be noted that Pelse returned to the proximity of the space station at 8:37 p.m., which happens to be the same time of the July 13th, 1977 'accident' responsible for the New York City Blackout. Eyewitness accounts of the incident at the Indian Point nuclear reactor have described the bright green flash in 1977 as very similar to the flash observed tonight upon Pelse's return.

CHAPTER 7

"Are you sure you want to do this now?" Sheila asked.

Leon was pacing the conference room floor, furtively looking out the glass wall to see if anyone was approaching. "I came to last night, ancient history. I'm plenty ready." He breathed through his teeth and bounced on the balls of his feet.

"For you maybe. I'll be frazzled for another month. But I'm sure this meeting will be fine, what's the worst that could happen?"

"I'm not worried about worst, I'm just hoping for the best. When my parents—I mean when my adoptive parents . . . man, that sounds weird to say after all these years, doesn't it? Anyway, after Mom and then Dad passed I figured that was it for extended family on my side. Thank God I had you and then the boys."

"Yeah, I still think about Nancy's meatloaf. Never could duplicate that recipe."

"Yours is fabulous, Baby. Different, but still fab. Mom couldn't get the bacon just right."

"She didn't have maple bacon to work with."

"Yeah, that's good stuff." Leon looked through the glass again, then checked his appearance in the ghostly half reflection.

"I have to ask, just one more time. Are you sure you want me here for this?"

"Of course, Baby. You're my other half. I even thought about bringing the boys in, but I was afraid nobody would get a word in edgewise." They shared a smile.

"That would change the dynamic, wouldn't it?"

"Sure would. Let's just ease into this one step at a time. Plenty of time for everyone to get to know each other."

"This must be so weird for you. I'm on pins and needles myself."

"Oh, it's weird alright. Weird ain't the half of it. I should be playing with hippos on the Luangwa right now, but instead I'm here in a conference room—"

The polyphone on the table beeped and lit up. Leon answered, and the security guard announced they were heading up.

"OK. Thanks." Leon disconnected the call. He inhaled deeply and said "This is it, Baby," with the exhale.

An excruciating two minutes and twenty-two seconds passed before he saw the elevator doors open across the office floor. A security guard came out first, then stepped aside to hold the door.

For as long as he could remember, Leon had imagined this moment. Not happening this way, but happening somewhere, somehow. His parents had told him about his adoption earlier than most. They said it was important that he know, but that they loved him like he was their own flesh and blood.

They didn't have to say it again, they just did it. He didn't talk about it in school, barely mentioned it to Sheila after they'd been dating a while. But it was always there; somewhere in the back of his mind he simply knew this moment would come.

He even tried searching for his birth parents. Twice on the paper trail and several times after the internet became the great reuniter of long-lost family and friends.

Now here she was, walking across the office toward him. Mr. Daxton had required her to pass a maternity DNA test before allowing her into the complex. That cranky old prick. The doctors would be more than happy to study a parental link in the complex before the upcoming tests on him and Ryder.

He couldn't hold himself back any longer. He bolted through the conference room door, met her halfway across the open space and swept her up in a giant bear hug.

~~~

"That's right. I lost track of James after he went away to college. I never did find out what happened to him." Jennifer sipped her coffee. "I know people always say mushy stuff at times like this, but you really do have his eyes."

Leon put Sheila's coffee on the table in front of her, and sat down again with his fresh cup next to his banana peel rhino.

"I actually got a call through to someone who used to work with Dr. Neubauer, but they said he'd never see me. Said there was no way he'd be part of this media circus. She said that of the thirteen kids in his study, three sets of twins and one set of triplets have found each other. Two still don't know they have a twin, and then there's you and Ryder. I swear to you, Leon, I had no idea they were going to put you in that study."

"I know, I know." He reached across the table for her hand. "You couldn't have. You were just a scared teenager doing the best you could. Really, I can only thank you for not doing the opposite."

"That was not an option. After I found out I was pregnant, I became a good Catholic and that's exactly what I've been ever
~~~

since." She looked around. "You know, I've been working in an office sort of like this for a long time, but I never imagined meeting my son in a conference room."

"Yeah, I know what you mean. I guess I didn't know how it would happen, I'm just glad it finally did." He took his hand back and stood up to pace again. "I wish we could spend all day catching up on all the years, but I guess we have to decide what to do about meeting Ryder."

"He's coming back from the space station now," Sheila said. "Should be touching down in about an hour, I think. They got special clearance to land at Cape Canaveral so they could get here sooner."

"I have to say; I never thought in a million years you boys would end up famous. I dreamed it, but I wouldn't think it. I'm so proud of you, Leon."

"Well . . . I'm proud of you, too. It takes a lot of guts to walk into a frenzy like this is going to be."

"That's right," Sheila said. "Mr. Daxton agreed to let you meet Leon in private—well, we didn't give him a choice. But he says if we want to meet Ryder here it has to be televised, and there's no way he's letting Ryder out of the complex until after his next mission."

"That's six weeks from now," Leon said.

"They can't keep him locked up, can they?" Jennifer asked.

"I guess that's up to Ryder."

~~~

"First time we've had a crowd on the tarmac." Tammy slowed Allison for a turn and Ryder looked out the cockpit window. "Think we should taxi around the block a few times,
~~~

just to mess with 'em?"

"I like the way you think, Tammy. Always have. How come we haven't hooked up?"

"Because I don't like you."

"That's fair. Had to be at least one of you."

"Yeah, that and the dozen years I have on ya."

"You said it, not me."

"You couldn't keep up."

"Try me after this little parade." Ryder leaned forward to look past her. "OK, time to get this over with. Let's go knock that news van's antenna over into the crowd. Whaddya think?"

"C'mon, ya big stud. I know you're all talk. Just smile and wave like the politicians do. And don't fall down the stairs."

~~~

The dignitaries and VIP tourists had all gotten off the plane and waved properly for the cameras, as had Tammy. Ryder waited just long enough to make everyone wonder, then popped out the door at the top of the stairs. The crowd went as wild as a group of official invitees and their entourages can go. Ryder found each news camera and gave a wave and a big smile directly into it. There, that'll be the promo shot you can recycle a thousand times until the next breaking story.

He descended the stairs and shook hands with the Kennedy Space Center Director, the Vice President, two Generals from the Army, the Governor of Florida, and lastly Daxton.

Ryder leaned close to Daxton's ear. "You're really pissing me off, old man."

Daxton smiled big for the onlookers. "Sounds like your problem, not mine."
~~~

~~~

"Ladies and gentleman, could I have your attention please?" Daxton was at the podium in the atrium lobby of his headquarters, reveling in another moment of glory. The crowd of media and VIPs quieted down slightly, then entirely.

"Thank you. As you all know, this has been a very exciting time, not only for us here at Dax Space Corp., but for all mankind. We have now been further into space than anyone believed possible in so short a time after NASA went to the Moon. Commercial space tourism is flourishing, and it won't be long before we head for new frontiers.

"But for the moment, let me introduce you to one of the men who made this triumph possible. It's been said that 'You can't build a reputation on what you are going to do.'

"This man has done many things, and he deserves your praise. He served his country valiantly as an airman, and he has served mankind as an astronaut on three monumental missions. First, he went to Mars. Then he breached the heliosphere. And today, he returned from almost a thousand AU out in space, having positively confirmed the gravitational lensing effects predicted by Claudio Maccone.

"Ladies and gentlemen of the entire world, I would like to introduce Mister Ryder Pelse." Daxton raised his hands to welcome Ryder to the podium amid a sweeping round of applause.

Ryder took the podium, smiled, and waved as the accolades continued. Let them have their fun.

"Thank you, thank you very much." The noise started to subside. "I guess you already know a lot more about me than I do about you." The crowd had a good laugh.
~~~

"Seriously though, I'd like to thank Mr. Daxton for providing me with these incredible opportunities. Without him I wouldn't have realized my childhood dream of becoming an astronaut. No disrespect to NASA, but those budget cuts really suck." He shared another laugh with the crowd.

"Anyhow, I'm not much for speeches, so let's go straight to Q & A. I'll start with you." He pointed to a sharply dressed young woman near the front.

~~~

"I'm surprised it took so long for you to go there," Ryder said to the reporter. "Everybody all done with the space stuff?" he asked the crowd. There was a mix of clapping hands and shaking heads.

"Enough time for both, I guess. The answer to your question is 'yes'. I've heard about my twin brother and my birth mother. The answer to the follow up is 'no'. I haven't spoken to them yet. The answer to the next follow up is 'as soon as we're done here'. See, I don't need you guys, I can do this by myself."

"Mr. Pelse, I'm Edward Linnehan from the *Nation's Inquiry*."

"I've heard about you, too," Ryder said.

"Thank you." Edward seemed to miss Ryder's point. "Could you please confirm that you also experienced loss-of-consciousness during the flights, much the same as Mr. Berger?"

"No."

"Excuse me? . . . You didn't lose consciousness, or you can't confirm it?"

"Just no. Who wants to talk more about light speed?" he asked the crowd.
~~~

~~~

"Alright folks." Daxton took over the podium. "I think we've pretty much covered the highlights of the missions. Let's all thank Mr. Pelse for his insights." He paused for applause. "Thank you. Thanks so much. There'll be more details forthcoming on our web-site shortly. But before we wrap this up today, I think we can make time for a surprise."

Ryder shot Daxton a look that could pierce him as easily as a ten-inch bowie knife.

Daxton smiled and returned to the mic. "We have two special guests here who'd like to meet Mr. Pelse."

All but two eyes turned to the door opening at the side of the lobby. They were so intently watching Leon and Jennifer approach that they missed Ryder heading the other way for the stairs.

~~~

"What the fuck was that?" Daxton caught up to Ryder. The demand continued echoing up and down the stairwell while Ryder considered how to respond.

"Not in the mood."

"I don't give a shit what kind of mood you're in. Get your ass back in there and meet your goddamn family." Daxton was holding Ryder by the arm, but let go when he saw Ryder's glare.

"I'm just a fly-boy to you, right? You picked me because I don't have any attachments, right? So let me ask you this . . . Why the fuck are you messing with me?" The fire in his eyes was like an afterburner.

"Hey," Daxton held up his hands, "I don't want to play

Family Feud any more than you do. But it is what it is, and we have to figure out what's going on between you two."

"What are you talking about? I haven't even met him."

"Take a step back for a minute. Let's go big picture." Daxton leaned against the wall. "Are you still up for Flight 4?"

"Ready and willing."

"Perfect. Look, you don't have to meet the woman. Be an asshole if you want. But we have to let the docs figure this shit out so we can focus on the mission. How's it going to look if we launch you out there and Monkey-Boy blanks out again?"

~~~

"That's some bad hat, Harry," Ryder said to Leon.

"You talkin' about *Jaws* or Singer's vanity card?"

"What the fuck is a vanity card? I mean that stupid bathing cap with all the wires coming out of it. You look like Gallagher."

"You mean Leo or Ron?"

"Let's just say you look stupid," Ryder said.

"Yup. Yours is nice, too."

"Gentlemen," Davies said over the intercom. The men could see the doctors through the control booth glass, but couldn't hear through it. "We're ready to get started. Please just clear your minds, we're taking a baseline reading to compare with previous scans."

"Yeah, I don't have anything on my mind. Nothing at all," Ryder said.

"Everybody's stressed out," Leon said. "Just relax for a minute, you might like it."

"You gonna start chanting?"

"Might."
~~~

"Oh, great. My own personal Buddha."

"Ever tried it?"

"I prefer killing bad guys. Gives me that same sense of enlightenment."

"You have to wind down after that."

"Depends on whether more bad guys are coming."

"Nice." Leon shut his eyes and started regular, rhythmic deep breathing.

Ryder looked around the room. The installers had left a pile of drywall scraps and a few paint cans in the corner. They managed to fit a second fMRI machine in the lab by knocking down the wall to the next room. He really didn't want to waste time in that giant magnet with a tiny hole in the middle. The capsule was cramped enough.

"Gentlemen," Gajra said over the squawk box. "Just a few more minutes and we will get you in the fMRI."

"You know," Leon looked at Ryder. "You really should have met Jennifer. She's great."

"I had a mom."

"Awww, did you have a bad childhood?" Leon was tired of being nice to Ryder.

"It was fine. Guess I just didn't bond like you and Winnie."

"You talkin' about *The Wonder Years* or 'the Pooh'."

"I really can't win this game, can I?"

"Occupational hazard. I have to hang with Hollywood types between shoots."

"Figured your hazards all had sharp teeth and claws."

"Yeah. Hollywood types."

"Whatever."

~~~
~~~

"It's really quite fascinating," Davies said. He spun the 3D holographic brain images over the conference table, and waved his hand vertically to select a cross-section. He then pointed to a highlighted area just bigger than a grain of rice in both.

"Their pineal glands are radically different from everyone else. See? Right here between the hemispheres, at the apex of the spinal cord. This tiny gland, called 'pineal' because it looks like a pine cone, appears at first blush to be normal in both subjects. Except theirs is not calcified like many adults'. They're also not functioning as per normal. Not even the biological mother has this condition."

"What does it do?" McKinley asked.

"Normally, it would just be sitting there secreting melatonin and regulating circadian rhythms. But in this case there are a few neuronal cells either adjoining or commingled with the gland itself. We can't tell without an invasive procedure."

"So go get your drill," Daxton said.

Davies stood up straight. "I'm afraid that would be completely unethical. These men present no symptoms whatsoever when one of them is not flying through space."

"What else is different about their glands?" McKinley asked.

"We just discovered this situation. We haven't fully mapped it yet," Davies said.

"What do you think is different?" Daxton asked.

"What we know at this point is that it's constantly and steadily active, in a way very similar to regular neuronal brain activity, such as the DMN. Of course, this is completely atypical for a gland, since glands merely secrete chemicals. We have seen no increase or reduction in the electrical activity regardless of what the subjects are doing." Davies consulted his folder. "Sleeping, resting, problem solving, testing, anything. Doesn't matter if one is sleeping and the other is active. It didn't even change when we had Ryder confirm a simulated return trajectory."

"Anyone ever had theirs taken out?"

"Um... yes. A partial and sometimes a complete pinealectomy is performed when the gland has a cancerous tumour, typically caused by a germinoma."

"So cut it out."

"There is no quick fix, sir. We must study this thoroughly. We can't just excise it like some benign cyst. There are myriad negative side effects and possible complications associated with even a partial pinealectomy."

"Look, I need those two decoupled in short order," Daxton said. "Bassett bailed on me. Cold feet. I have exactly one remaining pilot who can fly the next mission, and he can't take his twin brother along for the ride."

"I understand that, sir," Davies said. "What I'm asking for at the moment is some time to collaborate with my colleagues. I need to share our findings with the scientific community and determine (a) whether anyone has seen anything like this before, and (b) whether anyone can formulate a plausible theory we can pursue."

"How much time?" McKinley asked. "We're scheduled to announce Flight 4 tomorrow."

"I can assure you there won't be any answers tomorrow. Please, let me start this process and I'll report back to you in a week."

"You'll report to us daily," Daxton said. "We'll hold the announcement for a week, two at the most."

~~~
~~~

FOR IMMEDIATE RELEASE
Contact: Hanlon
E-Mail: Inquiry@IAskOfLife.com

DAX TWINS ARE INTERCONNECTED
Pelse and Berger Have Odd Pineal Glands

Neuroscientists studying the twins at Dax Space Corp. have discovered an abnormality in their pineal glands. The issue was not previously discovered because the gland does not normally produce electrical brain activity, and neuroscientists were focusing on the quieting of the DMN both men experienced while Pelse was in flight. The twins' glands are now thought to have shut down along with the DMN.

It appears so far that this condition cannot be reproduced unless Pelse accelerates to near-c again. Dax has delayed the announcement of their next mission, pending the results of further research.

The French philosopher, René Descartes studied the pineal gland extensively in the 17th century. Although many vertebrates also have pineal glands, he was first to suggest that only humans have minds and that the mind interacts with the body via the pineal gland.

Descartes described the mind (or soul) as a nonmaterial entity able to interact with the body only through the pineal gland. Cartesian dualism has set the agenda for most philosophical discussion of the mind–body problem ever since. However, the vast majority of contemporary philosophers have abandoned the concept of an immortal soul in favor of a physicalist view.

Another theory being discussed is that of 'quantum entanglement' or the 'quantum non-local connection'. It is thought that some kind of quantum particles or process has connected the twins, such that when one reaches near light-speed the connection is broken, leading to the loss-of-consciousness and silencing of the DMN.

Even Albert Einstein, who co-founded quantum theory, found it lacking or incomplete in key respects. He derided entanglement as 'spooky actions at a distance'.

~~~

"How the hell is Hanlon doing this, Sean?" Daxton swirled the scotch in his glass while McKinley poured himself another.

"Got me. He's always one step behind and sometimes two steps ahead of us." McKinley waved his way through a cloud of Daxton's cigar smoke and collapsed into the armchair across from him. "You think there's another leak?"

"Probably. Could be Davies. Didn't get a chance to run him all the way through the ringer." Daxton paused to consider this. "Nah, this place is locked down tight. I know. I pay the goddamn bills every month."

"What about Gajra? She met Hanlon and she's as obsessed as Davies with figuring out the linkage thing."

"She's good people, I vetted her myself. I just wish we could find Hanlon or one of his pissy little minions and beat it out of them."
~~~

"I suppose we could run through the list of possibles in here again." McKinley sipped his scotch.

"Make Wilcutt do it. That's what I pay him for. But you keep with him every step of the way. You're the only one I trust anymore."

"Kinda boring waiting for results from the lab rats anyway."

"Knock yourself out." Daxton saluted with his lowball.

"The only thing Wilcutt said is that Khrunov's been taking more smoke breaks than usual."

"Of course he is," Daxton said. "Fine. Go ferret out whoever's doing this and do it fast. But don't drop the ball on Flight 4. We held off announcing it, but that doesn't mean I'm not going ahead with it."

~~~

"You got a minute?" Leon approached Ryder and threw a towel over the hand rail of a treadmill.

"Kinda busy." Ryder finished a set of leg curls and flipped over to start with presses.

"What's your problem, man?" Leon took a bite of his banana.

"Nothing. Just not into chatting while I push."

"Well, you're gonna." Leon sat down on the bench press opposite Ryder's machine. "Aren't you the least bit interested in what's going on here?"

"Sure. I was a good little guinea pig and sat in the boxes." Ryder strained with the effort of one more rep.

"I get the feeling that's only because you want the all-clear for the next flight."

"No shit, Columbo."

"You can't go until we figure this thing out," Leon said.
~~~

"Says you."

"Seriously? You wanna be a dickhead forever?"

"It's my thing."

"So you don't even want to talk about us?"

"There is no us," Ryder said. "Our DNA is just a closer match than anyone else on this silly rock."

"Hey, man." Leon stood and tossed his banana peel in the trash can. "I just threw down the olive branch, you gotta pick it up." He grabbed his towel and turned to leave.

"You pullin' chocks?" Ryder asked.

"What?" Leon turned back. "Um, yeah. I'll work out later."

"No, dipshit. I mean are you packing up Cartman and Kenny to head home?"

"Haven't decided yet."

"The docs got what they need, they'll figure it out."

"Maybe. But it's so much fun hangin' with my new bro'." Leon turned to leave again. "We'll stick it out a few more days, see what's what."

"Oh goody."

"And how did you manage to piss off poor Leon today?" Christine asked as she strolled into the gym.

Ryder groaned. "Can't a guy push in peace around here?" He finished another set of leg presses and grabbed his water bottle.

"He looked pissed on his way out, and, what a shock, I find you in here. It fits."

"I'm an asshole. I get it."

"The burning question on my mind is 'why?'"

"Just born that way." Ryder started a new set of leg

extensions.

"He's hot, you know. I always wondered what you'd look like with hair and a beard."

"Go for it."

"What, and break up that perfect little family unit? Not my style." She sat down on the machine next to him and pretended to do some butterfly presses. "I prefer the strong silent type who'll ignore me."

"You got it."

"Yes, I do." She stopped to stare at him. "And you're pissing me off too."

"What's new?"

"Come on, Stud. You don't have to be that way."

Ryder stopped and planted his feet on the floor. He looked at her directly for a moment, then shook his head and grabbed his water bottle.

"What? . . . What are you not telling me?"

"Why doesn't anyone get this?" He positioned for another set of reps.

"Just fucking tell me what you're thinking."

"It's personal."

"I get that Leon screwed up the next flight. Fine. But why take it out on me?"

"He didn't screw it up. The docs will figure this out."

"And if they don't?"

"Don't push me."

"Oooh, the big secret-and-none-more-secret Flight 4. Very mysterious." She wiggled her hands beside her face. "What is it with you space-nuts? I'm supposed to be shooting a documentary on it and Dad won't even tell me where you're going."

"Classified."

"Ya think?"

"Let it go."

"You mean, let you go."

He looked her straight in the eye. "Yes, that's exactly what I mean."

~~~

Hanlon entered the room and surveyed the situation. Never before had so many outsiders been in his home at one time. All eighteen were seated at the large round table in the banquet hall, along with one stenographer. There was no discussion, no fidgeting, no movement at all. The huge room with its vaulted and ornate ceiling was so quiet they could all hear the muffled drag of his Victorian chair's legs along the plush Persian rug. Now seated, he placed his hands palms down on the massive oak table and indulged himself in savoring the sheer potential energy of the room.

"Ladies and gentlemen . . . You have been invited here to partake in what will one day be described as the most consequential meeting of minds since the signing of the Magna Carta or even the Declaration of Independence. For those who accepted my invitation willingly, please also accept my thanks. For the remainder, please accept my apologies, and my assurance that your participation will not go unappreciated.

"Someone I once respected would gather a willing but unthinking flock and provide them false answers. This reluctant and learned council will guide humanity to the truth. A truth I have been searching for throughout my life. *Quaero Vitae*—I Ask of Life. The Answer is before us, and we must find it.
~~~

"You were chosen as arguably the best from a long list of candidates in each of your chosen fields. Some of you know each other personally, others do not. Many of you will at least be familiar with each others' work to some degree. Some of you are diametrically opposed to one another, others' views are complementary. We are seated as were King Arthur's Knights of the Round Table, such that all have equal status and importance.

"As you may or may not have heard, two men have been under study at Dax Space Corp. for two weeks now. One is Ryder Pelse, an astronaut. The other is Leon Berger, a wildlife expert and explorer. These men are identical twins manifesting some sort of external linkage that has never before been observed between two living creatures. My concern is that the research appears to be stalled, and that competing theories as to the nature of their interconnectedness cannot be resolved through conventional means. Hence, your presence here.

"You will be given ample time this evening to review all empirical and theoretical information pertinent to their case, and to prepare your initial presentations. I have made every effort to distill said findings to the barest essentials in order to provide parameters without advancing any given theory over another. Should additional information come to light, you will be apprised and we will reevaluate our then current position.

"Before we begin, permit me to establish the ground rules of this discourse. First, there is to be absolutely no profanity of any kind whatsoever. It is critical that you comply with this rule before all others." Hanlon indicated the armed guards around the room. There was one in each corner, two at each of the large double doors on either end of the hall, and God knows how many throughout the estate.

"Second, there is to be absolutely no interrupting, talking over another participant, dismissing of concepts, or unsanctioned side conversations. Your well-deserved egos are not welcome at this table. I intend to facilitate the free and open exchange of ideas, but it is crucial for the transcript and general comprehension within this room that everything said be heard loudly and clearly. An adjunct to that rule is that all discussion will be conducted in English.

"Third, you will address me only as Hanlon. You will address and refer to the other participants only by their title on the placard in front of them. To emphasize and be clear, please allow me to make one round of the table." He began pointing at each of the participants while reading their placard. "Neuroscientist, Geneticist, Biologist, Physicist, Astrobiologist, Astronomer, Aerospace Engineer, Bishop, Reverend, Rabbi, Imam, Buddhist Monk, Hindu Monk, Atheist, Skepticist, Ethicist, Politician, and last but not least, General.

"Fourth, and also last but definitely not least, we will continue the discourse for as long as is required to reach a practical consensus. Appropriate breaks for meals and rest will be afforded on an as-needed basis, as determined solely by me. You must understand that time is of the essence, although I expect some enlightening discussion on that topic from the more esoteric disciplines.

"Suffice it to say that we have external pressures necessitating a swift conclusion to these deliberations. To that end, I will summarize each premise as it comes up, and you will be required to vote on its acceptability. I understand that 'voting' is not part of the scientific method, but it is the most expedient means by which we--here in this room—can reach consensus and move forward swiftly. If you feel strongly that a particular consensus was reached too hastily or without all relevant information, you will be encouraged to spark further deliberation.

"I realize that we have some of the best minds in the world assembled here, and that you all hail from diverse disciplines. Let me simply state that I will be the ultimate judge as to whether you are contributing wholly and in good faith, and I alone will decide when we have reached either a consensus or an impasse.

"These rules are neither negotiable nor flexible. Having said that, I do hope you can appreciate the profound significance of the task we are about to undertake, and that you will embrace the sheer potential of the outcome as fully justifying this exercise and my tactics in bringing it to fruition.

"I appeal to the curiosity and insatiable thirst for knowledge that propelled you to become foremost in your field. You are better at what you do than seven billion other humans sharing this planet. Work hard and then rest well tonight; we convene at first light. This is an unprecedented and unique opportunity to unlock the greatest mystery mankind has faced since we first became self aware."

CHAPTER 8

Ryder lay on the bed in his quarters and stared at the ceiling. When the door buzzer sounded, he reached for the intercom button and said, "What?"

"Got a minute?"

"No."

"Come on, open up."

"I'm busy jerkin' off with a handful of thumb-tacks."

The door slid open and McKinley holstered his badge as he walked in. "This I have to see."

"Not in the mood," Ryder said.

"Still playing the tortured soul?"

"It's not a game. You know that."

"I do know that. OK, what's up?"

"Nothing."

"Having second thoughts?" McKinley asked. "Cold feet?"

"No."

"Convince me."

"You calling me a liar?" Ryder resumed his stare at the ceiling.

"No, just a jerk." McKinley walked to the bedside. "All the civilians are worried about you. Should I be too?"

"I'm fine. Just want to be left alone."

"Plenty of time for that later."

"Depends on who's there."

"Good point." McKinley nodded.

"Did the docs figure it out yet?"

"Still inconclusive. Love that phrase. They're always just a minute away from nailing it—until they aren't."

"We still have time."

"Not much. If we miss the window, that's a big push."

"You don't think I know that?" Ryder looked at him. "But a lot can happen between now and then."

"Oh sure, we could find another perfect destination next week." McKinley wasn't very good at sarcasm.

"I mean now and launch."

"Daxton won't wait. He's all about this one."

"So am I. I'm go." Ryder turned away.

"No matter what?" McKinley leaned over to look at Ryder.

"Balls out. You think I came this far to bail now?"

"Of course not, but things have changed. You have a family now."

"No I don't," Ryder said. "They don't mean any more to me now than they did two weeks or twenty years ago."

"You sure?"

"Big picture. That's the Curmudgeon's line."

"Yes, but any court would issue an injunction based on what would happen to Leon."

"Sucks to be him." Ryder looked back to McKinley. "Let 'em try to arrest me at the space station."

"Alright then." McKinley gave Ryder's foot a pat. "Just wanted to make sure you're still on board."

~~~
~~~

(AT 10:17 A.M. TO 10:31 A.M., CONFERENCE AT RECESS)

HANLON: We are reconvened. Some of you have not yet embraced the intended spirit of this conference. As you have seen, such outbursts will not be tolerated.

IMAM: You cannot continue holding us here against our will.

UNIDENTIFIED SPEAKERS: (VARIOUS OUTBURSTS)

HANLON: Order. You will all come to order or be dealt with even more harshly. I am sorely disappointed that some of you cannot see the importance of what we are here to discuss.

GENERAL: Does anyone mind if I have a cigar?

HANLON: That is not acceptable.

GENERAL: I brought enough to share.

HANLON: Silence. Let us resume our deliberation.

NEUROSCIENTIST: May I request clarification on a particular point?

HANLON: Please do.

NEUROSCIENTIST: Are we to assume that the 1977 incident at the nuclear reactor is a fact?

HANLON: Yes.

NEUROSCIENTIST: More specifically, can we be certain that the birth mother was in fact present at the time of the incident? And if so, can we determine her proximity?

HANLON: Relevance, please.

NEUROSCIENTIST: Last night I was trying to satisfy as many aspects of causality as possible. I count only six of nine.

HANLON: Clarification, please.

NEUROSCIENTIST: From an epidemiological perspective, I'd like to run through the Bradford-Hill criteria.[4] I'm afraid we can't reasonably confirm causality yet.

GENETICIST: You have a statistical sample of one, how will this be helpful?

HANLON: Are you pursuing a biological cause and effect?

NEUROSCIENTIST: Yes. It seems to me that if the incident was antimatter rather than nuclear, and we confirm the girl was within unprotected close range of the pulse, we may advance further toward establishing plausible causality.

HANLON: Details, please.

NEUROSCIENTIST: The nine criteria, more accurately called 'viewpoints', are: (1) Strength—it's true that our sample size is one, so by default we assign a strong correlation. (2) Consistency—we believe this hasn't happened before so consistency is irrelevant. (3) Specificity—the girl and the incident. Check. (4) Temporality—the cart and the horse. We agree the pregnancy was probably normal until the incident. (5) Biological gradient—that's where I was going with proximity. Was she close enough to receive a large dose of radiation? (6) Plausibility—I think we can all agree that a dose of x-rays and/or gamma rays would affect a zygote in some way, the most likely being genetic damage. (7) Coherence—same argument as plausibility. (8) Experimental evidence—we can rely on prior studies of radiation poisoning and its effect on biology. And finally, (9) Analogy—where clearly there can be none. By my count, we have two irrelevant, and six fairly certain. I'd like to confirm proximity to complete the evaluation.

HANLON: She was in a park near a baseball diamond, approximately 600 meters from Unit 1. We do not have exact figures on the antimatter pulse, but it was a practical test.

NEUROSCIENTIST: Excellent. In that case, for purposes of further discussion, I propose we classify the incident as causal to the abnormality of the twins.

HANLON: Vote, please.

STENOGRAPHER: 10 in favor, 7 opposed, 1 abstain.

HANLON: Premise accepted. Further discussion?

GENETICIST: If I may?

HANLON: Proceed, please.

GENETICIST: We are presented with identical twins having an abnormality of the pineal gland.

HANLON: Stipulated.

GENETICIST: We have considered causality only in relation to the defect itself. My review leads me to believe the causal event was further back.

HANLON: Clarification, please.

GENETICIST: Human twins occur in approximately one percent of all pregnancies. Of that one percent, thirty percent are monozygotic; what is commonly referred to as identical twins. No one knows exactly why twins occur; it's a common misconception that the mother passes on the gene for having them.

HANLON: Direction, please.

GENETICIST: Referring back to the point made by the Neuroscientist regarding plausibility, is it not even more plausible that the antimatter pulse actually caused the blastocyst to divide?

HANLON: Details, please.

GENETICIST: Given the following: (1) The statistical improbability that this particular girl would already be carrying twins—three tenths of a percent. It could be even less since she was under twenty-five years of age. (2) The coitus was approximately ten days before the incident and the study records indicate that the twins were MoMo, that is, both monochorionic and monoamniotic. This is consistent with an implanted blastocyst cleaving between day eight and thirteen after fertilization. The chance of MoMo twins is between one and two thousandths of a percent. And (3) The fact that they have an identical abnormal condition, presenting identically in both subjects, presumably caused by radiation and coincidentally involving some kind of link between the subjects.

HANLON: Your premise?

GENETICIST: I submit that the event caused both the twinning and their abnormality.

HANLON: Vote, please.

STENOGRAPHER: 15 in favor, 2 opposed, 1 abstain.

HANLON: Premise accepted. Further discussion?

HINDU MONK: Yes, please.

HANLON: Please proceed.

HINDU MONK: We may be seeing Adrsta at work with the astronaut twin.

HANLON: Some in the group may not be familiar with that concept.

HINDU MONK: Adrsta is commonly confused with Karma, but it is closer to what you would call fate or destiny.

HANLON: Details, please.

HINDU MONK: I believe we should consider that the astronaut was predestined to pilot this ship.

HANLON: How so?

HINDU MONK: Since we agree that the antimatter event caused the twinning, is it not also logical that the twin who would not have otherwise existed is now pilot for the ship so created?

HANLON: Vote, please.

STENOGRAPHER: 2 in favor, 15 opposed, 1 abstain.

HANLON: Premise rejected. Further discussion?

~~~

"OK guys, five more minutes in the pool," Sheila said from the deck of the dophin tank. The handlers were guiding Nathan in another swim while Leon was off to one side snorkeling with a different dolphin. They were both loving every minute of it. She turned to Christine and said, "You got enough footage, right?"

"Plenty. Cute little guys, aren't they?"

"They're not little, the big one there is nine feet long."

"I meant your boys."

"Oh, thanks. Yeah, but they're a handful." She turned to check on Felix who was sitting under a lone potted palm tree affording the only shady spot on the deck. He had already complained several times about not being able to see his 3D game in the sun, and he was getting more frustrated as Nathan kept swimming.

"Don't bang it, Feely. That won't help." To Christine she said, "I can't wait to get back home and play with the dolphins. I miss Rip Torn."

"Who?"

"He's the sort of alpha-male patriarch dolphin in Sarasota Bay. They call him that because his dorsal fin got split by a boat prop."

"Ouch. I hope he's OK."

"He's fine, that happened when he was, oh, maybe five or six years old, but he's almost thirty now and his DNA is all through the pods."

"Horny little bugger, is he?"

"Aren't we all?" Sheila asked.

"This should tide the guys over though, shouldn't it?"

"Oh, it's fine I guess. Very nice of your father to let them
~~~

swim. It's just that Leon and I aren't big fans of seeing animals in captivity."

"Better than making them dinner," Christine said.

"Of course. Sure it is. But they suffer so much in these tanks."

"I heard most of them get along with their trainers like friends."

"How many have attacked without warning?" Sheila asked. "The inmates might get friendly with the guards after a while, but they'll still take one out if they get a chance."

"Harsh."

"What about the dolphin in Japan that threw itself out of the tank?[20] That doesn't sound like someone happy with their living arrangements. It sounds like a suicide attempt."

"I guess a dolphin can get depressed, too." Christine was wrapping cables and packing the camera gear.

"There's no proof, but it sure seems like it."

"How long are you sticking around?" Christine zipped a pocket shut.

"Probably just a few more days. Dr. Davies wants to get Leon to a better research facility," Sheila said. "Oh, sorry, it's fabulous here and all, I just think there's some different equipment he wants to try."

"Ryder won't leave."

"I heard. Dr. Davies thinks he can still get some insight with just Leon for now."

"What's he like?" Christine asked.

"Dr. Davies? He's nice—"

"No, I mean Leon. Is he anything like Ryder?"

"Not really. It's kinda weird, but they're sort of opposites in a lot of ways."

"You mean Ryder is an asshole," Christine said.

"You said it, not me."

"Yeah, I said it."

"You two have a thing, don't you?" Sheila asked.

"How did you know?"

"Come on, Christine. Everybody knows."

"Hmm. I guess we weren't as quiet as we should be. You'd think the walls in a fortress would muffle—"

"Nice try, but I saw the way you looked at him in the meeting. And I don't think you would have pissed off your Dad by blocking the feed for just anybody."

"Yeah, well." Christine bent down and moved some spare batteries from one pocket to another.

"Look, all I can tell you is that Leon is great, and I love him. We're a team. That's the most important thing for a couple: make sure you're on the same team."

~~~

The cafeteria was nearly empty, which was typical so long after breakfast and before lunch.

While waiting for his turkey club sandwich, Davies asked Gajra, "What next?"

She gave him a puzzled look.

"I'm sorry. I mean where do we go from here? I'm at a loss."

"As am I. I no longer believe that repeating the differentiation tests will yield new information."

"Fine with me, because Ryder is getting tougher to deal with."

"Yes, he has been difficult lately." Gajra was carefully constructing a salad to her liking. "When do you expect your colleague in Cairo to contact you again?"
~~~

"I doubt it will be soon, he left for an extended vacation."

They collected their food and drink, then walked to the dining area. Neither of them bothered to look out the four-story glass wall to admire the spectacular view of the mangrove swamp and Turkey Creek. As they sat down in a booth, Gajra asked, "Do you believe we are stalled?"

"Pardon me?"

"Mr. Daxton is very concerned that we have made no further progress in the past several days."

"So am I. But this isn't a race, it's a scientific inquiry. These things take time."

"I agree. However, there are certain time constraints within which we must operate."

"I know, I know. Everything is a huge rush." Davies took a bite of his sandwich.

"Normally, I would agree that Mr. Daxton imposes unrealistic deadlines. However, in this case there is an added dimension of urgency."

"What's that?" he asked with a turkey-filled mouth.

"I am not allowed to disclose the timeline, but I must tell you that we have less than two days with both subjects present."

Davies swallowed hard. "What do you mean?"

"It is very likely that Mr. Berger will leave with his family on the weekend."

"Oh, no problem." Davies wiped his mouth with a napkin. "I talked to Sheila. They want to leave, but I can get them to stay as long as it takes to figure this out."

"On what basis should we keep them here?"

"Because we haven't figured anything out yet. Everyone really needs to know what's going on." Davies saw her waiting for more, and said, "You mean, what tests should we perform next."

"Yes. It seems to me that the only way to induce any sort of reaction between the twins is to accelerate one to near-c."

"Have Daxton take Leon for a spin down Alligator Alley in that Ferrari of his. Then we'll see what happens to Ryder."

Gajra smiled, but only briefly. "I am frustrated by the lack of new direction."

"I understand. You left academia a long time ago, Gajra. In this palace with Daxton's unlimited budgets you can get almost anything done faster than a university prof can fill out a grant request."

"It is not that. I have this feeling that we are looking down the wrong road."

"Clearly. I just wish we knew which road to take next."

"Do you have any intuition about this?"

"Oh, let's not go down that road. This thing is confusing enough without bringing gut feelings and hunches into it."

"Many problems have been solved in this way."

"True. I just don't think we've scraped the bottom of the logical barrel yet."

Davies poured vinegar over his french fries. Gajra cringed.

"Oh, sorry. It's a Canadian thing."

"I see." But she really didn't. "Can you tell me your hunches? Perhaps they may spark a logical direction of enquiry."

"I just feel like we're missing something related to the abnormality of the pineal gland."

"How so?"

"We've been through every test we can think of, and they respond like any normal, healthy pineal glands would; except for the extra neuronal activity. I still say we should take the twins to UAB."

"I am afraid Mr. Daxton will not allow Mr. Pelse to leave the complex until after his next mission."

"But they're doing amazing things in Birmingham. They have the latest MagnetoLink. It has combined EEG and ERPs with fMRI in real-time, and a magnet with a Tesla rating out of this world."

"I really don't think—"

"I saw the current version in operation back at U of C. It was phenomenal. If we could get both of them in a unit like that, even separately, it would—"

"You can take Mr. Berger, but—"

"We need both, don't you think?"

"We do, but I am afraid that will not be possible."

"Gajra, they have a 10 Tesla fMRI there, fully integrated with 1024-channel EEG and ERP. State of the art stuff. How can we not take them there?"

"It is simply not possible."

"You can keep saying that, but I'll keep wondering if it's true."

"You need to accept that Mr. Pelse must remain here. Both Mr. Daxton and Mr. Pelse are adamant about this."

They both ate in silence for a minute, then asked in unison, "What if it's not just the pineal gland?"

~~~

"I'm Bruce Phillips, and the noon-hour news begins anew on the Wolfe Report—right now. Our top story today continues to be the possible mysterious disappearances of several prominent intellectuals from around the world.

"Officials from various countries have been collaborating to
~~~

determine if there's any link between key figures from many different walks of life who have allegedly disappeared or been reported missing in the past two days. With the addition of two more Nobel Laureates this morning, and the subtraction of a few actors who might like to be on this list, the total count now stands at eleven.

"That's four clergy, two scientists, two philosophers—who are probably just out thinking on a mountain—and as of late this morning an astronomer who missed his speaking engagement, along with an aerospace engineer who's become unreachable on vacation. The Army has also reported the possible disappearance of an unnamed General, but they also said that's not confirmed yet.

"For details on the astronomer, we turn to Margaret Atwan who is on location at Yale's Leitner Planetarium lecture hall with some very disappointed students and faculty."

~~~

AEROSPACE ENGINEER: It's a Fermi problem, but given the following: (1) The proven range of the Dax ship at one thousand AU. (2) The engineering data from Dax's web-site augmented with the few additional details provided as well as some assumptions. And (3) The limited time available for detailed analysis; I submit a first order approximation that the practical range of the Dax ship would be four orders of magnitude greater.

HANLON: Premise conditionally accepted without soliciting consensus.

ASTRONOMER: You're suggesting that the ship could travel ten million rather than just one thousand AU?
~~~

AEROSPACE ENGINEER: Yes, my first order is two exameters.

HANLON: Life support requirements, please.

AEROSPACE ENGINEER: Well, we typically factor astronauts with distances on this scale only in theoretical terms, but the Physicist calculated the relative ship time to be approximately nine months each way. Given that the astronaut in question is rendered comatose in flight, entertainment is not a requirement. An automated life support, feeding, and waste disposal system would be sufficient. Basically, a closed ecological system.

BIOLOGIST: Dr. Robert Fitts at Marquette found that muscular atrophy becomes a serious issue at six months.[3] An average astronaut would lose approximately twenty percent of their muscle mass even with regular exercise in the ship. In the worst case as much as forty percent. The loss in muscle power approaches forty-five percent as the muscles become not only weaker but slower. A thirty year-old becomes like an eighty year-old after a trip like that, although they can recover after returning to Earth. In a coma the effect would be far worse.

AEROSPACE ENGINEER: Agreed. Even though the astronaut is an exceptionally fit individual, we have to conclude that the practical range would be half of that postulated, or nine months total.

HANLON: Potential destinations within that range?

ASTRONOMER: The logical destination for a single-rider manned mission with no significant payload capacity would be an exoplanet.

HANLON: Clarification, please.

ASTRONOMER: An exoplanet, or extrasolar planet is one orbiting a star other than our Sun. Of primary interest for our discussion are those in what's called the habitable zone, more commonly referred to as the 'Goldilocks Zone' because it's just right for supporting life as we know it. There have been dozens of missions cataloguing such planets since the early '90s, and of course SETI has been around since the '60s. NASA's JPL maintains a catalogue at PlanetQuest[24], but to date they've found only a few probable Earth-like planets. There is one though, that might fit the bill.

HANLON: Details, please.

ASTRONOMER: Some idiot paid fifty bucks to name the star after his wife, but the IAU-recognized name is '30 Ari B'. I'll refer to it as 'Ari' for sake of discussion here. It's an F-type star, similar to the Sun but slightly warmer and larger. It has a planet called '30 Ari B b', having about ten times the mass of Jupiter and an elliptical orbit averaging close to one AU from the star. This means it's about the same solar distance and orbital period as the Earth in relation to our Sun. What makes this solar system unique, as far as we can tell, is the existence of a very Earth-like planet in a binary orbit with the larger planet.

HANLON: Is this widely known?

ASTRONOMER: It hasn't been publicly announced because several teams are working on confirmation, but it's tentatively been dubbed 'BiTerra', for 'second Earth' or 'two Earths'. There's an ongoing debate as to whether this is truly a double planet system or merely a planet-moon configuration. But the salient point is, that's the only place currently projected to be as close to perfect for carbon-based life forms as we've ever seen. Well, apart from Earth, of course.

HANLON: Could this be confirmed with a space-based telescope at Lagrange Point 3?

ASTRONOMER: That would depend on the type and capabilities of the telescope. I am not familiar with a mission in that space.

ASTROBIOLOGIST: I concur with the Astronomer's position regarding BiTerra. Many years of searching, even with the relatively new Kepler mission, and this is still the only viable candidate, assuming it turns out to be. If they could send the Dax ship close enough and return pictures and data as detailed as they took from Mars, they would advance our understanding tenfold.

ASTRONOMER: It should also be noted that SETI's Big Ear radio telescope received a signal just thirty-three days after Mr. Daxton's initial antimatter test in 1977. The seventy-two second pattern was dubbed the 'Wow!'[1] signal, but has not been detected since, so it can't be confirmed as non-random. The signal did not originate near Ari, and could have been a reflection of some kind.

HANLON: The group is to classify the SETI Wow signal as 'unlikely involvement; probable coincidence'.

PHYSICIST: Clarification on a prior point?

HANLON: Please proceed.

PHYSICIST: His relative ship-time would be 5.6 months each way to BiTerra; more than eleven months total.

HANLON: Stipulated.

PHYSICIST: Could he survive that?

BIOLOGIST: He would suffer severe deterioration, but given his initial level of fitness, I think he would probably survive.

HANLON: Vote, please.

STENOGRAPHER: 11 in favor, 3 opposed, 4 abstain.

HANLON: Premise accepted. Further discussion?

~~~
~~~

FOR IMMEDIATE RELEASE
Contact: Hanlon
E-Mail: Inquiry@IAskOfLife.com

DAX'S NEXT MISSION TO AN EARTH-LIKE EXOPLANET

Einstein's Twin Paradox Would Play Out

The fourth mission for Ryder Pelse in the Dax Space Corp. antimatter ship will be to an Earth-like exoplanet orbiting the star '30 Ari B', some 128 light-years from Earth. NASA's JPL PlanetQuest has confirmed the detection of this planet which appears to reside in the 'Goldilocks Zone' of its solar system, meaning conditions are just right for supporting extraterrestrial carbon-based life forms similar to those on Earth. PlanetQuest has not published the planet's discovery pending independent corroboration and confirmation. The planet is informally being referred to as 'BiTerra', for 'second Earth' or 'two Earths'.

Although 128 light-years from Earth, the flight to BiTerra will appear to last only 5.6 months from Pelse's perspective in the capsule, due to the ship's near-c capabilities and a phenomenon called time dilation predicted by Einstein in his Theory of Special Relativity.[2]

Former Dax astronaut Captain John Bassett has confirmed his withdrawal from consideration for the mission. He cited family ties and concern for astronaut safety on the mission itself, primarily due to the unexplained loss-of-consciousness and muscular atrophy during the journey. No other pilots have come forward.

This would not bode well for Pelse's twin brother, Leon Berger. Doctors have been unable to determine what is causing the loss-of-consciousness episodes both men experience during the flights. If they cannot and Pelse was to make this flight, Berger would surely perish while lying unconscious waiting for his brother to return.

~~~

Sheila plowed through the door of the workout center, then ran straight to Ryder and slapped his face as hard as she could. He didn't try to duck.

"You son-of-a-bitch! You're going to kill my husband so you can joy-ride around the universe?"

"To paraphrase Spock and Kirk, 'The needs of the many outweigh—'"

"We're not playing, dude." Leon caught up with and restrained Sheila.

"Neither am I," Ryder said.

"He's a father! You can't do this!" Sheila was shrieking through furious tears.

"I can, and I will," Ryder said.

"It's murder!" Sheila hit a frequency Leon knew only bats could reach.

"Involuntary manslaughter at worst. There's no intent, it's just bad luck."

"Oh my God! You're a fucking sociopath!" She struggled in Leon's arms, but he held her firm.
~~~

"Seriously dude, this is not cool."

McKinley and two security guards stormed in.

"Alright, break it up," McKinley said.

"I'll kill him!" Sheila said. Leon gave the guards a look that indicated he had her under control, and they should back off.

"Conference room. Five minutes." McKinley turned and walked out.

~~~

"Knock it off, Sheila." Daxton stormed into the conference room. "Everyone sit the hell down." They did. "OK . . . fucking Hanlon has gone too goddamn far this time. I want to know how in the name of anything holy he found out." Daxton waited a few seconds, then pounded the table. "Right now, 'fess up!"

"I really don't give a shit how anyone found out," Sheila said. "The point is, you're going to kill my husband."

"Not technically," Gajra, Ryder, and Daxton said in chorus.

"Bullshit!" Sheila didn't know who to slap first. She moved to stand up and Leon grabbed her arm. Their eyes locked and he managed to both reassure and calm her in an instant. She settled in her chair and began worrying her handkerchief.

"Listen folks," Leon said, "I understand it's real important to you that someone go check out this second Earth. But we haven't even figured out what's going on with this one yet."

"That's exactly why we need to go," Ryder said.

"Really? We made a mess on this one, so let's go find another one?"

"There's more to it than that," McKinley said.

"So what? You can't just light up a rocket when innocent people are standing under it." Sheila had somewhat composed
~~~

herself.

"Who's going to admit they snitched?" Daxton yelled which set Sheila off which pissed Leon off which made the guard come over which got Christine in between which got Ryder out of his chair which made Gajra and Davies scoot which made McKinley purse his lips and let out a shrill and sustained whistle.

"Come on, people." McKinley gathered their attention. "Let me address these things one at a time. If you'll all just take a deep breath and calm down, I can explain what the issues are."

Ryder wandered back to his chair.

"Everybody breathing in both directions now?" McKinley asked. "Good. First of all, nobody told Hanlon. Wilcutt and I have vetted everyone and can't find any evidence. Let's table that for a minute. Now, since you all know where Ryder is going, let me tell you why."

"This better be good," Leon said.

"BiTerra is important for several reasons, based on, but not limited to it being Earth-like," McKinley said.

"Earth-like," Davies said, "as in already having developed an oxygen-rich atmosphere?"

"That's right," McKinley said. "It's a common misconception that an Earth-like planet wouldn't already have life on it, because in our case it was early life here that developed the atmosphere we have now."

"What do you mean?" Christine asked.

"He means that our oxygen was developed as a byproduct of photosynthesis by the first autotrophs," Davies said. "It's a big stretch to expect an atmosphere like ours on a barren planet."

"Exactly," McKinley said. "Now, a couple of months ago, we detected radio signals we think originated from BiTerra. Nothing major, not enough to stir anything up, but we believe they are probably artificial. SETI can't confirm because they weren't listening there, and we don't intend to tell them until Ryder is on his way."

"I really need you to tell me why this justifies murder." Sheila was remaining as calm as she could.

"I'm getting to that," McKinley said. "As you heard, this planet is 128 light-years away. That means that Marconi's first radio transmissions haven't even gotten from here to there yet. The fact that BiTerra is probably Earth-like, and that we detected potentially artificial but still primitive radio signals from it would seem to mean there's intelligent life there."

"So what?" Sheila said. "They're not bothering us."

"Our thinking is that by some astronomical coincidence, they're on a similar developmental schedule to us, perhaps way ahead. Of course, that's a ridiculous stretch without confirmation, which is one reason we need to send Ryder."

"Who put you in charge?" Leon asked.

"I did," Daxton said. "The minute those morons at the U.N. formed UNOOSA, I knew they couldn't be trusted with the truth."

"Unoosa?" Leon and Sheila asked.

McKinley said, "It's the United Nations Office of Outer Space Affairs."[27]

"You're kidding," Sheila said.

"No, they're actually serious," McKinley said. "They even appointed a Malaysian astrophysicist named Mazlan Othman as Earth's ambassador to anyone who shows up and says 'Take me to your leader'."

"Oh my God." Sheila flopped her arms on the chair's arms and looked straight up.

"I know," McKinley said. "That was our reaction. We knew

these people couldn't be trusted with handling an actual ETI encounter."

"You mean, like E.T.?" Sheila asked.

"Yes, but with an 'I' for intelligence," Daxton said.

"Is it still illegal when a U.N. official takes a bribe with currency from another planet?" Ryder asked. "If a BiTerran and an Earthling get into a fight and neither is Jewish, how will the U.N. decide which one to condemn?"

"That's enough, Fly-Boy," Daxton said.

"No, wait. I got a million of 'em. To join the U.N., would an alien have to be a planetary despot, or is oppressing one BiTerran nation good enough?"

"Can I continue?" McKinley asked.

"The more important point," Daxton said, "is what happens to us if they get here first like Columbus, making us the natives? Even Hawking thinks that's possible."

"We're getting ahead of ourselves," McKinley said. "Let's table the ETIs for a minute, too. Now, as you all figured out, Leon will be in harm's way when Ryder launches."

"You mean *if*," Leon and Sheila said.

McKinley looked at Daxton and got a slight nod. "OK, if. Now, unfortunately there are two reasons why Ryder is the only one who can make this flight."

"I'm not sold on why yet," Sheila said.

"Fine." McKinley sighed. "The scientific knowledge we'd—"

"Don't go there," Sheila said.

"How about natural resources?" Daxton asked. "You green-weenies got a problem with us buying all of mankind a little more time? Or maybe even colonizing another planet?"

"Ah, the truth shall be revealed," Leon said. "He's in it for the money."

"Fuck you!" Daxton said. "I've spent more money on this thing than most countries' GDP for a decade. I've taken us from firecrackers to Ferraris. Don't get all pissy about saving the spotted owl when I'm in a position to save the entire fucking planet!"

"At what cost?" Leon asked.

"You want to lecture me on costs?"

"I'm just saying that if no one expected guys like you to bail us out of a jam, we might take better care of what we have."

"There's no talking sense to their kind," Daxton said.

"Let me keep trying," McKinley said.

"Why bother?" Sheila asked. "There's nothing you can say that makes it OK to kill my children's father."

~~~

Hanlon sat in his study with his headphones on. He listened carefully, rewinding and fast-forwarding as necessary. He took great pleasure in what he was hearing. Mr. Pelse's joke about UN officials accepting bribes was especially salient.

It was sometimes frustrating to wait for the bribed Dax guards to upload files from the voice-activated MP3 players they'd hidden in the complex.

With Daxton's constant bug-sweeps and monitoring of the airwaves around their building, the only safe place from which a guard could unidirectionally transmit was the outdoor smoking area.

~~~

(At 12:33 p.m. to 1:55 p.m., conference at recess)

Hanlon: We are reconvened. Please accept my apologies for the unavoidably extended lunch hour. It seems we have a new direction for the moment. We will now consider the possibility of alien life.

Astrobiologist: Dr. Richard Hoover, an astro-biologist at NASA's Marshall Space Flight Center, says he found evidence of bacterial alien life on a meteorite[5]—

Hanlon: Forgive my lack of clarity. We are to discuss first contact with an ETI, or extra-terrestrial intelligence.

Astronomer: Both the Drake Equation and the Dole Equation are fascinating thought experiments, made even more interesting by Dr. Claudio Maccone's SEH[8], which is—

Hanlon: For the record, 'SEH'?

Astronomer: Ah yes, it means 'Statistical Equation for Habitables', which is the most current attempt to determine how many planets could sustain life as we know it. But the Fermi Paradox still leaves us wondering whether we're alone in the universe.

Astrobiologist: Agreed. There are countless volumes and theories on the subject. May I ask which facet we are to explore?

Hanlon: Reaction of the public at large.

Astronomer: Our surveys indicate that the public at large is generally split sixty-forty in favor of believing that some form of ETIs exist. Of the sixty percent in favor, roughly three quarters believe ETIs are as advanced or more advanced than we are.

Politician: There is a reason that governments keep UFO investigations classified. The public could not deal with proof positive.

BISHOP: If I may?

HANLON: Please do, Bishop. Good of you to join the conversation.

BISHOP: I have had many such discussions within my diocese, and I believe people can generally be categorized in one of two ways. Either they accept the notion that ETIs, as you call them, exist, or they do not. Both sides present a significant challenge.

HANLON: Details, please.

BISHOP: Genesis 1:1

In the beginning, God created
the heavens and the earth.

HANLON: Relevance, please.

BISHOP: Note the distinction, 'the' Earth, as opposed to 'an' Earth.

HANLON: Continue.

BISHOP: John 10:16

I have other sheep,
which are not of this fold;
I must bring them also,
and they will hear My voice;
and they will become
one flock with one shepherd.

BISHOP: Some people infer that God has indeed created races of other humans on other planets. However, the Church interprets this verse as differentiation between Jews and Gentiles. Physical life cannot arise from non-life. Every race would have its Adam, and if another Adam has not yet fallen into sin, then his race must be under strict Divine orders to avoid contact with humans until the hour of temptation comes to pass.

HANLON: The Church's position is understood. Please explain the two categories of people within your diocese.

BISHOP: Those who believe man is a singular miracle simply denounce the very notion of ETIs. Those who do not are frankly unprepared for the reality, if it were actually presented to them.

IMAM: I disagree. In America there are many interfaith marriages and interfaith friendships that were historically forbidden by doctrine.[14]

HANLON: Relevance, please.

IMAM: Many people are growing to believe whatever they wish to believe. Even the Pope finally declared that Purgatory is not a 'place', it's now called 'condition of existence'.[13]

SKEPTICIST: And even more recently the Pope approved a theological report that freed the souls of un-baptised babies from limbo.[12]

HANLON: I must insist upon relevance.

IMAM: If this Mr. Daxton says he found life on another planet, those who wish it to be so will believe, and those who do not will deny it.

SKEPTICIST: There's no convincing evidence of ETIs, and no convincing probability that society will freak out. It's a non sequitur.

ASTROBIOLOGIST: I must concur with the majority view. We in the scientific community are well accustomed to discussion of ETIs as accepted but eventual fact. However, for the public at large it would present another Copernican revolution.

~~~
~~~

"It's like we started a pissing contest with a skunk," Christine said. "Let's go back to why it has to be Ryder."

"Up the ante," Sheila said to McKinley, who was watching Leon's banana peel eel begin to take shape.

"Well, as I stated," McKinley said. "There are two reasons Ryder is the only one who can make this flight. One, he's physically fit enough to handle the atrophy."

"Bullshit," Sheila said. "Are you saying none of NASA's guys have the right stuff?"

"Bassett could have done it," Christine said.

"Bassett is a coward," Daxton said.

"It's true," McKinley said, "John could have handled the flight. Unfortunately, his withdrawal and a lack of qualified volunteers bring up the second reason Ryder is best for this mission. He's the only one who is willing and able."

"Why?" Christine pleaded with Ryder. "Why?"

"Because it's there."

"Not buyin' it." Leon scrapped the peel eel. "I've been there, and I've risked my life there . . . and there isn't the same there you're talking about."

"OK, fine. Everyone wants to roll around in the space-jockey's head, then fine. How about I rattle off the obvious reasons first? I get to be the first human being to outlive his lifespan. I won't get back 'til two thirds through the 23rd century, and maybe things will be better, maybe they won't. But I'll get to see it. I'll be Rip Van Winkle without the wrinkles."

"Well hoo-ray for Botox," Sheila said.

Ryder ignored her. "I might be the first human to see an alien civilization. Maybe they're bad guys, maybe they're not. But if they're scary, I get to be the guy who sounds the alarm. It's Paul Revere time, planetary-style."

"Nope. Too selfless. Doesn't fit." Sheila shook her head.

"Cork it," Ryder said. "I'll decide what matters to me, you just keep trying to save your hubby over seven billion other people."

"Don't get personal, dude," Leon said.

"Why not? This whole thing is absolutely personal. From the Curmudgeon building his legacy to McKinley tagging along to the docs Jonesin' for a Nobel Prize. Why can't I play?"

"Because they're not killing anyone!" Sheila said.

"Don't be so sure. Besides, collateral damage happens all the time, and you're just fine with it," Ryder said.

"What the hell are you talking about?" Sheila asked.

"If you can't back it up, don't spit it out," Leon said.

Ryder turned to McKinley and said, "They're so cute when they're young, aren't they?" To Sheila he said, "We sacrifice thousands every year so we can drive to the mall. We kill thousands of innocents so we can keep the right dictators in place and keep the oil flowing. We let millions starve because we're afraid to take out the warlords who keep the aid for themselves. We sacrifice friendlies in an unwinnable drug war to keep assholes back home from committing pharmaceutical suicide. In the grand scheme of things, how is losing just one TV-guy really going to collapse society?"

"You're right, Baby. He is a sociopath," Leon said to Sheila over Christine's sobbing. To Ryder he said, "If you're right, I don't want to be."

"Of course I'm right, but I'm an optimist too. And I still think this Pale Blue Dot is worth saving."

Chapter 9

Hanlon: Very well, I believe that concludes the lion's share of our precursory discussion. We shall now move toward the meat of the matter as it were. The primary idea that prompted me to assemble this conference. Based on the secret ballots cast earlier this morning, I have rearranged your seating into three groups under admittedly broad labels. It surprises me to see where some of you now sit.

Politician: If I may?

Hanlon: Please hold questions until I am through. Those of you starting to my left have identified yourselves as dualists, in the sense that you firmly support the concept of something like a soul as an entirely separate entity from the body. Some of you ascribe a form of incorporeal immortality to the soul, along with the existence of a higher power, supreme being, or universal intelligence.

Imam: Clarification, please?

Hanlon: Not at this time. Those to my right are self-described physicalists, in the sense that you fundamentally subscribe to the theory that everything, including man's mind, thoughts, consciousness, morals, and subjectivity can be explained through physical phenomena, most likely brain function.

Hanlon: (Off the record discussion at sidebar.)

Hanlon: Those roughly across from me at this round table have equivocated in one way or another, so I have grouped you as agnostic in the sense that you have either not made a specific decision regarding this premise, or you believe the answer is unknown or unknowable. Unfortunately, your input will be less valuable to the upcoming discussion, so I must ask that you participate only when you have firm convictions that can shed light on the topic at hand.

POLITICIAN: If I may?

HANLON: Yes.

POLITICIAN: I'd like to change my seat.

HANLON: Have you received new information or reconsidered your position?

POLITICIAN: I misunderstood the ballot.

HANLON: That is irrelevant to our purpose. Everyone here is encouraged to argue for or against a given hypothesis regardless of their stated position. The seating arrangement is simply a means to facilitate like-minded collaboration during formal subcommittee discussions, such that the dualists and physicalists may elect a spokesperson to present their group consensus succinctly.

SKEPTICIST: If I may?

HANLON: Yes.

SKEPTICIST: I understand the two primary theories put forth, one that the twins have a single soul between them, the other that there is some form of quantum entanglement. I'd like to propose a third option.

HANLON: Direction, please.

SKEPTICIST: We're all familiar with the falsifiability arguments around religion, theism, and the supernatural, so let us stipulate those issues as a matter of individual faith. I'd like to examine your claim that the 'twins are manifesting some sort of external linkage that has never before been observed between two living creatures'.

HANLON: Details, please.

SKEPTICIST: Yes, thanks. A basic example of a falsifiable statement is 'All humans live forever'. Produce one dead human, and the theory is debunked. A more practical example would be something like 'The fossil record validates the Theory of Evolution'. The fact that no one has yet discovered a Jurassic fossil in Cambrian rock strata is taken as evidence that all fossils are ordered chronologically. But imagine a human fossil in the same sedimentary layer with a trilobite, or even a Tyrannosaurus rex. That would certainly throw the Darwinians for a loop.

REVEREND: That's why it's still referred to as the *Theory* of Evolution.

GENETICIST: Don't get carried away now, Reverend. Evolution is a fact. Hopefully, everyone understands that species change genetically over time. The theory is just our attempt to explain how and why it happens.

REVEREND: It hasn't been proven.

GENETICIST: Technically, no theory has been *proven*. No one should doubt that gravity is a fact—even if Newton and Einstein can't explain it fully. We attempt to explain facts with theories, which are always subject to revision in light of new evidence.

REVEREND: Evolution still has its problems.

GENETICIST: I understand you're still worried that it negates Christianity because you can't figure out exactly which two hairless apes were Adam and Eve.

HANLON: That is enough. Direction, please.

SKEPTICIST: Thanks again. My point is that simply because we haven't seen anything like the twins' external linkage before doesn't make it relevant on its own. It manifests only when the astronaut gets to near-c, which is the first time anyone has done that before, but we can't say for certain that it's a unique condition.

HANLON: And the alternative?

SKEPTICIST: It's just as likely there are thousands or even millions of linked people or animals all over the planet right now. A very small percentage of the world's population has been in an MRI machine.

HANLON: Vote, please.

STENOGRAPHER: 6 in favor, 9 opposed, 3 abstain.

HANLON: Premise rejected. Further discussion?

HANLON: Very well, moving on. What I would like at this time is for each subcommittee to confer separately and elect a foreman to present the consensus view to the overall conference. Please begin.

~~~

"This is torture," Ryder said. "How many times do we have to go over this?"

"As many as it takes to keep you out of that ship," Sheila said.

"That ain't gonna be long."

"What's he talking about?"

"He means we have to launch Flight 4 very soon," McKinley said.

"Like the day after tomorrow," Daxton said.

"Why?" Leon, Sheila, and Christine asked altogether.

"I thought we had another month," Christine said.

McKinley looked to Daxton for approval and got it. He said,
~~~

"BiTerra is either in a binary orbit or it's a moon to the larger planet. Either way, it presents significant challenges in determining the clear-path."

"Like what?" Leon asked.

"Like the view of the clear-path I got on Flight 3 was over a hundred years old," Ryder said.

"And?"

"And there's a lot of stuff between us and BiTerra. It's risky enough even factoring in orbits and viewable asteroids."

"Then don't go," Sheila said.

"You wish," Ryder said.

"People," McKinley said. "Ryder has to come to all stop within close enough range of the planet to collect usable data."

"So what?" Christine asked.

"So if we don't go now, it'll be sixty-plus years before we can try again," Daxton said. "It's now or never."

"Doesn't sound like never," Leon said.

"So you'd rather play wait-and-see with our planet," Daxton said.

Christine smacked the table. "Would you please quit with all the flashing-red-light we're-all-gonna-die this is an immediate emergency proclamations!"

"How about educate-and-hope?" Leon asked.

"Hope doesn't move the ball forward," Daxton said. "We already told you we don't know who's out there, friend or foe. You already admitted that people here are hopelessly determined to chew this planet up and spit out the pit. You really want to ride that out when we have options?"

"Selfishly, yes," Leon said. "I don't want to spend the rest of my days in a coma."

"Typical one-finger flag-saluter," Daxton said. "Everyone else stop your destruction and recycle your tin foil while he flies around snapping pictures of tree frogs. It's all about him; do as he says not as he does."

"You're really starting to piss me off," Leon said.

"I've been pissed at him for a long time," Sheila said.

"I'm pregnant," Christine said.

Ryder stopped twirling his pen and stared at her. His expression morphed from disbelief to shock to anger in an instant. "Why are you telling me this?"

"Because it matters," Christine said. "You have obligations here. You can't go."

"She's not pregnant," Daxton said. "Gajra would have told me."

"That is correct," Gajra said. "Your pregnancy test was negative."

"OK, fine." Christine's voice cracked. "But didn't it make you think for even a second that you shouldn't go? Can't you imagine how brutal this is for Sheila and their kids? What kind of monster are you?"

"No room for baggage on this flight," Ryder said.

"Are you kidding me right now?"

"Lesser of two evils."

Christine put her head in her hands and started sobbing while Sheila moved to console her.

Leon said, "Glory built on selfish principles is shame and guilt."

"Oh, so you want to play some more."

Leon gave Ryder a long once-over, then said, "No, I don't want to play. I want to know if a jury would buy self-defense if I killed you right here, right now."

~~~
~~~

HANLON: Have the dualists reached a consensus?

BISHOP: Tentatively.

HANLON: Proceed, please.

BISHOP: We conditionally agree that the evidence presented suggests the sharing of a single soul between the twins. However, we cannot endorse this hypothesis.

HANLON: Clarification, please.

BISHOP: For lack of definitive proof, we feel this could not have happened. As a result, we reject the notion that it has.

HANLON: Justification, please.

BISHOP: Notwithstanding the various positions regarding origination of the soul: whether one supports creationism, traducianism, pre-existence, or any of the non-Christian conceptions of the soul; and understanding that this conference is far from an ecumenical council; we are all in agreement that there is always one soul to one body. Therefore, we feel the evidence is incomplete.

HANLON: You must have some theory that could address the facts as presented.

BISHOP: You really should have brought the Pope for the definitive Church position.

HANLON: Indeed. However, his security detail is somewhat more extensive than yours. Now please, continue with the alternative theory.

BISHOP: It has been suggested by the Reverend that Satan has created this situation to cast doubt upon God's infallibility.

HANLON: Details, please.

REVEREND: If you agree that God is infallible, and that He has intended one person to have one soul, then the evidence to the contrary must indicate a ruse.

HANLON: Please assume the facts as presented, and discuss

potential ramifications.

BISHOP: For the record, none of us are willing to question God's infallibility. Having said that, in a hypothetical situation in which two physical bodies actually shared a single soul, the result would be simple. The single soul would be judged according to the actions and sin of both men while on Earth. That is to say, while in the flesh. This would occur when one or the other of them dies.

HANLON: Is it your prediction that when one body dies, so goes the other?

BUDDHIST MONK: Anatta: The skandhas will contribute to the arising of a new group of skandhas. These men are clinging to a single aggregate.

HANLON: Clarification, please.

BUDDHIST MONK: Hypothetically setting aside for a moment the Buddhist doctrine of 'no soul', I will consider the concept of soul in one of the ways the 14th Dalai Lama described it. If we think of the soul as a 'continuum of individuality from moment to moment, from lifetime to lifetime', then we may think these men are experiencing life through a single soul, so they might experience death at the same time.

HINDU MONK: Samsara: The body cannot live without the soul. If these men have not attained moksha, the consciousnesses will move on to inhabit their next biological construct.

NEUROSCIENTIST: How does that address brain-death or near-death experiences?

HANLON: Please hold that question until this line of inquiry is complete. Would it not be possible for the remaining body to encompass the entirety of the single soul?

BISHOP: This is really an exercise in futility given that the situation will work out according to His plan.

HANLON: I understand the religious perspective and deference to a higher power. I am attempting to ascertain which set of circumstances would prove or disprove the church's position.

BISHOP: In this purely hypothetical situation, if one of the twins dies, most of us believe the other would die simultaneously. If that does not occur, then it can be said that they both possessed their own individual souls all along.

BUDDHIST MONK: Anatta: 'All phenomena are not *Self*; when this is seen with knowledge, one is freed from the illusion of affliction.'

HANLON: Or that the single soul continued in the remaining body.

BISHOP: If that pleases you.

HANLON: What would please me is a definite answer.

REVEREND: God works in mysterious ways.

HANLON: Given. But I am asking your group to take a position as to what would constitute proof or disproof of the existence of an immaterial soul.

RABBI: We cannot presume to interpret God's will.

HANLON: You cannot be serious. Theologians have been doing that since the Nicene Creed. Please excuse my outburst and disregard that comment. I need for the dualists to take a position with regard to the twins' soul in this situation. The premise is that they share a single soul between two bodies. Dualists only, vote, please.

STENOGRAPHER: 5 in favor, 2 opposed, 1 abstain.

HANLON: Premise accepted. The next premise is that if one twin dies, the other will die as well. Vote, please.

STENOGRAPHER: 4 in favor, 3 opposed, 1 abstain.

HANLON: Premise accepted. The next premise is that given the previous two, the second twin dying at the instant of the first, and in the absence of causal medical or physical symptoms, would constitute proof that there exists an immaterial soul. Vote please.

STENOGRAPHER: 7 in favor, 0 opposed, 1 abstain.

HANLON: Premise accepted. The last premise is that if one twin dies and the other does not immediately die, this can be said to disprove the existence of an immaterial soul. Vote, please.

STENOGRAPHER: All abstain.

HANLON: Please, we are discussing the answer to the most crucial question mankind has ever faced. Re-vote, please.

STENOGRAPHER: All abstain.

HANLON: I am very disappointed. I am not asking you to accept anything as specious as Pascal's Wager. I implore the dualists to reconsider their position while we move on to the physicalists.

RABBI: An additional point of order?

HANLON: Proceed.

RABBI: It should also be noted that, as much as we might like to hope it would, proof of the soul's existence does not extend to prove or disprove God's existence.

~~~

The security guard knew he was outmatched on both sides. Even so, he gripped his Taser in shaking hands and stood his ground between Leon and Ryder.

"Knock it off boys," Daxton said. "Sit down and let's talk this through like grown-ups."

"I gotta hit the head." Ryder turned to leave and the security guard flinched. Ryder patted him on the shoulder and said, "Holster it, man. No showdown at the OK Corral today."
~~~

They all took their seats as the door closed, and the security guard breathed a heavy sigh of relief, then did his best to pour a cup of coffee without spilling.

"I get it," Daxton said. "It's a shitty deal for everyone. But we have to go big picture here."

"My big picture shrinks a lot when you're planning to kill me," Leon said.

"Socrates still gets kudos for taking one for the team," Daxton said.

"You honestly believe this is the only way to save the world?"

"I know it," Daxton said. "And don't go all philosophical on me with 'What *is* knowledge?' and 'How can we *know* anything?' It's a fact that this little blue marble is in danger from within and without. And it's a fact that I'm in a position to bail us out."

"Sorry, but I don't buy it," Leon said. "We can debate the possibilities all day, but if I wanted to die for my country I'd have joined the Army like my jarhead brother."

"Wow, you really don't get it, do you?" McKinley asked.

"Get what?"

"Honor and sacrifice. First, he was Air Force—"

"Kicked out," Leon said.

"And second, a jarhead is a Marine. You only make those mistakes if you're ignorant or trying to get a rise out of him."

Daxton answered his cell phone. "What? . . . Oh, sure. Tammy will take care of it." He winked at McKinley and hung up.

"I'm real sorry I can't be the big picture hero here," Leon said. "What I want to know is how I can stop him from sealing my fate."

~~~
~~~

NEUROSCIENTIST: We cannot reach a consensus.

HANLON: Is there any common ground?

NEUROSCIENTIST: We agree that there exists a unique link between the twins, that it is biologically observable, and that the connection was broken when the astronaut accelerated to near-c. We are split on the issue of whether one twin's death would precipitate the other's.

HANLON: Arguments for?

NEUROSCIENTIST: Based on the data gathered to date, primarily the complete silencing of the DMN in both twins when the link is severed—

HANLON: Reference, please.

NEUROSCIENTIST: Yes, my apologies. DMN, or Default Mode Network, is the name given by Dr. Marcus Raichle to a recently discovered brain system.[15]

HANLON: What is its function?

NEUROSCIENTIST: The DMN functions in such a way as to keep us ready for immediate response to a sudden threat, and it's what helps suddenly remind us we need to pick up milk on the way home. It may also help you roll over without waking up. Most interesting though, is the formulation of long-range goals and actions by prioritizing our needs and wants through the filter of prior experience. A clearer indication of the biological seat of consciousness has not yet been found.

HANLON: Details, please.

NEUROSCIENTIST: The old view was that the brain shows little or no activity when at rest, and high levels of activity when consciously focused. The contemporary view is now that the brain has high activity when at rest, and higher activity when focused, but perhaps as little as a five percent increase. It is thought that the DMN represents sub-conscious activity, as well as the brain's ability to organize memories, process prior stimuli, and prepare for future action.

HANLON: Further details, please.

NEUROSCIENTIST: One of the things that has intrigued Dr. Raichle is the fact that a key component of the DMN, specifically the part along the midline in the back of the brain, has never been destroyed by a stroke. This is quite remarkable given the fact that most other parts of the brain have suffered such a fate. It's also of interest that this area actually has a dual arterial supply, as if designed with an insurance policy against the loss of blood supply as occurs in a stroke. Given these curious facts, and that this area seems critical to the overall organization of the brain, it would not be too much of a stretch to suggest that suddenly reducing its activity drastically might have major consequences with regard to consciousness.[16]

HANLON: Premise, please.

NEUROSCIENTIST: The majority of us believe it is likely that the death of one twin would sever the link in much the same way that near-c travel seems to have done.

HANLON: Causing death for the other?

NEUROSCIENTIST: Not necessarily. But several believe that the death of one would likely cause the other to at least enter the same coma-like state observed when the link has been severed on prior occasions.

HANLON: Arguments against?

NEUROSCIENTIST: Some believe that permanently severing the link would not cause any adverse reaction in either twin.

HANLON: Clarification, please.

NEUROSCIENTIST: The analogy is that of a telephone call. Under normal circumstances, the conversation continues uninterrupted. Traveling at near-c is like one party setting the phone down, but not hanging up. At that point, the conversation ceases but the line is left open and unusable. However, if one party hangs up, the other is free to carry on unfettered. It should be noted that this is not a majority view.

HANLON: We will retain the original premise and add that when one twin dies, the other will simultaneously die. Physicalists only, vote, please.

STENOGRAPHER: 4 in favor, 3 opposed, 0 abstain.

HANLON: Premise accepted. Please discuss the involvement of the pineal gland.

NEUROSCIENTIST: As yet undetermined. The DMN is spread throughout the brain. It involves constant background activity in several regions. The twins' abnormality of the pineal gland appears to be the seat of their linkage, and that is what makes them unique.

HANLON: In addition to the silencing of the DMN?

NEUROSCIENTIST: Yes. Both aspects are fascinating. We must study these men thoroughly to determine how they differ from the rest of us, and what they can reveal about consciousness itself.

HANLON: Can these studies be done without a space ship?

NEUROSCIENTIST: We have a great deal of information from the existing data obtained by doctors Davies and Ranayan. However, now that the linkage has been identified and isolated, the next logical course would be a detailed study when the connection is severed.

HANLON: But not over hundreds of years.

NEUROSCIENTIST: Exactly. Dax Space Corp. must be convinced that their next mission should be delayed until more practical testing means can be exhausted.

~~~

"We still have time to conduct further research into the anomaly," Davies said.

"That is correct," Gajra said. "We have not completed all the possible lines of inquiry."

"So you've been holding out?" Daxton asked.

"No, sir. I am merely suggesting that we should make the best use of our remaining time."

"What can you figure out that you haven't already?" McKinley asked.

"Well," Davies said, "there is the possibility that—"

The conference phone in the center of the table rang.

McKinley answered the phone on speaker. "Yes?"

"Is Mr. Daxton still present?"

"Who is this?"

"You may call me Hanlon."

"We meet at last. You rat bastard," Daxton said.

Hanlon paused, then said, "I would appreciate your restraint from profanity."

"I'd appreciate you keeping your nose out of my business," Daxton said.

"The intrusions have been necessary. The stakes are high."

"Of course they are. What do you want?"

"I would like for you to postpone Mr. Pelse's next mission."

"No can do. Sorry, gotta go." Daxton moved to disconnect the line.

"Mr. Pelse will die on that flight."

Daxton stopped. "Why?"

"I have it on very good authority that the connection between the twins works both ways."
~~~

"Meaning what?"

"Meaning that even if Mr. Berger perishes due to old age, it will be long before Mr. Pelse reaches his destination. As goes one, so goes the other. Mr. Pelse will be dead on arrival at BiTerra."

"Says who?"

"Believe me when I tell you we have given this serious consideration."

"Who is 'we'?"

"My collaborators are many and learned. You should heed their warning."

Daxton muted the phone and said to McKinley, "Jesus Christ, this guy's a fuckin' riddle-machine."

"He's been right about everything else," Sheila said.

"Not everything," Daxton said, then unmuted the phone. "Tell me how you figured out the other stuff. You got a mole in here?"

"You really should intercept Mr. Pelse. It is imperative that he remain in the complex."

"Where is he going?" Sheila asked.

"I do not know for certain, but I assume he is attempting to leave the complex and go to the space port."

"That son-of-a-bitch!" Sheila slammed her hand on the table.

Daxton said, "Sorry Hanlon, you can't always get what you want," then disconnected the phone. He flopped back in his chair, let out a low whistle, then said "Go get him," to McKinley. "And take Monkey-Boy with you in case he puts up a fight. They can't kill each other until we figure this out."

~~~
~~~

Leon held the elevator door and asked, "Where are we headed?"

"Lower level, East Wing." McKinley punched the button and the doors closed.

"He won't just walk out the front door?"

"He hates the press and there's still some camped out front."

"This place has a secret exit?"

"Yes, it does."

"If I have my bearings right, it's a wet exit."

"Yes, it is."

"Mind telling me what we're in for?"

"The East Wing is a fully encapsulated section of the complex suspended over Turkey Creek."

"That's swampland, river, and mangrove trees. Christine told me this place was built back in the '80s."

"Yeah, Reagan gave us a special exemption to sink the pilings down to bedrock and clear out some wetland."

"Why would he do that?"

"We were an integral part of SDI."

"Star Wars?"

"Yep. That's what the press called it."

"So, what? That gives you free reign to destroy protected wildlife habitat?"

"It does if you're responsible for a big chunk of national security. And besides, do you really think all cities were built in the barren desert? It's not like we're the first to displace a few trees and birds."

"Big juicy rationalization."

"Whatever. Come on, it's down this hallway." McKinley badged his way through another secure door.

"So what's the exit?"

"It's a double-barrier hatch in the floor that'll get him down to the river."

"And why would you need one of those?"

"We may have done some testing on a few alligators and manatees over the years."

"You're kidding." Leon stopped in his tracks.

"Oh come on, you big fuzz ball. You think we keep dolphins in that tank for swimming lessons?"

"I guess not, but—"

"I noticed you're wearing a leather belt."

"No, it's Vegan Leather."

"Ever had a cheeseburger?"

"Fine. Point taken."

"Anyway, this is the only way in or out aside from the portal between the East Wing and the rest of the complex. Here we are," He badged his way through the remaining door.

They entered and found Ryder prostrate on the floor, looking down through the open hatch. He looked up at McKinley and asked, "Where the hell is the boat?"

~~~

"Give it up Hanlon, you're not invited to this party," Daxton said to the conference phone.

"Mr. Daxton, please do not hang up again. You must understand the gravity of this situation."

"I understand you'll get my boot up your ass if you don't back off."

"What are you proposing that the doctors haven't already tried?" Sheila asked.

"There are several options still left to be explored. I would
~~~

like to collaborate with doctors Davies and Ranayan and suggest next steps."

"We have come up with only one possible option," Davies said. "It involves a detailed analysis of a shorter flight, with enhanced monitoring equipment aboard the craft."

"Unfortunately," Gajra said, "it is not feasible to install anything beyond an EEG in the capsule without a significant overhaul."

"There is another option," Hanlon said.

"Yeah, we ground Ryder and skip the trip to E.T.'s house," Sheila said.

"Mrs. Berger, you do not seem to fully grasp the magnitude of scientific breakthrough in which your husband is able to participate." Hanlon's voice was steady, but insistent.

"I'm over it. Now that we know Ryder dies if he flies, that's good enough for me. We just have to keep him out of a stunt plane so he stays safe long enough for Leon to play with his grandchildren."

"Hang on." Daxton muted the speaker phone as he answered his cell. "Slow down Wilcutt . . . you're sure? . . . Holy shit!" He spun out of his chair and bolted to the console on the wall. "Chrissy, get over here and bring up the feeds from the security cameras."

A moment after seeing the feeds, Daxton shoved Christine aside and began frantically punching the keyboard. A digitized woman's voice echoed over every P.A. speaker throughout the complex, "Allison to the cafeteria, please. Allison to the cafeteria."

~~~
~~~

"That's weird. I didn't know you guys had a P.A.," Leon said.

"You think?" Ryder asked McKinley.

"It's on a fail-safe. No way he tripped it by accident." McKinley began rummaging through the storage cabinets.

"Gotta be a false alarm," Ryder said.

"No chance. You have to get the hell out of here." McKinley slammed another cabinet and started on the next.

"Excuse me, guys. You mind filling me in?" Leon asked.

"Time to go, Monkey-Boy." Ryder opened a cabinet McKinley hadn't checked yet.

"Here, this is it." McKinley triumphantly held up two sets of swim fins, masks, and snorkels.

"You're coming with." Ryder started stripping. "Come on, hop to." He nudged Leon to do the same.

"Not me," McKinley said, "I only dog paddle."

"Come on, you'll be fine." Ryder was taking off his pants.

"Dudes!" Leon said. "What is happening?"

"The complex is under siege," Ryder said. "Bad guys with bad attitudes are here. Now, strip down and get in gear or you're on your own."

"I'm going to get Sheila and the boys." Leon moved toward the door.

McKinley stepped in his way. "Too late for that now. Daxton's coded alarm said the equivalent of a platoon has already breached the perimeter and taken control of the complex. You really have to go." He tried again to hand Leon the mask and fins.

"We have to help," Leon said.

"We are helping." Ryder was now down to his skivvies and working into his flippers. "We're going to go get some real help. You can't take on a platoon by yourself and McKinley is useless."

"Thanks, asshole," McKinley said.

"No way, I'm not leaving them behind," Leon said.

"Come on, even Aristotle said it's not always cowardly to retreat."

"That was Socrates, but—"

"Whatever. Regroup and counter-attack can be braver."

"Why should I let you leave so you can fly away and kill me?" Leon reluctantly started undressing.

"Because I'm the only one who can get your wife and kids out of this building now," Ryder said. Then to McKinley he said, "You can still come."

"Not a big fan of 'gators. I'll stay here and cover your tracks. Both of you just stay underwater 'til you're across the river."

"Why?" Leon asked.

"Jesus, why did I get all the brains in the family?" Ryder asked. "*Dude*, bad guys is in *da house*. They stole our boat which means they're patrolling the river. Now shut up, take a deep breath, and swim like you mean it."

"You got another knife?" Leon pointed at the bowie strapped to Ryder's calf.

"Nope, but you can wiffle the bad guys with your snorkel."

"Hah." McKinley laughed.

"I'll take the lead." Leon grabbed the gear from McKinley. "And I'll tell the 'gators you're with me. Turns out you need me as much as I need you."

~~~

"That's right Bruce, just moments ago a large Winnebago with a manatee montage on the side pulled into the parking lot, along with a brown UPS delivery truck," Yvonne said.
~~~

"We don't have an accurate count," she continued, "but it seems like as many as thirty men and women streamed out of the vehicles and entered the front door of the Dax Space Corp. headquarters."

"Did they say why they were there?" Bruce asked from the studio.

"They didn't talk to anyone," Yvonne said. "And none of them responded to the CBN reporter who approached them. They just walked through the front door."

"How were they dressed?"

"They were all wearing gray jumpsuits, and the CBN reporter said they had earpieces like the ones we use on location." She pointed to the clear curly tube leading into her ear.

"Did they bring anything with them?"

"Yes. Many of them were carrying large black duffel bags. Four of the men wheeled two big carts out of the delivery truck, and they took those through the front door as well."

"Very strange," Bruce said as he turned back into the camera. "If you're just joining us, Yvonne Forrester is in Palm Bay at the scene of a strange—... Just a minute, Yvonne has another update. Can we cut back to her?"

The live feed showed a man in a gray jumpsuit in front of the Dax entrance, firing a machine gun into the air. He had a bullhorn and raised it to indicate he was about to make an announcement.

"We are in now control of this facility and the people within it," he said. "Make no attempt to breach the perimeter of this complex, or there will be further loss of life."

~~~
~~~

Leon's lungs were starting to beg for air, so he figured they were just over half way across the first part of the river. The late afternoon sun and murkiness of the brackish water kept visibility low, which was good for hiding from the patrol boat, but bad for seeing alligators. He felt something brush his arm and turned to see Ryder swimming alongside. Ryder used his index and middle finger to indicate 'look there'.

It was a shadowy figure paralleling them, but it was too big around to be an alligator. He gave Ryder the 'OK' sign, knowing that a manatee was no threat but might still get the astronaut quaking in his flippers. The manatee swam closer, made eye contact, and dove deeper. Leon motioned to Ryder that they should follow the beast down. They heard the whine of a boat prop pass by overhead and Leon once again gave thanks to a giant baked potato.

When they reached the shallows of the narrow mangrove island bisecting the river, they swam under the canopy and surfaced among the tangled roots slowly enough not to make any splashing sounds. They inhaled deeply but quiet enough to avoid detection if anyone was nearby.

The tangled and arched roots of the trees were covered with sharp oysters and barnacles, which made for slow going. Ryder was surprised to see silver-dollar-sized spiders all over the roots, but soon realized they were just small black crabs. Both men slid quietly back into the water to traverse the second half.

Leon surfaced early to choose a landing spot, chancing cover from the treed island. When Ryder came up to see why they were stopped, Leon pointed to two alligators, roughly nine or ten footers, catching the last of the day's heat.

The men landed ten yards east of the scaly sunbathers and crawled slowly up the bank through the mud. Ryder indicated that Leon should stay put while he checked the area. He went for his knife as one of the alligators stood and turned toward them. Leon motioned for him to freeze and hold back. The prehistoric lizard slithered slowly into the water. Ryder figured he must have already eaten.

They both stayed silent as Leon followed Ryder up the bank to swampy ground firm enough to stand without sinking past their ankles. There was a walking trail thirty yards further in, and after they completed a sweep of the area they felt it safe to start running, so they ditched the swim gear and hopped to it.

They emerged into an open field at full sprint wearing only their underwear, splotches of mud, and red rings left on their faces by the masks. They ran straight toward the school parking lot, past the cheerleaders' after-school practice. Leon noticed a couple of kids in the bleachers aiming cell phones at them. He was sure the muddy streaking twins would have been the top-of-the-hour lead if there wasn't a hostage crisis across the river.

Chapter 10

"So good of you to invite me in." The three dimensional image of Hanlon's disembodied head and shoulders floated two feet above the conference room table.

"Call off your dogs, Hanlon." Daxton stood to address the hologram at eye level.

"I am afraid you left me no choice, Mr. Daxton. It would be unconscionable to allow Mr. Pelse to leave and take with him our best chance to unlock the mystery of the human mind."

"You'll be locked up—"

"Please, we mustn't waste our time with idle threats. My guards have reported that most of your security team did not resist forcibly. For that I am grateful. For the others, please accept my sincerest condolences."

"How many of my guys are in your pocket?" Daxton glared at the guard by the door and three others outside.

"It is true that some on your team are not singularly loyal, but that should not reflect poorly upon you."

"I knew it!" Daxton said.

"Hanlon," Sheila said. "What do you think you're doing?"

"I am merely ensuring that we take full advantage of such a monumental occurrence. You should thank me for preventing Mr. Pelse's departure."

"Where are my boys?" Sheila asked. "They were in the daycare center, and if your thugs touched them—"

"Rest assured Mrs. Berger, your sons are safe."

"Safe, as in waiting outside with the police?"

"They are safe."

"If you hurt them—"

"I understand your concern Mrs. Berger. Now, shall we get down to business?"

"There is no business until you back off," Daxton said.

"That is not possible at this time," Hanlon's head said. "My guards are escorting doctors Davies and Ranayan to the medical lab. You, your daughter, and Mrs. Berger are to remain in this conference room until further notice."

~~~

Ryder and Leon jumped out of the car, thanked Principal Durrance for the ride, and apologized again for the mud on the seats.

"Who's in charge here?" Ryder asked.

"Over there." The rookie officer recognized the twins and gave them a once-over chuckle. He pointed through the gathering crowd to a squad car parked askew among several others, all with lights flashing. Three more rolled up, followed by two more ambulances, another fire engine, four more media vans, and a SWAT truck.

Ryder made a beeline for the SWAT team, arriving just as they were piling out the back and assembling their gear.

"I'll suit up," Ryder said to the officer in charge.

"Who the hell are you?" Sergeant Weitz asked.

"I'm the guy who's gonna get this thing handled for you."
~~~

Ryder climbed into the van and started toweling off.

"Get him out of there," Weitz ordered one of the officers.

"There are thirty well-armed pros holding a hundred hostages in the fortified wing of a secure complex specifically designed for lock down. You really wanna go in there blind?"

"Looks more like several hundred," Weitz said. He pointed to the stream of people flowing out the lobby doors with several of Hanlon's guards.

"He's just clearing out the chaff," Ryder said. "Let the blues handle the crowd. Hanlon's going to hole up with the core team and some bargaining chips in the East Wing."

"How do you know it's Hanlon?" Leon asked.

"Who else?"

"What does he want?"

"How should I know? What matters now is that he doesn't get it."

"Hey, who the hell *are* you?" Weitz asked.

"I'm Pelse, and that's my kid brother Leon. I'm combat-ready and I know that facility like my own dick. We'll make a surprise incursion and retake this place before dinner." Ryder grabbed a uniform from the rack and started dressing.

"Whoa there fella, we don't even know what they want," Weitz said. "That whole wing is one-way glass. No sniper cover."

"I just told you what's what. They're digging in while we chew the fat. Let's take charge and get this done."

"Jesus," Weitz said. "Make way for the famous astronaut. You're not going anywhere." He turned back to his team and started barking orders.

Leon hopped into the van and started toweling off. "He probably wants us, and when he figures out we're not there, he'll back off."

"Yeah, right," Ryder said. "I'd say he's pretty committed, and probably should be."

"We can't run right back in there. Why don't we wait and see if he'll trade us for the hostages?"

"You're not going anywhere. You stay out here and negotiate; I'll go solve the problem."

"Don't you think we should let the SWAT guys get their bearings?"

Ryder jammed the clip into a borrowed Sig Sauer and said, "I have a plane to catch."

~~~

HANLON: My apologies for the delay, I was unavoidably detained by a premature turn of events. Neuroscientist, you were about to propose a new line of inquiry.

NEUROSCIENTIST: I merely stated that practical means of experimentation should be exhausted.

HANLON: Such as?

NEUROSCIENTIST: I haven't had a chance to formulate any kind of coherent program.

HANLON: Initial thoughts?

NEUROSCIENTIST: We should adhere to standard scientific method. Nothing meaningful can be done ad hoc.

HANLON: Please, we are under significant time constraints. Give me your conjecture.

IMAM: ibn al-Haytham was a pioneer of the scientific method. But we must remember his words: 'God, however, has not preserved the scientist from error and has not safeguarded science from shortcomings and faults.'

NEUROSCIENTIST: We need to consider the ethics involved in
~~~

human trials, especially non-consensual. There are risks to the subjects.

HANLON: As Alhazen also said: 'Truth is sought for its own sake. And those who are engaged upon the quest for anything for its own sake are not interested in other things. Finding the truth is difficult, and the road to it is rough.'

ETHICIST: You sound like a relativist who also thinks torturing babies is not always wrong.

NEUROSCIENTIST: Who said anything about torturing babies?

ETHICIST: No one. I just think we need to define the parameters of inquiry, so we can choose where to draw the line.

HANLON: I will draw the lines, thank you. What I need to know is how to direct the experiments. I must insist that you provide your guidance.

NEUROSCIENTIST: Well, um, we have observed that both twins enter a coma-like state when the astronaut accelerates to near-c.

HANLON: Stipulated.

NEUROSCIENTIST: Yes. And, um, given that. Well. It seems. I'm sorry. I'm just not ready to proceed along these lines.

BIOLOGIST: The next logical step would be to replicate the situation without having to launch one of the twins into space.

HANLON: And how could this be done?

BIOLOGIST: I have no—

GENERAL: Put one in a coma and see if the other one passes out.

BIOLOGIST: That doesn't—

GENERAL: Look, Hanlon over here is obsessed with consciousness, which is all fine and dandy. I tend to see things more practically, like how does this link-thing work?

POLITICIAN: To what end?

General: Can you imagine battalions with biological communication capabilities? No dead batteries, no encryption, no interception. Just platoon after platoon operating in perfect lockstep.

Imam: You are not serious.

General: I'd rather have my boys rigged like that than fight an enemy with such a huge tactical advantage.

Politician: I'll dip right into the pork barrel for that.

General: And let's not forget to dip into the soul of this issue.

RABBI: General, please.

General: Come on now, don't tell me y'all haven't gone down that road.

Imam: Which road is that?

General: If we can find the soul, we can kill it. Or if we can't kill it, maybe we can shut it off and save our boys some PTSD.

Hanlon: General, you have overestimated my interest in military application. We need to focus on the task at hand. The twins are isolated in a facility with ample scientific equipment and qualified medical personnel. I have done my part, now you all must do yours.

~~~

"No can do, Pelse," Weitz said. "No way I'm going to jump the gun in broad daylight, and no way I'm going to deputize you. It'll be dark enough in two hours, we'll use that time to go over the assignments."

"Hey Sarge, we could use that site plan," the SWAT officer wearing black elbow pads said.

"I told you, there isn't one," Ryder said.

"Why not?" Weitz asked.
~~~

"That place was built hush-hush in the '80s, and I'm the only one out here who knows it well."

"Draw us a picture," Weitz said.

"Fine." Ryder pushed his way toward the impromptu command table and grabbed a pen. "The whole wing extends out over the water. It sits three feet above high tide to allow for a storm surge. We had lots of head room when we came out, so I figure high tide is late tonight."

"Twenty-three hundred, sir" the officer with the purple bandana said.

"Great. So there's plenty of time to get us under the wing in a couple of RHIBs."

"Why?" the officer with the eagle tattoo asked.

"Because that's the only place to sneak in."

"Why not full-frontal?" Eagle asked.

"We're not prepared to sacrifice hostages," Weitz said.

"We'll be sitting ducks in single file," Elbow Pads said.

"Let the skirt bring up the rear," Ryder said. "I doubt Hanlon knows about the hatch. It's in a sealed utility suite at the end of a dead-end hallway."

"Hey," Bandana said. "If that whole wing is on pilings, there's probably a single conduit for telcomm and power. Cut that and the whole thing goes dark."

"Got it." Weitz switched gears and said, "Oh, shit," as a man in a suit approached with his entourage.

"Special Agent Rex Kerwin, FBI," the suit said. "We'll take it from here, and you won't be going in right away."

"Back off. We have a plan," Ryder said. "You go negotiate and keep their eyes forward."

"They already made contact," Kerwin said. "They want you and your brother toot-sweet."

"They don't know we're out here?" Leon asked.

"I'm on my way. He stays out here," Ryder said.

"I know the building too," Leon said.

"Not like I do; and you've never worn a uniform. Besides, that wingnut thinks we're both toast if you bite it, and I don't want to prove him right."

"Oh sure, I'll just sit on the curb while you get us both killed."

Kerwin stepped between them and said, "You're both benched and so is SWAT until we get some more details out of these dickless wonders."

~~~

"Mrs. Berger, if you have the means to contact your husband I would greatly appreciate your asking him to report to the medical lab," Hanlon's head said.

"Why should I?" Sheila asked.

"It is imperative that he and Mr. Pelse submit to additional testing. If we can determine the function of their abnormality, Mr. Pelse may be able to make his journey safely."

"We figured it out," Daxton said.

"Not true," Hanlon said. "If that were the case, Dr. Ranayan would have informed me."

"No way," Christine said. "She's not with you."

"No, she is not. But she is similarly motivated to solve this quandary."

"I doubt she's got a gun to anyone's head," Sheila said.

"There are times when the end justifies the means."

"Tell that to the widows of the security guards."

"A regrettable consequence for the greater good."

"How many have to die so you can solve your riddle?"
~~~

"As few as absolutely necessary."

"As many as it takes."

"One and the same, Mr. Daxton. You, of all people, should realize the scope of what we're on the verge of discovering."

"My hands are clean," Daxton said.

"Hardly," Hanlon said. "You have many skeletons in your closet, as do I."

"I'm out to save the human race; you just want to dissect it."

"Have you truly considered the possible ramifications of your discovery, if it were to bear fruit?"

"Of course I have."

"Au contraire. What would happen to humanity in this day and age if an advanced alien culture were proven to exist?"

"It'll be 256 years 'til we find out. They'll be fine by then."

"Perhaps. But what of religion? Do you truly wish to take that away from people?"

"What are you talking about?"

"An alien race and a second Earth are not consistent with any of the three major Abrahamic religions of *the Book*. Would aliens have souls? Would killing one be a sin? Would we have dominion or be relegated to walk with the animals? How could multi-thousand-year-old texts purport to address such issues?"

"God is on life support and the candy stripers are out to lunch."

"Sadly, I cannot disagree. Let us only hope He is either resuscitated or ultimately replaced with knowledge and understanding of even greater confidence, import, and facility."

"Had you figured for a true believer."

"I am many things, Mr. Daxton. But I no longer succumb to any sort of faith-based epistemic obligation. I believe the twins can provide The Answer, but time is running short. You must tell me where they are."

"You can forget about testing Ryder and Leon," Christine said. "They'll never sit still for the likes of you."

"I can be very persuasive."

"Go find them yourself," Daxton said.

"My guards are searching your premises as we speak. You could expedite the process by revealing their whereabouts."

"We're in no rush," Sheila said.

"Ah, but Mr. Daxton is hoping for a speedy resolution so he can meet the launch deadline."

"Jes-! Would you please just tell me how you know all this? No way a few guards got those kind of details."

"A magician never reveals his secrets."

"A pure consequentialist," Daxton said. "Damn the categorical imperative."

"Mind your language, please. Yet again, you label and categorize me at your own peril. The philosopher Kant and his ilk are certainly entitled to their opinions, some of which I have found quite helpful. Not lying to you, however, is yet another imperative to which I no longer subscribe."

~~~

After two fruitless hours of back-and-forth in the standoff, darkness fell and the FBI decided to drop the hammer.

Weitz sat point in the first inflatable boat, with five of the SWAT team crowded behind him and one more manning the silent trolling motor. He couldn't hear or see their other RHIB in the black of night, but he knew they were following close.

With guns drawn they hugged the shore along the mangroves, still hoping to get under the East Wing undetected.
~~~

Two police helicopters kept the rooftop snipers down, and the news choppers were kept at a safe distance so as not to interfere.

All good so far. Weitz moored to the piling by the hatch ladder and the other boat came alongside. He ducked under the hatch tube rim and climbed onto the ladder, waist deep in water now. He was relieved to see the outside hatch was still open, but he banged the inner hatch in frustration when it wouldn't budge.

He whispered to Eagle, "They must have locked it on the way out."

"Blow it," Eagle whispered back.

"Negative! We'll be—"

The hatch wheel released and started turning slowly, and after a painstaking fifteen seconds it opened to reveal McKinley's smiling face. "Took you long enough," he said.

"Thanks for leaving the light on." Weitz climbed the ladder.

"Couldn't chance them finding it." McKinley stood up stiffly and stretched.

"You catch a nap?" Weitz asked as another SWAT officer came through the hatch.

"Couldn't get comfortable in the cupboard."

"Did they get in here?"

"I don't think so."

"Good."

"How many did you bring?" McKinley asked. The room was getting cramped and the first boat wasn't empty yet.

"Enough. You get down to the boat. When we're set, haul ass outta here."

"My pleasure," McKinley said.

"Just stay low. The choppers will keep snipers off your back, and the inflatables are Kevlar just in case."

“I disabled the camera after Ryder left.” McKinley pointed to the broken lens hanging in a corner of the ceiling.

“Great. Let’s just hope they think it was down before they got here.” Weitz turned to Eagle and said, “I’ll take out the first camera in the hall. You be ready for a sentry.”

The last of the SWAT team squeezed into the room, which was now overflowing with testosterone, muscle, and ammunition. McKinley wiggled his way to the hatch, and squirmed down into the inflatable boat.

Weitz threaded a suppressor to the barrel of his Sig Sauer while Elbow and Bandana did the same. He crouched low by the door and they took up positions behind him.

He slowly released the latch on the door, cracking it just enough to get a bead on the camera in the top corner of the hall. With one muffled shot the three of them were in the hall before the broken glass hit the floor.

~~~

Weitz snuffed the last security camera and kept his gun forward as he looked over his shoulder for a quick headcount along the length of the hallway. All in, Eagle bringing up the rear. He crept along the last few feet and held up a fist to indicate everyone should stop. He motioned for Bandana to get on the opposite side of the door.

He was poised to charge when he noticed what looked like a hockey puck-sized sticker blending into the tile in the corner. He looked across and saw another by Bandana’s foot. He looked up and saw two more on the walls. He did not have time to look back and see them scattered throughout the hallway.

The blinding flash of light stunned everyone while a
~~~

thunderous boom reverberated up and down the hallway, knocking every last man to the floor.

~~~

"You continue to perform honorably."

"For your glory, Hanlon."

"For humanity. Are any officers deceased?"

"No, Hanlon. Just unconscious."

"Very well."

"What should we do with them?"

"Secure them in a room and post a sentry."

"As you wish, Hanlon."

~~~

"So perish every one that shall hereafter leap over my wall."

"What did you do, Hanlon?" Kerwin asked.

"You should not have tested my boundaries."

"Are there any wounded? You can gain some ground by letting them go for treatment."

"I have all the ground I need, Agent Kerwin. What I am lacking are the twin brothers. I am now convinced they escaped and you are withholding them from me."

"What if I am? I could give you Pelse in return for half the hostages."

"I will surrender all but ten hostages if you send both twins this instant."

"You know I can't do that."

"That is indeed a shame."

~~~
~~~

“That sonofabitch Kerwin would hand me over.” Ryder pulled Leon back behind the tactical van so they wouldn’t be seen.

“Maybe he should,” Leon said.

“Maybe he should,” Ryder mimicked. “OK, Monkey-Boy, here’s the plan. We’ll—”

“Wait a minute,” Leon said. “What are you talking about?”

“SWAT is down, and the FBI is gonna wait for CIRG.”[26]

“Who is Sirg?” Leon asked.

“Jesus, are you playing catch-up for missed years of being a pain in my ass?”

“Just tell me what you’re talking about.”

“Critical Incident Response Group. They’re the bad boys on the block when there’s a kerfuffle.”

“When will they get here?” Leon asked.

“Depends on who and when Kerwin calls,” Ryder said. “The FBI Director deploys the nearest team.”

“That could take hours.”

“So go get a banana.”

“You got a better idea?” Leon asked.

“Yeah.” Ryder pointed to the gun in his belt.

“Oh, wow.” Leon leaned on the van.

“Yeah, wow,” Ryder said. “I’ll get you one too, and we’ll go get your wife and kids.”

“We’re not qualified—”

“Is the mountain man afraid of a few zealots?”

“You’re just a pilot and I’m—”

“—just a point-and-shoot picture-taker. Listen, *dude*, I trained with the PJs and I went through some nasty shit in Colombia. These hacks are no tougher than guerrillas and drug lords.”

"But this is diff—"

"Come on, man up," Ryder said. "You really want to live with no wife and kids when you could have stopped it?"

"No."

~~~

Leon could see the headline and subhead now: 'Wildlife Expert Mauled by Alligators. SWAT Team Smart Enough to Use Boats'. He was breast-stroking alongside Ryder as quietly as he could, keeping close to shore and wishing the helicopters would drown out his pounding heartbeat.

They made it to the outside piling of the East Wing, and could barely see the two inflatables tethered to the ladder. The hatch was closed.

Ryder swam ahead and scaled the ladder. He opened the lower hatch and pounded the inner one when it wouldn't budge.

"Should I check under the mangroves for a spare key?" Leon asked.

"Shut up, man. Let me think," Ryder said.

"SWAT probably locked and covered it so Hanlon's thugs wouldn't find it."

"Shut up."

"Let's get out of here."

"I swear I'll shoot you right where you stand if you don't shut the fuck up for one minute," Ryder said.

"Suicide by proxy?" Leon asked.

"Goddammit." Ryder slid off the ladder and splashed down. Leon took a defensive stance. McKinley opened the hatch from above. Ryder scrambled back up the ladder.

"What the hell are you doing?" Ryder whispered.
~~~

"Playing doorman, what does it look like?" McKinley said.

"Looks like you're soaked too."

"Yeah, well, after the SWAT guys blew up I hid in the mangroves for a while, and when nobody came to the hatch I figured I'd better go hide it."

"So they didn't get into the hatch room?" Ryder asked.

"I don't think so."

"Why don't you know?"

"I was hiding in the cupboard again."

"Again?" Ryder asked.

"Are you coming in or not?" McKinley asked.

"You get your ass down and out first," Ryder said.

Ryder and McKinley traded places, and Leon helped McKinley into one of the RHIBs. They fumbled around trying to start the electric trolling motor, but eventually found the switch.

Leon was just about to give the boat a push when McKinley stopped him and handed over his access badge. Leon waved his thanks and started back toward the ladder.

The boat was almost out of the building's ambient glow when Leon heard the gunshot. He was so startled he lost footing as he saw McKinley slump over the inflatable pontoon. He stared in disbelief as the boat glided silently into the enveloping darkness. He figured the second gunshot took out the sniper, and he knew it was high time to get up this ladder.

~~~

Ryder was crouched with his ear pressed to the door. Leon thought about how far out of his league he was, and looked back at the hatch. Nope, not that far out. It was time to get Sheila and the boys.
~~~

He squished over to the door and Ryder shushed him. He put his ear to it and assumed Ryder could hear the muffled speech outside as well. He couldn't make out the conversation, but based on the pauses he figured this was just half of it.

Let's hope there's only one out there.

He pulled the gun from its holster and out of the plastic bag. He'd only fired tranquilizer darts in the past, but this couldn't be much different.

Leon reconsidered and holstered the gun, surprised yet again at how heavy it was. Good thing it wasn't just stuffed into his belt. No time to learn something new; better stick to basics.

The twins crouched as both prepared to storm the door when the conversation ended.

Ryder barged through and rolled, intending to cross the hallway as fast as possible. What he didn't intend was crashing into the shins of a guard and sending him to the floor amid a hail of lead.

A bullet pierced his arm, but Leon was so amped on adrenaline he was still able to drop to his knees on the guard's gun arm.

The guard kicked and struggled, but Leon knelt fast. Ryder sent an elbow to the guard's bladder and folded him like a rusty lawn chair.

While the guard was still disoriented, Ryder was able to use a hammer-fist for a brachial stun. That stopped his struggling.

They stood up, took the gun from the guard, and Leon kicked him square in the face . . . for McKinley.

"Jeez, you're a little jacked up." Ryder said.

"Dude had it comin'," Leon said.

"I'm outta here." Ryder started toward the door at the end of the hallway.

Leon heard muffled shouts behind the door across the hall, and figured it was the SWAT team. "Hey, the good guys are in here."

"Great, go save the day," Ryder said over his shoulder. He paused by the exit and must not have heard anything, because he barged right through and was gone.

Leon swiped McKinley's badge across the door lock and swung the door wide, shouting "I'm on your side!" and kept to one side in case they were set for an ambush. He was relieved when they didn't attack.

"Where the hell did you come from?" Weitz asked.

"In there." Leon pointed to the hatch room, and noticed the smashed keypad by the handle, which was also covered in blood.

"Ouch. Who took that out?" he asked.

Bandana came through the door with his bandana tied as a tourniquet around his bulging bicep. "That would be me."

"Got another one of those?" Leon grimaced as he proudly showed off his bullet wound.

~~~

"Oh my God!" Gajra put both hands over her mouth as the guards wheeled Ryder into the medical lab.

"What happened?" Davies rushed to the gurney.

One of the guards restrained Davies and the female guard said, "He's just unconscious."

"What are you going to do?" Davies asked.

"We're going to find out where his brother is. Wake him up."

A guard waved smelling salts by Ryder's nose. He inhaled sharply and strained to sit up but the straps held firm.

"Where is Leon Berger?"
~~~

"What?" Ryder shook his head and tried to focus.

"Your brother. Where is he?"

"Pretty sure I don't qualify as my brother's keeper."

The guard brought down the butt of his machine gun into Ryder's gut. "I won't ask you again."

Ryder groaned. "Yeah . . . you will. It's gonna suck, but I'd be disappointed if you gave up too easily."

The guard grabbed a scalpel and pressed it into the flesh under Ryder's eye. "You don't need to see for these experiments," he hissed.

"Please," Ryder said, "please don't let my last vision be your butt-ugly face. Show me her titties."

The guard tossed the scalpel back on the tray in disgust. "You must tell us where he is."

"Hey, I don't even like the guy. I'd tell you if I knew."

The female guard held up Ryder's bowie knife and said, "Let me cut off his fingers. He will talk."

"Very well," the guard in charge said.

She came alongside Ryder and took his hand. "Which one first?"

"Go for the pinky. I can't type, so I don't need it."

"He escaped," Gajra said. "He was with Mr. Pelse when you took the complex, so he must have escaped as well."

"Is that true?" the woman asked.

"Do I get to keep my fingers?"

"Maybe."

"Then I'll gamble on yes. I left him with the cops outside." Ryder tried to glance around at all the guards and said, "Can't say he didn't go home to shit, shower, and shave; but that was the last I saw of him."

~~~
~~~

"Listen Hanlon, this has to end now," Kerwin said into the phone.

"It will end when I am satisfied."

"I can't send in the twins. No way."

"It seems you already sent Mr. Pelse, so why not Mr. Berger?"

"What do you mean?" Kerwin asked.

"My guards subdued him," Hanlon said.

"Holy shit." Kerwin looked around frantically, and realized he hadn't seen Ryder or Leon in quite some time. "Hanlon? Are you still there?"

Dead air.

"Hanlon?"

"I need you to avoid profanity, Agent Kerwin. For my sake."

"Oh. OK," Kerwin said. "What did you do with Pelse?"

"There is something else you should know about the situation."

"What?" Kerwin waved off an agent.

"The building contains sufficient explosives to cause its collapse," Hanlon said. "I can detonate at any time, and I cannot be held responsible for what happens to anyone remaining inside."

"You're responsible for this whole thing!" Kerwin said. The other agent was still in his face, indicating he should keep Hanlon on the line.

"True statement. I misspoke. What I meant to say was that the East Wing is mine to do with as I please. So again, I implore you to send in Mr. Berger."

"What do I get?"

"You get to save the lives of sixty innocent civilians, as well as Mr. Daxton."

"Give me half now."

"I already sent four hundred out the front door. Am I not entitled to just one in return?"

"Hang on for a second."

"No, I will not. I am aware of your efforts to trace this call, but surely you would expect me to have anticipated your every countermeasure."

"Yes," Kerwin said. "Thought we had a lead."

"You must not underestimate me. I am quite capable of controlling this situation from my present location. I grow weary of your stalling."

"I just can't do it."

"So be it," Hanlon said. "Please advise Mr. Berger that we shall commence experimentation on his twin sons forthwith."

Chapter 11

Ethicist: I wasn't serious about torturing babies.

Hanlon: I have no intention of torturing the twin sons, I merely intend to see if they exhibit the same abnormality as their father. The Geneticist thinks the trait may be heritable.

Geneticist: I didn't say that. I just wondered out loud if their offspring would also manifest the same symptoms.

Hanlon: And that is precisely what we shall determine. The doctors are preparing to scan the boys via fMRI, and we should have the results shortly. In the meantime, we need to discuss expected outcomes if they do share the trait. Neuroscientist?

Neuroscientist: This is absurd. It's gone too far. I can't—

Hanlon: You will regain your composure and resume participation in this conference immediately. Very well. Now, assuming we observe the same pineal abnormality in the twin boys, is it logical to assume they would share the same linkage as their father and his brother?

Neuroscientist: I. I, um. Suppose so.

Hanlon: Excellent. And how best to verify the connection?

Neuroscientist: It's not. Well. I guess that. It should—

Hanlon: I have two neuroscientists on location with the twins. You are excused from this conference and remanded to your quarters until its conclusion. Does anyone here have any suggestions, or shall I contact the other doctors at Dax?

ASTROBIOLOGIST: It seems to me that we should await the results of the fMRI and further testing. 'An extraordinary phenomenon such as this demands an extraordinary investigation.'

HANLON: Agreed. Assuming the results are positive, what should be the next step?

GENERAL: Knock one out and see what happens.

BIOLOGIST: I'm afraid that is the only viable option at this point.

HANLON: And how best to accomplish that?

BIOLOGIST: You'll have to induce a coma in one, and see if it affects the other.

~~~

"Hold still Nathan," Davies said over the lab intercom. "The machine can't read you if you move. He cut the mic and said to Gajra, "I think we'll have to sedate him."

"We need to find a way out of here," Gajra said.

"Are you kidding? Those guards are playing for keeps. I really thought they'd cut Ryder's fingers off."

"He was provoking them."

"Holy shit, you're on their side?"

"No, I am not. I am merely suggesting that if we give the appearance of cooperation, we may be able to lull them into providing us an opening for escape."

"No chance against three of them." Davies turned the mic back on and said, "Come on now Nathan, this will just take a minute. You need to hold still."

Nathan's scream echoed through the MRI tube and throughout the lab when the lights went out.
~~~

The auxiliary lighting came on moments later, and the lab was a quarter as bright as before. Nathan continued screaming, now in concert with his brother.

"Oh, shit." Davies and Gajra hurried out of the control booth. "I bet the police cut the power."

"So it would seem," Gajra said. "At least we can't bother the boys any longer. There, there. You are safe now."

"You haven't figured where Hanlon is going next?"

"Without our equipment, what kind of testing can we possibly do?"

Davies slid Nathan out of the tube and walked over to whisper in Gajra's ear. "My guess is he'll make us induce coma in one of the boys to see how it affects the other."

"That's ridiculous!" Gajra stood up from the wheelchair in which Felix was strapped. "What could he hope to gain from such a thing?"

"It might tell him if they're linked. Then it's anyone's guess."

~~~

"OK, let's roll," Weitz said in the dimly lit hallway. He held the machine gun from the guard Leon and Ryder had subdued, and Leon had given his pistol to Bandana.

"You really think he should go?" Eagle asked.

"He's my problem now," Weitz said. "He bailed our asses out and his plan makes sense. We'll assume Pelse won't screw things up. You two have to take the lab at exactly 20:50, which is right when the rest of us will hit the gym." Then he asked Leon again, "You're sure that's the biggest room in the wing?"

"It's the biggest one I've seen. The conference room could probably hold twenty, but if he kept more than that it would
~~~

make sense to move them to the gym."

"Yeah, especially with the bathrooms right there. Clock sync on my mark . . ."

~~~

"Agent Kerwin, I demand that power be restored to the wing immediately." Kerwin recoiled and Hanlon's voice could be heard even by the agents not listening on the other lines.

"Not gonna happen, Hanlon. It's over."

"I told you it would be over when I am satisfied."

"Well, you can't run tests without equipment."

"Chemicals work the same in the dark, Agent Kerwin."

Kerwin muted the phone and said, "Get the power back on!"

"We can't," the agent next to him said. "We cut the hardline."

~~~

"I can't do that," Davies said into the wall phone. "No way. It's just too risky."

"Dr. Davies," Hanlon said. "My patience wears thin. You will administer a sufficient dose of pentobarbital to one of the twins such that a coma ensues."

"They're just little boys!" Davies said.

"Their youth does not make their potential contribution to society any less significant. Do it now, or face the consequences."

"We can't monitor his vitals. It's too risky."

"As you should be well aware by now, I am not averse to risk when it can further our progress. Guard, please encourage Dr. Davies to administer the drug."

Gajra cleared her throat. "I . . . will do it."

~~~

"It's a good thing long-hair brought a few extra clips," Bandana whispered as the two of them crept up the stairs.

"Cut it." Eagle motioned for him to flank the door. No sign of bad guys, one more flight to go.

They approached the door to the third floor, from which Leon had told them the lab would be thirty yards west. It was past a series of cubicles in the open office area.

Bandana cracked the door from a crouch, and eased his way through. Eagle followed, and waited for it to shut.

They crawled through the cubicle aisles, keeping low all the way. Bandana peeked around the corner, and was able to see one guard outside the lab, with two more inside.

Bandana pointed to his watch, and they both knew it was three minutes 'til they could go medieval on the bad guys.

~~~

"Did you see Sheila?" Leon whispered as Weitz was lowered to the floor of the maintenance room.

The sergeant shook his head. He should have sent Leon back out the hatch while he had the chance, but it was good to have a guide in this maze.

Weitz didn't know what Sheila looked like even with a description, and couldn't have picked her out of the crowd anyway. It's tough enough trying to keep quiet while standing on your buddies' hands and peering through a ventilation grate. He wasn't about to review the who's who of the hostage roster; it was enough to get a headcount and a layout.

"Standard four by four in the main gym," he whispered.

"Two more by each john, they're probably letting people go in shifts. Who knows how many outside the swinging doors. No way we can breach. Gotta fall back."

"No dice, dude," Leon said. "We're going in."

"They have one gun for each of us, and we have one gun between us. It's a suicide play. We're outta here."

"We gonna go hide in the basement?" Leon asked.

"Not cool. I don't like this either, but facts are facts. We have to contact the outside, get them a sitrep. Then we'll provide backup at the lab."

"Can we at least check Daxton's conference room before we bail?" Leon asked.

"Do not open the door!" the guard shouted through it. "You are surrounded. Do you understand?"

Weitz's shoulders sagged, and he hesitated before replying, "Yes."

Leon moved toward the back of the maintenance room.

"Very slowly, open the door just enough to slide out your weapon. On the floor. Do it now."

Weitz complied.

"Very good. Now, everyone lock your fingers atop your heads."

"Done," Weitz said when everyone but Leon was.

"We're going to open the door, and anyone who moves will be shot along with two others. Do you understand?"

"Yes."

"Good. We are opening the door now."

The guards shepherded the SWAT team into the open, then marched them single file into the gym to join the other hostages.

Weitz could only hope the sweep guard didn't dig too far into the laundry bins. Especially the one with Leon hiding in it.

~~~

"Mrs. Berger, I wish to verify that Mr. Berger is indeed the biological father of your children," Hanlon said over the speaker phone.

"What do you care?" Sheila asked.

Christine raised her head from the table.

"I am truly sorry, and perhaps I should have verified this earlier."

"Oh my God, what have you done?" Sheila knocked her chair down as she jumped to her feet.

"Please calm down, Mrs. Berger. We have nothing to gain from hysterics."

Sheila put her mouth directly over the speaker phone and launched into a vicious tirade of expletives, curse words, and foul language strung together seamlessly and eloquently enough to make a rapper blush. It ended abruptly when the guard knocked her out.

Hanlon was silent for a long while before he was heard to say anything.

"Sorry, *dude*, couldn't quite make that out." Daxton winked at Christine.

"I asked if you can confirm whether Mr. Berger fathered his sons." Hanlon's voice was meek.

Daxton could barely contain a smile, but through pursed lips he managed to say, "Nope. Never came up."

~~~

"Now!" Bandana said from the guard's left.

Eagle sprinted from behind the cubicle divider to the guard's right and hit him full force with a sacking tackle. They both plowed through the glass wall of the lab and crashed to the floor. Bandana took up a firing stance and capped the male and female guard with clean headshots before they could raise their weapons.

Eagle pushed the gun aside and ground his guard's cheek into the broken glass. "How many more?" he said through his teeth right next to the guard's ear.

Bandana side-stepped the divider and swept the remainder of the lab. "Clear!"

"What?" the guard asked through the pain and Felix's crying.

"How many more jumpsuit-motherfuckers roaming this building?" Eagle leaned harder on the guard's head and gave it a slide.

"Twenty-nine."

"Where?"

"One first floor." The guard could barely speak through the half of his mouth not smeared to the floor. "Fourteen in the gym, um, ahhgh."

"Shit," Eagle said to Bandana. "That's a heap of trouble for the main team." He resumed his interrogation, "Keep talking."

Bandana was checking Gajra and Davies, who were each unbuckling a boy. Gajra swept Felix up in her arms and ran back to the control booth. Davies stayed with Nathan, who remained motionless on the extended MRI table.

"Four at the top floor . . . conference."

"Come on, I know you can do it."

"Four on the roof . . . ahhgh. One . . . was watching cameras."

"That's twenty-seven. You're doin' great."

Bandana freed Ryder who grabbed his knife, his pistol, and her machine gun from the dead guard, then headed out through the shattered glass wall.

"Hold up, Pelse," Bandana said. "The main team is at the gym."

The shredded guard cried out, "Five on perimeter . . ."

"You sure that's all? Perimeter sounds light." Eagle twisted a handful of hair to emphasize his point.

"It's a . . . bottle . . . neck," the guard said. "Limited access."

"And?" He increased downward pressure on the guard's skull.

"Artillery . . . they're . . . fortified."

"Very good, shit-for-brains. Now it's time for nigh-nigh." Eagle pulled up the handful of hair and thumped the guard's head on the floor, then took his earpiece.

"Pelse, what's up?" Bandana asked as Ryder resumed his egress.

"Gotta spring my boss so he can get me off this rock."

"Come on, man," Eagle said. "This is a team sport. Stick it out." He finished handcuffing the guard to the MRI.

Ryder stopped and turned around. "Fine. But we hit the conference room next."

"No good," Eagle said. "I like three-on-four better than fourteen any day, but the gym has a truckload of hostages, including Weitz and our guys."

"No shit?" Bandana asked.

"Grab an earpiece, man. They stomped 'em and the whole team is in corral with the cattle."

"Do they know you two are here?" Ryder asked.

"Doesn't sound like it." He grabbed the gun from the floor, then paused halfway to standing. "Oh shit, they're calling for the lab rats to check in."

~~~
~~~

"Come on, Hanlon, you just told me we have the lab. Now give it up."

"Agent Kerwin, This turn of events is completely unacceptable. You will order your men to stand down immediately."

"I wish I could," Kerwin said. Then he added, with more spite than intended, "But your goons took my team's comm gear."

"There is a little boy in need of medical attention," Hanlon said.

"I doubt our guys killed the docs. As long as yours didn't, they'll take care of him."

"Neither of us knows exactly what transpired there, now do we?"

"No, we don't. So call it off and we'll clean it up."

"It is likely that your men would be wearing my guards' earpieces. Do you agree?"

Kerwin looked around the command post for feedback. There was no consensus as to whether he should confirm. "Maybe."

"Thank you. Good-bye."

~~~

It's not like rock climbing in here, more like caving an extended overhang. Leon carefully made his way along the plumbing trunk line above the drop ceiling. He was glad Daxton had scrimped on the firewalls so he could easily transition over the truncated drywall and studs between rooms.

The grip was way better than rock, and he could shimmy along the length of one pipe at great length before transitioning
~~~

to another. He missed his Petzl lighted helmet, but there was some ambient emergency light coming through various slivers and gaps in the ceiling. If only the fluorescent ballasts were on, he could possibly make do without a penlight in his mouth.

He figured he was over the southwest corner of the gym now, and wrapped his legs around the pipe so he could hang down and get a good look at the flexible foil air duct leading to the ceiling tile. He thanked the engineer for specifying pinch clamps rather than worm screws. He was able to remove the duct and look through the ventilation grill. Just enough to get a look, but not enough to get caught.

Most of the hostages were sitting or lying on the aerobics dance floor. Many, mostly the SWAT officers, were strewn about the various universal workout stations, apparatus, and a couple of chairs. A few were standing or leaning against a wall. None of them were Sheila, Nathan, or Felix.

The guards were positioned six by six now, with only one at each bathroom. The bathroom shifts were presumably stopped, dormant, or at least down to a trickle. Once the SWAT team had settled in, the overall mood of the gym had mellowed to tense melancholy.

What to do now? The odds were significantly worse than before. There were still eleven SWAT guys, but now no gun and a badly reduced element of surprise. He wondered how Bandana and Eagle had fared.

Think, Leon, think. Even if Sheila were here, it would be like a lone researcher with nothing but a loud voice and waving arms trying to spring one gazelle from a herd overrun with lions. That scenario hadn't played out well for the researcher, and went especially bad for the gazelle.

Two of the guards suddenly broke formation and moved

swiftly toward a group of SWAT guys. They grabbed one by the arms and escorted him to the small raised platform at the front of the aerobics floor. Several other guards raised their guns and encouraged the remaining SWAT guys to sit back down. The SWAT officer, Leon thought his name was Bowen or Bowman or something like that, was faced away from the other hostages and forced to kneel.

~~~

"Jesus Christ, they're gonna shoot Borman." Bandana put a hand to his forehead and started pacing excitedly.

"No way," Ryder said. "It's a power play to flush us out."

"Shut up, man," Eagle said. "We gotta think this through."

"Nothing to think about," Ryder said. "Always go down swinging."

"That's not how we roll," Eagle said.

"That's because you're pussies," Ryder said. "City has you hamstrung so you don't get sued."

"Not cool." Bandana was grinding his teeth. "Not now."

"Do we fold?" Eagle asked.

Bandana continued pacing feverishly. He smacked a wall cabinet and heard Felix start to cry again.

"Fifteen seconds, man," Eagle said.

"Pelse." Bandana grabbed the wall phone. "How do I call the gym?"

"Don't do it," Ryder said.

"Fuck you!" Eagle moved toward Ryder who moved toward him.

"Just fuckin' tell me," Bandana said.

"Don't think so." Ryder was now toe to toe with Eagle.
~~~

Eagle growled then bent over the dead guard. He tore her jumpsuit open and started searching for her comm mic.

"Motherfucker!" Bandana slammed his fist into the cabinet. "What's the goddamn extension?"

"It is in the list on the phone," Gajra said from the booth.

Bandana searched the list frantically, found the number, and started to dial. All three hardened men flinched as they heard the gunshot through the earpieces.

"Hello?" the guard said.

"That better be a fuckin' warning shot you prick!" Bandana said.

"I'm afraid you missed the deadline."

Bandana kicked the wall with enough force to break through the drywall and get his leg stuck. He wrenched it free and bellowed, "Motherfucker!" from his gut into the phone.

"We have ten more of your team here, and over forty hostages. Will you be joining us?"

"Yes, godammit, yes!" Bandana slammed the phone down and turned to Davies. "You. Stay here with the kids. And here, hide these guns where you can get to them."

Bandana dialed Kerwin and traded sitreps as fast as possible while still providing useful intel.

"Come on, asshole. You're coming with us," Eagle said to Ryder who was now walking away.

"Hey, dickhead!" Bandana said. "The building is wired to blow. We can't piss this guy off any more than we already have."

Ryder turned back and raised his gun. "You may as well let me shoot you now. Head or heart?"

With that, Bandana and Eagle sprinted out of the lab and back toward the stairs.

~~~
~~~

"You should not keep me waiting, Agent Kerwin," Hanlon said.

"I was being told about your ruthless murder."

"Nothing emboldens sin so much as mercy."

"'Tis mightiest in the mightiest," Kerwin said.

"I trust your officer's report has shown you the folly of resistance. He failed to mention our fortified artillery position at the main junction to the rest of the complex. I wish only to complete the testing, then my guards will leave."

"They can't just walk away."

"You would sacrifice so many innocents to punish a few guilty?"

"You kill innocents for experiments."

"Touché. When can I expect the power to be restored?"

"I'm afraid that's not going to be easy."

"I did not request a difficulty assessment; I need a timeline."

"Four hours."

"I will grant two. I will even mercifully round forward to 11:15 p.m. There are fifty-seven hostages remaining. Do not force me to expend their lives frivolously."

"I won't."

"Very well. I understand Mr. Pelse is in possession of an earpiece from one of my guards. Do you have the ability to communicate with Mr. Berger?"

"I don't."

"Now is not the time for deception."

"I'm serious. We can't find him."

"I will remain merciful until the power is restored. By that time, you must also produce Mr. Berger, and deliver him into my custody."

~~~
~~~

"Don't move."

Leon froze.

"What are you doing?"

"Nothing."

"Bullshit."

"What did you want me to say?"

"Turn around slowly."

Leon turned and found Ryder leaning on a cubicle divider. "You scared the crap out of me."

"Figures. Where you goin'?"

"Looks like the same place you are."

"You gonna be a hero?" Ryder asked.

"Might die trying."

"I hear that's bad for me."

"Bad for both of us."

Ryder held out his left hand and said, "Bad for humanity according to Hanlon." Then his right hand, "Bad for the world according to Daxton."

"Not my problem," Leon said.

"I'm getting over it, too." Ryder came out of the cubicle and stood facing Leon. He looked into a mirror of what could have been. "You really wanna do this?"

"Have to."

"Don't."

"Can't not."

"Well," Ryder said, "I guess we better go in together. Two heads beat one even if one's a shithead."

"What's the plan?"

Ryder leaned on the cubicle divider again, and considered the situation. "It's two on four. I say we go in spikes high."

"You'll get everyone killed."

"Hang on." Ryder focused on the sound from the earpiece. "Message for you from Hanlon: Give it up or the kids get it."

"Where are they?" Leon asked.

"In the lab. It's locked down by now."

"You saw them? Are they OK?"

"They were when I left," Ryder said.

"You bastard! You could have gotten them out?"

"Not really. How could I drag a load of doctors and kids through the gauntlet?"

"You could have hidden them."

"I don't play hide-and-seek, and they would have lost that game anyway."

"You really are a cold-hearted bastard," Leon said.

"I am what I am."

"I have to give in."

"I'm not, so you can't."

"Another standoff?"

"No need. You can accept it."

"So we take the conference room, then what?"

"Get the hell out."

"The gauntlet?"

"Sneak out."

"But not with my boys?"

"They can't get me off the planet."

"Neither can Daxton now."

"There's still time."

"McKinley is dead."

Ryder revealed a chink in his armor. "How?"

"Sniper."

"Goddammit. Come on, we're going in."

"We need a better plan than 'spikes high'."

"You fight?"

"I do OK."

"Two on one?"

"Sure."

"There's a hole in your arm."

"I'm fine."

"Good with a knife?"

"Better than a gun. Where can we hide them?"

"Daxton has a panic room in his office."

"Paranoid."

"Careful."

"Let's go." Ryder handed over the bowie.

"And when we're done there?"

"Clear out the gym."

"Fourteen guards."

"Good guys inside."

"Unarmed."

"Motivated."

"Other guards?"

"Eventually. Something else you should know."

"What?"

"Hanlon starts executing hostages in," Ryder checked his watch, "an hour forty-five."

"Why then?"

"Only if the power isn't back on."

"If it is?"

"He wants us back in the lab."

"More tests?"

"Yup."

"Not good." Leon familiarized himself with the weight and balance of the knife.

"Let's fix it."

"Not sure we should."

"Jesus, what now?"

Leon paused for a moment. "What if we let Hanlon figure us out?"

"Can't."

"Might."

"Hasn't."

"We haven't really given him a chance, have we?"

"Don't want to end up like your boy."

"What happened?" Leon tightened his grip on the handle of the knife.

"They put him in a coma."

"Why?"

"See if they're like us."

"They're adopted, for Christ's sake!"

"Oops."

"We're going to the lab."

"He'll be fine. They just drugged him."

"They can undrug him then."

"Probably have by now."

"Is Davies there?"

"Gajra too."

Leon was wound up like a four-way spring with only one option.

Ryder asked, "What'll it be?"

~~~

Leon made his way carefully along one trunk pipe and transitioned to another, then another. Almost there. He checked
~~~

his watch: three minutes to breach at 9:43 p.m.

This was it, time to pop the duct and take a peek. He assumed the bat-position and carefully reached down for the pinch clamp on the flex duct. But there wasn't one. Some idiot had used a worm screw, and forgot to leave a screwdriver behind for Leon.

He looked around, found the next one and prayed for a pinch clamp.

There, that was it. He could make out a table top and two empty chairs. He strained for a better angle, but couldn't see enough through the grill at this end of the room to be sure.

He hurried as quietly as he could along the pipe and came to where he expected to get the best view with the least probability of being seen by someone looking up.

Leon got a finger in between the ceiling tile and the support frame, and pried as slowly as he could, trying to make sure it didn't pop free.

When there was enough clearance, he hung back to get a good look.

He saw Ryder reclining in a chair with his feet up on the head of the conference table. Ryder looked up at the cracked lid and said, "Keep it up. You're almost as quiet as a couple of skeletons screwing on a tin roof."

Leon grabbed the pipe, let his legs swing down and kicked through a ceiling tile. Then he dropped down onto the conference table, and hopped to the floor. "What happened?"

"All gone."

"Where?"

"The gym, I guess."

"What now?"

"Try the lab?"

~~~

"What a mess." Leon stood in the dimly lit lab and surveyed the broken glass, strewn wheelchairs, empty gurney, damaged wall, busted cabinet, and dead guards.

"At least they took their wounded." Ryder shook his head over the left-behind bodies.

"Huh?"

"We had one cuffed to the big white donut box over there."

"Oh."

Ryder began rummaging through the cabinets and drawers.

"Need something?"

"More guns."

"Here?"

"Stashed."

Ryder produced the two MP5 machine guns and a Glock hidden by the doctor, then checked the ammo.

"Can we take it?" Leon asked.

"Not likely."

"Too many?"

"Yup."

"Odds?"

"Bad."

"Let's not."

"What then?"

"Call Hanlon."
~~~

CHAPTER 12

"Excuse me, Hanlon?" The Atheist poured most of the coffee into a cup, and some onto the break table while standing in line alongside the conference hall. Hanlon's bodyguard stepped in, but was waved off.

"Yes?"

"May I speak with you privately?"

"You are among the few who accepted my invitation willingly. Why have you not participated thus far?"

"I, uh, well; I contributed on the physicalist committee. But overall I feel the others have been providing what you need from the group."

"They have." Hanlon checked his watch. "But time runs short."

"I understand. I was hoping I could help you personally."

"In what way?"

"Is there somewhere where we can talk?"

Hanlon considered the proposal. "I have some time, yes." He motioned for a guard to follow and led them both into one of the large rooms adjoining the main hall to the west.

The two men took their seats in antique wingback leather chairs beside the grand piano, and amid more books than a municipal library.

Hanlon broke the silence first. "I'm quite familiar with your books, lectures, and public persona. Yet you never state what kind of an atheist you are, specifically."

"Ah yes, everyone needs their source bias. Typical and understandable. I was a rebellious atheist in my youth; a lazy agnostic in mid-life; and now I describe myself as a well-reasoned, wide and positive atheist. Until something changes my mind, that is."

"Forgive me. *Wide* and *positive*?"

"Correct. An example of a narrow atheist would be your typical Christian, Jew, or Muslim. They deny that the other's conception of god exists. A negative atheist is simply one who has fallen out of belief or never had it, but hasn't quite yet realized there really is no Santa Claus—for sure—at least until He shows up."

"How can you help me?" Hanlon asked.

"This is a wonderful estate." The Atheist overtly looked around. Floor to vaulted ceiling blackout drapes prevented a view outside, but he pictured lush gardens, fountains, and acres upon acres of rolling old-growth forest.

"To the point, please."

"You seem conflicted," he blurted.

"As are we all." Hanlon sipped his espresso.

"To one degree or another, I suppose. But I gather you are somewhat more so than most."

"I merely have the means that others lack. It is refreshing to finally focus all my resources directly toward The Answer."

"I bet." He catalogued the various original paintings, classic first editions, statues, sculptures, and other priceless art he'd seen in the mansion. "But why not just sign on with Gates and Buffett in *The Giving Pledge*?"[30]

"Their view of contributing to society differs from mine."

"Philanthropy sucks. Is that it?"

"'Charity sees the need, not the cause.'"

"I think you'll like where I'm headed." The Atheist could only hope. "Please allow me to offer you some clarity."

"I am quite familiar with both sides of the teleological fence."

"I see that. But I'm wondering if you have thoroughly evaluated the arguments against."

"Certainly."

"Certainly?"

"Yes."

"Then why the agnosticism?"

"The question has remained unanswerable. Greater minds than mine have struggled with it for millennia."

"And why is that?"

"My apologies." Hanlon stood. "I misunderstood your intent. I will not be proselytized by an evangelical atheist." He added "Guard," indicating she should open the door.

"Had enough of the Evangelicals, have you?"

Hanlon stopped, as did the guard with her hand on the doorknob. Without turning around he said, "Pardon me?"

"Only God can really do that. Right?"

Hanlon turned and faced the still seated man. "You antagonize me at your peril."

"Hey, I don't mean to drag the lion back into the Colosseum." He summoned the remaining bravado from the tips of his toes, "But I'm guessing you are the bastard son of some long-dead revivalist preacher or a televangelist-type. I can offer you some insight you may not have considered."

Hanlon regarded the Atheist carefully. Please let him see anxiety rather than scorn.

"What do you know about me?" Hanlon asked.

"I don't presume any details, but the indicators are there."

"Such as?"

"Must I state the obvious?" He put his coffee on the table and pulled up his socks.

"Please do."

"Well, you're very wealthy. Extremely wealthy by any standard. You're enigmatic, secretive, and reclusive. It seems no one but you and God know your background."

"Stipulated."

"Yes. And the pseudonym you've chosen is indicative of your leanings."

"How so?"

"'Never attribute to malice what can adequately be explained by stupidity.' It's beautiful. Couldn't have said it better myself."

"You assume too much."

"Maybe." The Atheist took a deep breath and said, "But you also exhibit the classic cognitive dissonance of a person with significant intellect having been raised in an overwhelmingly oppressive funda-mentalist household of some kind."

"Why would you say that?"

"Am I wrong?"

"Indulge me."

"Well, you've swapped the accent, but a few of the mannerisms persist. And your guards. They're not mindless drones. At least those I've spoken to appear to be both intelligent and well educated, although committed beyond any reasonable stretch. It seems to me that a loyal volunteer army such as yours could only be assembled with a significant degree of fundamentalist pursuit."

Hanlon was still listening.

"And only a person skilled in attracting such folks would be in a position to select the best from the herd, as it were."

"Many people are motivated to do God's will and save their immortal soul."

"Yeah, like Islamic Jihadists." Give me back my sarcasm! Nope, too late. "When was your crisis of faith?"

"You seem to have all the answers; you tell me."

"Oh, I don't know," the Atheist looked around briefly, then directly at Hanlon. "Maybe you killed your father and didn't get caught, so you started questioning God's existence?"

"You paint a pleasant, albeit convenient fiction of my circumstance." Hanlon gave a wry smile and took another sip.

"May I proceed to my point?"

"Please do."

~~~

"You're sure about this?" Ryder asked.

"Sure as I can be," Leon said.

"Has to be a hundred percent."

"Nothing is."

"Then let's not."

"Have to."

"What about your family?"

"They'll understand. They have to."

"Doubt it."

"No choice."

"Not for me."

"Me neither."

"Waffler."

"Yeah," Leon said. Then he thought for a moment and asked, "Why'd you join the Air Force?"
~~~

"Thought they'd let me kill bad guys."

"Why?"

"Because some need killing."

"No, why did you want to?"

"Some need killing."

"Like the Colombian guerrillas?"

"Yeah, them too."

"Insightful."

"Right."

"Might is right?"

"Always has been."

"And Hanlon?"

"He might be right, too. Let's hope he doesn't kill us to prove it."

~~~

Relief never tasted so sweet. He was making progress with Hanlon, he just knew it.

"I know," the Atheist said, "that you don't need me to run through all the epistemic arguments debunking religion on reason alone. That's been done to death."

"Interesting choice of words." Hanlon squinted over his espresso cup.

"Unfortunate choice. The point is that I think believing in God is unreasonable because it's not supported by the evidence—that is, it's simply not true. My position is that if believing makes people happy, then the truth makes them unhappy."[11]

"It is a bold stance, but not unfounded."

"Don't get me wrong, I'm not saying that there are no
~~~

benefits to religion, and that no one does good things in the name of it. Some of my best friends are Christians and Jews. My premise is that in a cost-benefit formula, it's off the charts in terms of cost."

"Contemporary Christianity has moderated and focused more on education and easing suffering than holy wars and coerced conversions."

"See? That's just it. I'm not talking about baggage from the Crusades and the Inquisition." He shifted in his seat and leaned forward. "Allow me to compare and contrast."

"By all means."

"Most religions historically kept people in their faith through guilt, fear, and sometimes coercion. 'Leave the Church and you leave your family', 'Believe or your immortal soul will burn forever', 'Lose your faith, lose your life'. The latter being more Muslim short-term and Christian long-term."

"And your point?"

"Religious leaders used to force-feed belief, now they're just trying to keep up with the flock's ever-changing beliefs—and those beliefs persist despite reason and facts from either side."

"How is the flock at odds with the Church?"

"People can no longer force themselves to believe that their best friend or spouse or kids are going to Hell just because they didn't pick the right brand of religion. And this flies in the face of what they've been told by their leaders and elders to be an incontrovertible fact."

"Then you and your brethren are succeeding."

"Sadly, no. True atheists and even agnostics are still an extremely rare breed—at least those who'll admit it on a survey. And of course, we don't have cool clubhouses. The fact is, people are not searching for truth, they just want to believe in God—

in whatever manifestation suits their mood."

"They are merely reacting to a lack of sufficient evidence." Hanlon seemed resolute.

"No, no, you misunderstand," the Atheist said. "I'm saying that everything, including new evidence, is subject to revision in the faithful mind—as long as it suits their need for immortality."

"The general public does not need immortality, they need truth."

"No disagreement there. But I believe the Church secretly admits to itself that there may not be a God, and seems to think humanity can't handle that truth. Moreover, they lean on the notion that believing makes people happier and better neighbors, so they've tried to sustain the lie to protect the public at large from that truth."

"Why would they do that?"

"I don't know, but it's just patronizing, nihilistic, and deeply pessimistic on the Church's part."

"And the contrast?"

"Well, and again with all due respect, you are in some ways like God should be."

Hanlon tried, but failed to hide his keen interest.

"What I mean by that, is you force people to come to you or not leave you under threat of death. Analagous to religion, but I'm still not a fan of the intimidation. The difference is, at least in this house anyway, you require that people bring their own minds to the party."

"I do."

"Yes. You want them to think for themselves—in fact you demand it—rather than brainwashing them with some divine but out-dated rule book."

"This would be an interesting debate, time permitting.

How can you help me?"

"You must understand that I mean no disrespect here. For my own safety, that is."

"Please, continue to speak freely."

"Thank you."

"You are welcome."

The Atheist put his hands on his knees and leaned forward again. "The answer you so fervently seek is . . . 'What then?'"

Hanlon's disappointment echoed off the bookshelves in a way that sound could not. "A question does not provide an answer."

"Never has. Listen, I know you had a lot longer climb than most going up Olympus only to find Zeus didn't really live there. I applaud you for reaching the summit, but you still don't appreciate the view."

"How so?"

"Let's suppose you manage to prove the twins share a soul. Or not. Or, for that matter, this Daxton guy says he found intelligent life out there. Will that really change anyone's mind?"

"It cannot be otherwise." Hanlon now seemed wide and positive.

"Really? You need to gut-check the phrases 'scientific fact' and 'clinically proven'." He sat up straight so he could talk with his hands. "Now hear me out and know that I'm speaking generally: Minds poisoned from birth don't recover. The statistics say we're making progress with those who got a lesser dose, and maybe future generations won't accept religion blindly."

"That time will come."

"But the ongoing appeal of something greater than ourselves and our continuance after death—to people indoctrinated from childhood—is simply too powerful for most adults to deny."

"I disagree."

"Of course, you're an exception as am I, and a growing number of others. But to change things on a societal level we need to eliminate or at least discredit the source of the poison."

"Why do you think that?"

"Short of the Almighty Himself descending on Times Square in a hail of fire and brimstone, then proceeding to actually demonstrate his omniscience, omnipotence, and omnibenevolence—beyond mere parlor tricks—I won't buy it. And as far as consumers of what you're selling, I place myself squarely in your target demographic."

"And the other side?"

"Same thing. Dogmatism trumps reason every time. You heard the dualists. They simply reject the premise that scientific evidence can actually be what it is. Six out of seven billion people can't be wrong—that sort of thing."

"Then we remain at an impasse." Hanlon set down his cup.

"Hey, I'm not saying we shouldn't figure out the twin link. That's fascinating stuff. And exoplanet exploration? Hoo-ra and Amen! I'm just worried that you and Daxton are pushing the limits of acceptable practices."

"Acceptable to whom?"

"'Ay, there's the rub.' No afterlife, no consequences, right?" The Atheist sat back in his chair. "Contrary to worldwide popular theist belief—thankfully less entrenched in the U.S. recently[14]—atheists in general do have a strong moral compass, and the prescription isn't written on some really old scraps of paper."

The door opened, and a guard poked his head in to say something to the guard already in the library.

"Shall I summon the Ethicist?" Hanlon asked the Atheist.

"No need." The Atheist sank further back in his chair. "I was just hoping an appeal to reason could slow down the kidnapping and murder and other such things."

"You disapprove of my methods."

"Yes."

"Excuse me, sir," the guard said. "You have an important phone call."

Hanlon stood and regarded the Atheist for a longer moment than the other man would have liked. He merely said, "Thank you for your input. You may rejoin the conference," and left the room.

~~~

"I have a gun, and I'm not afraid to use it," Ryder said into the dead guard's cell phone. He added, "On myself."

"That would be tragic," Hanlon said.

"So are all the dead people."

"'Et tu Brute?' How ironic."

"Every man has his limits."

"As you can see, I am determined to find The Answer."

"Yeah, I get it," Ryder said. "What do you have in mind that won't get me killed?"

"Both you and Mr. Berger are willing to cooperate?"

"I wouldn't say willing, but we will . . . with conditions."

"Where is Mr. Berger? May I speak with him?"

"No."

"What are your conditions?"

"He wants his family and the civilians released. I want Daxton and Christine out, too."
~~~

"Not the SWAT officers?"

"Come on. I know you need them to keep the cops out," Ryder said.

"Good of you to understand."

"Are we going to do this or not?"

"Which of you will submit to the pentobarbital?"

"Doesn't matter much, now does it?"

"That depends upon your estimation of the odds."

"He'll take it," Ryder said. "I fly out tomorrow and don't want to be groggy. Do we have a deal?"

"In principle, I believe we do. Conditional, of course, upon power restoration and live television coverage of the experiment. Doctors Davies and Ranayan will join you in the lab. My suggestion to you would be to leave your weapon at the entrance to the stairwell, then return to the lab and wait."

"We're going to a window so we can watch everyone walk past the perimeter. And don't bother asking which window. We'll come to the lab when everyone is out of the building. Oh, and Leon needs a few minutes on the phone with his family. After they're safe."

"He will have several. I would like to thank you for your cooperation."

"Yeah, right." Ryder disconnected the call. "And don't forget to fuck right off."

~~~

"How is he doing?" Sheila was holding a fresh ice pack to her head, and Felix's head in her lap.

Davies checked Nathan lying under a blanket on the bench press and said, "He's still out, but I think he'll be OK."
~~~

"I can't thank you enough," Sheila whispered to Gajra, who shook her head.

Christine sat up and whispered to Gajra, "Are you kidding? Giving him a sedative instead of a coma was a stroke of genius."

"Hush." Davies glanced at the guards around the gym. "You know what they'll do if they find out."

"They can't hear us over Dad's snoring," Christine whispered. Then she saw one of the guards watching them closely and said at a conversational level, "Yeah . . . I've been stuck in this complex for ten months, and now this. Feels like the Hotel California."

The group's muted laughter ceased as a guard started walking toward them.

"Dr. Davies," she said, "when can this child be ready to move?"

"Not on your life!" Sheila stood quickly, leaving Christine to catch Felix waking up and rolling off her lap.

The guard smacked Sheila squarely across the face and ordered her to sit back down. Sheila did not. Sheila received a punch to the gut. Sheila doubled over, then kneeled and continued gasping.

"We cannot move him again, unless it is to a hospital," Gajra said.

"They can take him to the hospital after they get out," the guard said.

"And when will that be?" Davies asked.

"Ten minutes" The guard walked away.

"Your attention, please." The lead guard was standing by the swinging doors to the gym and addressing the crowd. "Some of you, but not all will be leaving here shortly."

The crowd considered cheering, but decided collectively that this was not the time. Daxton stirred among the chatter.

"Quiet, please," the guard said, "quiet. Thank you. In a few minutes, when we announce it, the police officers are to gather by the stage. You may prepare your fallen comrade's body, say your good-byes, and place him on a gurney for a group of civilians we choose to wheel him out."

"What's this all about?" Daxton asked.

Three guards wheeled two gurneys and a wheelchair through the swinging doors. The shredded guard who'd been interrogated earlier in the lab took a gurney to the aerobics stage. The other and the wheelchair were for Nathan and Felix.

"Strap them in," the guard ordered the doctors.

"Why?" Sheila asked.

"Because you're leaving, and you'll be moving through a very dicey situation along the way."

"Felix can walk." Sheila was catching her breath.

Felix nodded sheepishly.

"Do you want to get out of here or not?" one of the guards asked, but didn't wait for an answer. "Doctors," he said, "when they're ready, you will join us at the doors."

"Why them?" Daxton asked.

The guard scoffed, but decided to answer. "Because they're staying here for now."

Both guards walked away and one said to the other, "Take your kid to Disney if you want him to run wild."

"Anyone know what's going on?" Daxton asked.

"Looks like they're letting everyone go but docs and cops," Christine said.

"Did they say why?"

"No."

"Did they find Ryder?"

Christine gave him a dirty look. "Yeah, he's in the john."

"Great. That's a relief."

"Jesus, Dad. You're getting thick in your old age."

"What?" Daxton shrugged sleepily.

"How the hell would we know if they found Ryder *or* Leon? Do you see them sitting here?"

"Never mind that," Daxton said. "Where are you going, Gajra?"

"I do not know," Gajra said.

"I think I do," Davies said. "My guess is we're headed back to the lab."

~~~

"That is correct, Agent Kerwin. You will be permitted to send one reporter and one camera operator. My preference would be Ms. Yvonne Forrester; she has a certain *je ne sais quoi*. They are to be at the lobby doors in ten minutes time."

"But we still have an hour to get the power back on," Kerwin said.

"You needn't use all the allotted time if it is not necessary."

"We're scrambling. It'll be tight."

"Do not miss the deadline."

"And I get all the hostages except the doctors and the SWAT team."

"Also correct," Hanlon said. "Be advised that the television personnel and their gear will be as thoroughly screened as if they refused an x-ray body-scan at the airport."

"What about Pelse and Berger?"

"They are no longer classified as hostages. They are staying in the complex voluntarily."
~~~

"Can't be."

"Semantics aside, they will participate in the most important experiment since Rutherford split the atom. Wolfe News must share their feed with all the networks. Do we have an agreement?"

"I'm thinking." Kerwin considered whether this could be construed as negotiating with a terrorist. He could hang his hat on 'voluntarily', but that was a flimsy peg when Hanlon still had thirteen cops—well, twelve now. At least he'll get the civilians out. And maybe the world actually wants to see this big breakthrough. Who was he to stifle that kind of progress?

"Agent Kerwin?"

"Fine . . . fine. Get the civilians out here, right now."

"Very well. They will be down shortly."

~~~

"Wow, Yvonne, are you sure you want to do this?" Bruce asked during the commercial break.

"Are you kidding me? This is big, Bruce. And they said this Hanlon guy asked for me by name. No way I'm going to pass this up."

"If you say so," Bruce said. "Good luck. OK, in five."

"Hello again, I'm Bruce Phillips and you're watching the Wolfe Report. We're back with more breaking news on the hostage standoff at Dax Space Corp. Our own Yvonne Forrester is still on the scene, and she has a remarkable and exclusive update for us. Yvonne?"

"Thanks Bruce. That's right, we've just been informed that the reclusive Hanlon, who is apparently orchestrating this standoff from somewhere outside the complex, has agreed to
~~~

exchange all of the civilian hostages in return for a TV crew. We'll be covering an experiment he'll be conducting on Ryder Pelse and Leon Berger. We don't know the exact nature of the experiment, but yours truly will be covering it live from within the Dax headquarters medical lab."

"When you say *civilian* hostages, does that mean the SWAT team will stay in the building?"

"That's right. They have not released the name of the officer killed, pending notification of his next of kin. However, there are still twelve officers in captivity, and they'll be staying behind as Hanlon's insurance that the experiment will not be interrupted."

"When do we expect the hostages will be released?"

"We're told they'll be coming down to the lobby soon, and we're to meet them in about five minutes from now."

"Excellent. You be careful in there, Yvonne. And there you go. You heard it here first and exclusively on the Wolfe Report . . ."

~~~

"I could kill you now." The guard raised his gun. Everyone in the gym, including the SWAT team gasped at least a little.

"Dad, I'm begging you," Christine said. "Please don't do this. It's not worth it."

"Just get him on the phone, will you?" Daxton asked the guard for the third time. The guard grudgingly complied.

"Hey, Hanlon," Daxton said.

"Ah, Mr. Daxton. And how may I be of service to you?"

"I want to be there for the experiment."

"You are in no position to ask any favors of me."

"Yeah, yeah, I know." He gave the guards a dismissive
~~~

glance. "But this is my building, and my legacy. You wouldn't have found the twins without me."

"Hardly a valid reason for stealing my proverbial thunder."

"You owe me!"

"In what way?"

"You can't be serious. You Tasered two of my detail last month, and killed a bunch today. Now you have my pilot on an operating table. First you blow the whistle on Flight 4, and now you've all but scuttled it. Give a guy a break over here."

"It does seem as though you've been greatly inconvenienced by our opposing desires. For that you have my sincerest apology. However, since I cannot risk having you interfere on such an important occasion, I respectfully refuse your request. My guards will escort you outside along with the others."

Daxton disconnected the call with his thumb, but still held the phone to his ear. "Great! Thanks so much Hanlon. This doesn't square us, but it goes a long way."

Daxton hit the disconnect button again, then tossed the phone back to the guard and said, "Take me to the lab."

~ ~ ~

"You have any problems in the head?" Ryder asked.

"You should know," Leon said. "Apparently we have the same brain."

"I mean the can. The pisser. The—"

"I get it. Nope, everything came out fine." Leon looked through the window into the parking lot at the myriad flashing lights and huge crowd gathered. "What have you been doing?"

"Jackin' off and calisthenics."

"Quite a circus down there."

"One more for the year in review." Ryder took another bite of a Three Musketeers bar he found in someone's desk.

"Here they come."

They saw the reporter and cameraman walk toward the building, but couldn't see the lobby entrance from this vantage point.

"Any minute now." Leon put his hands on the window and leaned close enough to fog it, straining to get an earlier look.

Time slowed down for Leon. Each second brought more doubt into his mind. Bucket by bucket he was now starting to overflow with dread that they'd made the wrong choice. That Hanlon wouldn't let his family go after all.

Then he saw the gurneys wheel out, and inhaled sharply. The first person was entirely covered in a sheet, but Nathan's head was uncovered. Sheila wheeled Felix next to the gurney, and they were followed by the crowd of Dax personnel who eventually sprinted past the police and into the arms of their loved ones waiting behind the barricades.

Leon slapped Ryder on the shoulder and said, "He actually did it! See? Christine is out there too."

"Time for some bad news," Ryder said. "This place is a powder keg."

"No doubt." Leon nodded.

"Probably Semtex. Maybe C-4."

"Seriously? Why?"

"Hanlon took a belt-and-suspenders approach."

"You sure?"

"Yup. When you call your wife, tell her to take your kids to the hospital. Tell Chrissy to ride along."

~~~
~~~

"Hey there, Little Man. How are you holding up?" Leon tried to sound as upbeat as he could.

"I'm scared, Daddy." Felix was barely audible over the phone.

"That's OK, Buddy. I'm kinda scared too."

"They killed the bad people."

"Who did?"

"The police man. He killed that bad man and the bad lady, but Nate was already sick."

"He'll be OK. Don't worry—"

"He won't wake up, Daddy." Felix began to cry again. Through intermittent gasps he continued, "Mommy says he'll wake up, but we can't wake him up, and—"

"It's OK. It's OK." Leon's eyes blurred. "Listen, Felix. OK? You need to be a big man and take your brother to the hospital. Can you do that for me?"

"Why can't you come with us?"

"I have some things to do here, but I'll be out soon, OK? We'll go back home and see Ralph. I'd like that too—"

Leon cut himself off in mid-snivel. Gotta be strong.

"Daddy? Daddy where are you?"

"I'm here," Leon said. "Can I . . . talk to Mommy now?" He added, "Love you, Little Man."

"I love you too, but I'm still pissed at you," Sheila said. "Christine, no . . . you have to pick him up and . . . hang on Baby." Leon heard the phone rattle on the asphalt.

"Baby? You still there?" It was Leon's turn to panic. It was surprisingly the first time tonight, but he was pretty sure it wouldn't be the last.

"I'm here," Sheila said. "I'm so sorry Baby, but we are freaking out here."

"We'll get through this, just like we always do."

"When? . . . When have we ever been through anything like this?"

"I don't know, Baby. But we'll get through it. We just have to."

"Why did you go back in there?" Sheila was calmer, but he knew she was still crying. "They said you got out with Ryder, but then you went back in. Why?" The word got sucked back into her throat as she sobbed again.

"You know I had to."

"No I don't! These aren't hippos and crocs, Baby. What were you thinking?"

"I wanted to get you out."

"The cops can handle it."

"You know that didn't go so well. Listen, Baby." Leon switched to serious-mode as leader of the expedition. "I don't have much time here. There's something I need to tell you."

"I know, I know! They're going to put you in a coma like they did my poor little Nate."

"There's more."

"Oh, my God! What now?"

"Ryder thinks the building has explosives in it."

"Jesus Christ, I can't handle this, Baby. I am so losing it out here . . ." She had moved on to weeping.

"I know. But you have to . . . are you there? . . . Sheila?"

"What?" She was exasperated and exhausted and barely audible.

"Please go with the boys to the hospital. Take Christine, too. Will you do that for me? I need to know that you're all safe."

"I . . . "

"Baby, I'm begging you. Please get out of here now."

"I. We will. We will, Baby." Sheila's voice was building up like a wave heading for the beach, "But you have to get out of there. You have to come home. I want my Leo back! I love you so much, Baby."

"I know, Baby. And I love you bunches. I know you know that. That I love you. We both know I'll get out of here . . ."

~~~

"Dammit, man. That was brutal." Ryder shook his head as he finished off a stolen Mountain Dew. "And you wonder why I want to go."

Leon grabbed some tissues from a desk and started wiping away the emotion. "Guess I got all the love for both of us."

"Is it worth it?"

"Absolutely."

"Never a doubt?"

"Nope. She's my other half. You suck."

"I can live with that," Ryder said. "You ready to do this?"

"I'm not really ready, but I'm Ready's calf."

"Close enough."

~~~

"I would like to see the broadcast now," Hanlon said.

"We don't have the power back on," Kerwin said. "They're getting close."

"I understand that, but the reporter should be ready to broadcast. I'm told Ms. Forrester agreed to cover the story. I appreciate that."

"What are you asking for now?"

"She can merely do a preliminary teaser setting the stage for the main event. I wish to ensure that all networks will break in."

"I'll see what I can do."

~~~

"That's right, Bruce. We're coming to you live from inside the medical lab at Dax Space Corp. This is the first time any media have been allowed past the lobby in this top secret facility, and we're told the experiment to be conducted here will be a game-changer."

"It looks awfully dark in there, Yvonne."

"It's not too bad, really. The building still has emergency lighting, and as you can see there's been some damage in the lab itself. The damage allegedly occurred when the SWAT team temporarily retook the lab, but they were later captured by the terrorists. We're told the power should be coming on around 11:15 p.m., just about thirty minutes from now."

"Have they told you what we'll be seeing?"

"We can hear it from the source!" Yvonne was always so perky. "Go ahead and zoom out, Roger. Good? OK. I'm here with Dr. Jeremy Davies, Chief of Neurology at Foothills Medical Centre in Calgary, Alberta, Canada. He's also an adjunct professor at the University of Calgary."

Davies nodded to the camera.

"Dr. Davies was Leon Berger's attending physician after the ill-fated ice climbing expedition near Banff last February. As you'll recall, world-famous ice climber Todd Healey and two other members of the party lost their lives while climbing with Berger when he experienced his second coma-like incident."

"Also with us tonight is Dr. Gajra Ranayan." Yvonne stepped
~~~

across Davies and Roger panned, following her.

Gajra nodded slightly, and it was obvious she'd rather not be seen.

"She's the primary Flight Surgeon here at Dax, and has been working closely with Dr. Davies over the past two weeks as they've tried, so far unsuccessfully, to determine exactly what links Leon Berger with Ryder Pelse, who is the astronaut scheduled on an upcoming flight to BiTerra, the Earth-like planet 128 light-years from us. Of course, we should note that Dax has not confirmed the details of the upcoming flight, because they've been more than preoccupied since the press release earlier this afternoon." Yvonne punctuated with a strained laugh.

"Lastly, and perhaps here to officially confirm the upcoming flight to BiTerra, we have with us William Daxton, the eccentric billionaire founder and financier of the commercial space tourism company headquartered here. He's also the long-time manager of the incredibly successful hedge fund that bears his name. As you'll recall Bruce, you covered the stunning world-wide phenomenon just twelve days ago, when Mr. Daxton proved that anti-matter space travel was now officially science fact."

"Hello, World." Daxton waved proudly. "Of course, I'd rather be speaking to you from mission control as we prepare for our next launch, but we here at Dax feel that it's in everyone's best interest, and especially Leon's, to get the link between he and his brother sorted out properly so the flight can go forward as planned. In fact, the doctors here have been collaborating extensively with many specialists around the world, and we were very close to solving this riddle before Mr. Hanlon decided to crash the party, so to speak."

"Well, it's been quite an exciting day for all of you here, I must say." Yvonne almost flashed her perfect pearlies back to the camera, but didn't go full grid as she was mindful this was not a puff piece. "So you were close to finding the answer?"

"Before we get to that, Yvonne, let me send out my sincerest condolences to the families of our brave Dax security guards who lost their lives in this senseless and brutal terrorist attack today. I would also like to commend Sergeant Borman of the Palm Bay SWAT unit for making the ultimate sacrifice in the line of duty.

"And of course, our prayers are with the remaining members of his team who are still currently being held hostage in this very building. I know they did their level best, but when someone as evil and despicable as this Hanlon conspiracy whacko makes a surprise attack with a private army, he can't always be stopped even by our most highly trained professionals."

"Absolutely," Yvonne said. "We should point out that all of us here in this medical lab are technically hostages. The terrorists holding us refused to be shown on camera, but I can tell you that our exclusive investigation has revealed . . . hold on, I'm getting something here." Yvonne tilted her head and listened to her producer through the earpiece.

"I'm very sorry, Bruce, but I'm being told that's all the time we have for now, so we won't be able to discuss any of the details on the upcoming experiment. We'll check back in less than half an hour, assuming the power comes back on, when we're ready to broadcast the experiment live as it happens. Until then, this is Yvonne Forrester with another Wolfe News exclusive alert, live in Palm Bay as one of the hostages in the ongoing incursion at Dax Space Corp.'s headquarters."

~~~
~~~

"What is Daxton doing in that lab?"

"I'm so very sorry, Hanlon. But Anton said you had approved him to stay on."

"Absolutely not! This is an outrage. He is making a mockery of our quest for The Answer."

"How shall I handle it, Hanlon?"

"Let me collect my thoughts."

"Of course, sir."

Hanlon returned to the line after a full minute and said, "I will call you back."

CHAPTER 13

HANLON: So you understand the problem?

ETHICIST: I believe so, but allow me to restate it.

HANLON: Quickly.

ETHICIST: You're concerned that Daxton's presence and his attempts to discredit you will undermine the efficacy of the experiment.

HANLON: Yes.

ETHICIST: Because you're being depicted as a terrorist, you feel neither the scientific community nor the public at large will accept the results as valid.

HANLON: Yes.

ETHICIST: May I speak my mind?

HANLON: Yes.

ETHICIST: This should not, and even may not, affect the validity of the experiment in the eyes of the scientific community. Pending proper peer review and the ability to reproduce the results, of course. Having said that, we must face the fact that you *are* a terrorist—in the truest sense of the word. I don't think the general public will accept results obtained under duress as valid under any circumstances.

BUDDHIST MONK: Your akuśala-karma will determine the realm of your rebirth.

HANLON: Enumerate.

ETHICIST: Pardon me?

HANLON: Rattle off the positions. And do it quickly.

ETHICIST: As you wish. An absolutist would say what you've already done is wrong, period. A deontologist might give you some leeway, assuming your motives were pure. A utilitarian would want to quantify the evil done versus the potential upside for humanity. You may get some traction there. An objectivist might grant you clemency as well, assuming you could prove that finding the answer is a metaphysically real and true good. As for the subjectivists, well, it's all relative.

HANLON: That is all?

ETHICIST: There are others I'm leaving out, but this should get us started.

HANLON: This does me no good.

ETHICIST: If it did, I'd be out of a job. But there is another option.

HANLON: What is it?

ETHICIST: We could wait until one of the twins dies of natural causes, and see what happens to the other.

HANLON: The premise is that the general public will accept the findings from this experiment as factual and true—assuming they can be independently corroborated later—regardless of Daxton's characterization. Vote now.

STENOGRAPHER: 5 in favor, 7 opposed, 6 abstain.

HANLON: Premise rejected.

~~~

Ryder was almost down to the third floor where the lab was, but froze when the stairwell door opened on the level below him. He looked at the MP5 but pulled the Sig Sauer and leaned over the railing barely enough to get a glimpse of two people
~~~

stumbling onto the landing. A guard shoved Daxton against the wall and said, "Hold still."

"Fuck you!" Daxton's expletive was still echoing up and down the column as the guard took a step back and raised his gun.

"Hey!" Ryder shouted as he jumped down the remaining steps. Now there were two guns, one aimed at a heart, one at a head.

The guard was momentarily stunned by the intrusion, and Ryder said, "Bad idea."

"Hanlon wishes it so." The guard appeared to be wondering if he could get a quick shot at Ryder then finish Daxton before going down himself. He could not, so he seemed resolved to finish Daxton one way or another.

"So do I. Let me do it."

Daxton's shocked expression matched the guard's, and they were both perplexed enough to miss that Ryder's change in aim was not directly at Daxton.

Ryder's bullet caught the guard square in his gun hand, and the guard's reflex shot came fast enough to seem as one.

Daxton went down amid a spray of blood and concrete shrapnel from the wall.

Ryder's second shot pierced the guard's brain and prevented a fourth shot from either gun.

"Keep quiet," Ryder whispered as he rushed over and took the guard's gun.

"I'm hit." Daxton grunted.

"Wasn't me. Let me see." Ryder lifted Daxton's jacket lapel and saw the entry wound was in his right pectoral muscle, just before the shoulder. He said, "Clean shot. Walk it off."

"Fuck you, too!" Daxton seethed.

"What? No thank you?"

"Sticking with fuck you," through clenched teeth.

Ryder hauled Daxton to his feet and pushed him back against the wall. "Steady?"

"No."

"Good. How many guards?"

"Five, I think."

"Shit. Get your ass into your panic room and stay put."

"What are you going to do?"

Ryder pulled the dead guard to his feet, then bent over and hoisted him over shoulder. "Get rid of this." He grunted as he stood and bounced to shift the weight more evenly. "Just like he would have done with you."

"Where?"

"Just get in your box and don't come out."

~~~

"OK, Bruce, we're back." Yvonne was visibly shaking. She composed herself as best she could and continued. "Sorry about the technical difficulties. Yes, ah, we're here in the Dax lab with Dr. Davies, who is going to explain the experiment we're about to see. Dr. Davies?" She pointed the microphone toward him.

"Yes, sorry." Davies cast an uneasy glance toward the stairwell. "We, uh, well, when the twins arrive we will be administering a sufficient dose of pentobarbital to one of them, Leon I think, so as to induce a coma."

"And what will that do?" Yvonne asked.

"It will put him into a coma."

"Yes." Yvonne tried to giggle and failed. "I mean, what will that show?"

"That depends on what happens."
~~~

“What do you think will happen?” The mic went back and forth like a tennis ball.

“It could go either way, really. We think this may simulate the conditions necessary to break the link, just as it was broken by the space ship.”

“What will happen to Mr. Pelse?”

“If our hypothesis is correct, Ryder should lose consciousness as well.”

“And what then?”

“Of course, the power needs to be back on first, so we can monitor both men with an EEG while they're in the fMRI machines.”

“I believe Bruce and our panel of experts back in the studio were discussing those machines in detail while we were away. What should we expect to see?”

“Sorry, but you won't see the readouts from the instruments themselves, as I'm afraid we're sort of . . . technically constrained in the lab at the moment.”

“If Mr. Pelse does black out, what would that prove?”

“I'm really not prepared to say.”

“Can you give us a hint?”

“I'm sorry, but not at this time.”

“Oh, now Dr. Davies,” Yvonne tilted her head with a hint of the perkiness that had landed her this gig. “Tell us what we're in for.”

“Alright . . . I guess. Uh, there are some who think this will tell us if the twins share one soul between them, and others who believe they can help reveal the physical seat of consciousness in the brain.”

“Now that *would* be something!” Yvonne tilted her head without pertness, and listened to her producer.

"OK, Bruce, it looks like we're going to send it back to you in the studio while we await the arrival of Leon Berger and Ryder Pelse. We'll bring you the exclusive coverage as soon as it breaks. This is Yvonne Forrester for Wolfe News, live on location at Dax Space Corp."

~~~

Step up, old man. No time to quit now.

Daxton braced himself against the wall of his office, then took another two steps forward and left a long red smear behind.

He made it to his executive en suite bathroom and turned the water on. Hot soap for the hands, cold splash for the face. Leave the bullet hole until he got to the first aid kit.

Daxton looked in the mirror.

How the hell did it come to this? He should have been standing amid VIPs at the airport three days ago, every one gazing in awestruck admiration as Tammy took off in the space plane with Ryder.

He would have waved to Ryder like Isabella sending off Columbus. The Daxton name would echo the halls of history for a thousand years after Ryder got back.

But no. That pissy little shit had fucked everything up.

"All my possessions for a moment of time." And he would spend that moment stomping on Hanlon's neck until his eyes popped out.

Better sit down. He stumbled into the panic room and fumbled around for a battery lamp, then shut the door. He was too dazed to remember how or even if he should lock it with the power still out.
~~~

He found the first aid kit and dressed the wound as best he could, then wilted into his reclining leather chair and promptly passed out.

~~~

Kerwin was pacing the command post, not wanting to discuss either of these issues.

"Mr. Pelse and Mr. Berger are late," Hanlon said.

"When were they supposed to arrive?" Kerwin asked.

A pause. "I suppose we did not specify an exact time after all."

"As long as they're back when the power comes on, it's OK?"

Another pause. "That will suffice."

"One more thing?" Kerwin asked.

"Proceed."

"We, uh, have the power ready, Hanlon."

"Then why is electricity not flowing?"

"It's my turn to make a request."

"I am still in control there."

"I know, I know. But this might be in your best interest. I think."

"What is it? My patience wears thin."

"The media . . . they've requested that we wait until 11:15 as planned."

"Unacceptable. Turn it on now."

"It's only twelve minutes."

"Now."

"It's the broadcast networks. They said they can't break in now because they've already shuffled things to accommodate 11:15, and they've been teasing it for then. They're not 24/7, you
~~~

know. They're assuming they can still cover the experiment without bumping Leno and Letterman." Kerwin held his breath awaiting the response.

A long pause. "That will suffice."

"Thank you." Kerwin exhaled. "Lights on at 11:15 sharp."

~~~

"I can't. I just can't leave him in there." Sheila slammed the door of the ambulance.

Christine opened the door again and said, "You told me the building might explode."

"Keep your voice down." Sheila shot an eye toward Felix sitting next to Nathan's stretcher.

"Let's get out of here. The boys need you."

"I can't do it."

"We waited long enough, the paramedics need to get Nate to the hospital, and they need to get the ambulance back here."

"What if the experiment goes wrong? What if they can't wake him up again?"

"He's been in a coma before, he's good at it just like Ryder is. We need to leave. Right now."

"You go. Take the boys and when Nate wakes up, tell him we'll be there as soon as we can."

Christine snarled, retreated into the ambulance and slammed the door.

As it drove off, Sheila wandered closer to the barricade. The flashing lights bounced off the mirrored glass building like so many memories blinking in and out of consciousness.

"Come home, Baby . . ."

~~~

Elbow was getting on everyone's nerves. He had lost it. The sounds in the gym-turned-hostage-corral had gone from quiet, controlled, and courteous weeping to full-fledged blubbering and sniffling and wailing like an Italian mother at her first born's funeral. Weitz tried, but Elbow was simply inconsolable.

"Leave me be!" Elbow slobbered as he stood up from the workout bench and brushed Weitz's hand off his shoulder.

One of the guards broke formation and stepped toward them.

"Come on, man," Weitz said to the guard. "He's all busted up about Borman. Let me take him to the head."

The guard shook his head.

"Borman was his best man, for Christ's sake. They played college ball. Don't let the guys see him like this. Just give him a minute to pull himself together."

The guard acquiesced, but indicated Elbow should go alone.

The sentries parted ways so Elbow could stagger into the bathroom, but blocked Weitz from following.

From the tiled bathroom emanated the wail of a man who had lost his best friend, younger brother, and favorite dog in one senseless tragedy.

"For the love of God!" Weitz said. "He can't be alone right now."

The sentries looked at each other, then at the other SWAT officers who were, in solidarity, standing at attention with their backs to the room. The sentries locked eyes for a moment, then the one to Weitz's left stepped aside and allowed passage.

"I can't hack it, man." Elbow bawled as he grabbed another handful of paper towels and blew his nose like an elephant in heat.

Elbow continued howling and moaning and blathering

nostalgia while Weitz looked around. He quietly took the lid off the garbage can and started digging.

He retrieved a small, yellow and crumpled piece of paper like the tiny wadded one that fell from the ceiling almost an hour ago. A Post-It from Heaven. It had hit Bandana's shoulder and he almost gave it away as it bounced to the floor. Weitz had retrieved it while the guards were busy watching the one-sided cat fight with Sheila.

Weitz hadn't chanced reading it until he was kneeling and bent over Borman's body, softly humming *A Fond Farewell*. They had passed it down the procession via handshakes. Squeezed onto the original tiny note was:

23:05—2 men to head
OK? Go. Not? No-go.
23:07:00—flash bang
23:07:01—spikes high

The new note in the trash was much less formal:

Welcome back to the party.
Happy hunting.
Please don't shoot me.

The plan would have been much less viable had there not also been two MP5s and a Glock hidden in the trash.

~~~

It's just like setting camera gear in a blind. The trick is to be silent and invisible, and set the gear in such a way that you can still control it when you get downwind.

Leon was back for yet another round of hanging from the pipes above the gym, getting ready to pull the trigger. The trigger in this case was a string of towels knotted together, with
~~~

the last of them tied to a five gallon jug of laundry detergent. He'd checked the label to make sure it wasn't flammable, because things were about to get hairy enough.

Last he looked, he was directly over a small group of guards, but the rest were scattered around the room in their typical formation, with two guarding the mens room and one blocking the ladies. He could barely make out Elbow's reminiscing, as it had subsided to a low and steady murmur.

Let's hope everyone is ready for this. He knew he wasn't.

He gave the towel-rope a yank and several predictions came true in rapid succession. The detergent jug crashed through the ceiling tile. Check. Several guards opened fire on the opening in the ceiling. Check. Leon wasn't there to receive the bullets. Double-check.

The SWAT stun grenades—the ones the guards were confident enough to stash in the maintenance room with the rest of their weapons—detonated one after another as he threw them through the hole in the ceiling. Check.

Leon grabbed the few towel-wrapped guns he could carry in the last trip back to caveland, and his legs released their hold on the pipe, sending him crashing through a ceiling tile and onto the guards clustered below. Check.

That was as far into the future as his prescience would permit him to peer. The rest would be a blur for anyone left standing when the dust settled.

~~~

Ryder lobbed two of the stun grenades Leon had given him. They'd buy about five seconds of blindness for everyone in the lab. Better get this done quick.
~~~

He charged, taking the same line Eagle had used to crash through the glass wall. His MP5 released controlled bursts, targeting the two guards outside the lab, but the three inside were not readily visible through the smoke. Shit.

He tossed the Sig Sauer on the floor next to the cameraman, who he was really really hoping was a cop masquerading as a cameraman. Get up, man, go to work! A bullet winged his calf. Then another hit him in the left shoulder, the one facing the control booth.

Ryder turned to fire on the guard he could now see to his right. He jumped over the pile of doctors and a reporter, and managed to take cover behind one of the MRIs long enough to take that guard out before she could do any more damage.

Camera-cop shot the other guard, and then there was one.

That one was holed up in the control booth and not quite as stunned as the others.

Ryder came out from behind the MRI in time to see the remaining guard's machine gun protruding from the busted window and taking aim at Camera-cop.

Both men launched a hail of bullets into the control booth, which bought Ryder enough time to make a run for it. He dove through the booth window just as the guard was standing up again. Several bullets grazed the left side of Ryder's torso. Then several more found his left arm as the barrel got stuck in his armpit when they crashed into the wall at the back of the booth.

Ryder strained to get up on his knees, but couldn't get any leverage with one busted arm and the other clinging to his MP5.

His last resort would be to head-butt the guard's face, and just as he recoiled came the blessed discharge of a Sig Sauer to his left. Camera-cop stood motionless in the doorway, still in his stance and waiting to see if the guard was finished.

~~~

Leon came down like an avalanche on the guards in the gym. Two of them crumpled under him and were kind enough to cushion his landing. He heaved the towel-wrapped guns in the direction of where the SWAT guys were, but they had already spread out like a swarm of bees repelling a bear attack.

Weitz and Elbow bolted from the bathroom and shot the two sentries, plus the one by the ladies room. They opened fire around the formation closest to them, but couldn't safely distinguish gray jumpsuits from blue SWAT garb behind the clearing smoke in the middle of the room.

Dumbbells flew like mortar fire, the lighter ones first, then the heavier denominations from the lower rack. Even two big purple exercise balls became effective diversionary projectiles.

Four of the SWAT guys charged the rear formation and took heavy fire as they advanced at full throttle.

Leon's objective now was to delay the entrance of the not-stunned guards outside the swinging doors. He delivered his best debilitating blows with one good arm before rolling off the two beneath him and lunging toward the doors. He came in spikes high just as two guards approached from the outside, and bullets came at him from the inside. His momentum carried him through horizontally and they were slammed between the doors and the walls. The last thought through Leon's mind was what a bummer it was that his head would hit the floor before his body did.

~~~

Nothing is as far away as one minute ago.

Hanlon listened in on the panicked chatter of his guards at the front line and those on the roof before they were gunned down from on high.

One minute ago he was ten minutes away from The Answer. An order of magnitude. What had seemed preordained was not meant to be. He craved no details of the Battle at Dax.

Ignorance was the victor from the start if the twin ambassadors of knowledge would be unable to participate in the experiment.

His finest hour was to become his greatest failure. His greatest failure would leave mankind in a continuing dark age indefinitely. None could fathom the repetition of such a grand coincidence as commingled twins. And now the fortuitous chain of events was to end unfulfilled.

Unanswered.

He needed to be without others. Alone so he need not face the arrogant superiority of the conference attendees. Alone so he need not face the heartfelt condolences of his loyal protectors and followers.

Hanlon walked slowly and deliberately into the conference hall. All were still seated at the large round table, just where he'd left them when they still had the power to receive and decipher The Answer.

The potential energy was every bit as great as when he had convened the meeting just the prior night. Perhaps even greater. But now it would be relegated to just that: potential.

The shuffling of his shoes on the plush Persian rug echoed softly through the ornate hall and closed the loop. The dream was not to be realized.

He came to a stop beside the Stenographer.

Looking around the silent room he saw seventeen intellectuals and a dozen guards staring intently at him with the perplexed look of a dog wondering what he must do to receive his bone.

Hanlon bent over and whispered to the Stenographer, who proceeded to add one final line to the conference transcript:
(AT 11:14 P.M., CONFERENCE ADJOURNED)

~~~

Ryder had said two words before losing consciousness on top of the wounded guard: "Panic room." But that's not what the room did.

Camera-cop had righted a gurney and cleared the guards' bodies so he could roll it over to Ryder.

Gajra and Davies had untangled themselves from atop Yvonne and checked all the guards for signs of life. The one in the control booth was the only soul still clinging to its body.

Yvonne had remained curled on the floor, wishing she still had her medical coverage blanket.

They hauled Ryder onto a gurney, his bleeding slowed by various bandages and a tourniquet at the shoulder. Then they hauled the control booth guard onto a gurney and strapped him down tight.

It was time to move.

"Where's the panic room?" Camera-cop asked Gajra.

"How do you—"

"Where is it?"

"It adjoins Mr. Daxton's office on the fourth floor," she said.

"That's where we're going," Camera-cop said.

"Why not out the front?" Davies asked.
~~~

Camera-cop barked at Gajra. "You. Call the gym and tell whoever answers to get the hell out of this building anyway they can."

"We should too," Davies said.

"No time," Camera-cop said. "This place is rigged to blow."

~~~

Leon heard the phone ringing and wondered why. It didn't sound like the ring at his house. Wasn't his cell phone. Who'd be calling at this hour anyway? Oh. Consciousness and pain crashed over him like a point break on the north shore of Kaua'i.

I get it: I'm dead and that's the taxi calling to say they're at the curb.

"Get that!" Weitz said to Elbow.

The overhead lights came on like a silent stun grenade, revealing the devastation in high definition. The functional SWAT officers were tending to their wounded and confirming their dead. All told, the plan went better than Ryder had predicted, but certainly not how the SWAT team wanted.

They were the victors, and had managed to repel every last perimeter guard. Those leaderless guards had each made the same tactical error in not regrouping to mount a cohesive offense that stood any chance of retaking the gym.

Three dead, four including Borman. Two severely wounded, including Bandana. Everyone wounded to one degree or another. Heartbreaking losses, all. Leon wondered if submitting to the experiment would have yielded a better outcome. He and the living SWAT members would have to live with that question, but live they would.

Their friends and family would comfort them with the
~~~

reminder that they were united. Everyone had signed on for the operation; a single 'no-go' would have squelched it.

But the time for reflection and mourning was not upon them.

"She says the building is wired to blow," Elbow said.

"Oh shit," Weitz said. "When?"

"When? . . . She doesn't know." He slammed the phone down and went back to Bandana who was in desperate need of a surgeon.

"It's up to Hanlon." Leon stumbled to his feet and hugged the corner. He had a few more holes than he used to, plenty of cuts and gashes and future scars for his collection, along with a wicked margarita headache. But other than that, he was feeling better than expected, because it was almost over.

Weitz barked at Elbow, "Wakata! Get your ass up there and see if you can disarm it. Check the struc-frames on three and four."

Weitz barked anew. "Morgan! Call EOD. Have them see if the portal to the main complex is rigged."

~~~

Why did I adjourn the conference?

Yet another mistake, but comparatively miniscule. Hanlon sat alone in his study, the radio and television respectively silent and black. News reports would be merely speculative; they could not have yet discovered the extent of his crushing defeat.

He longed for the counsel of the intellectuals. But they were under the watchful eyes of his faithful, all busy collecting their belongings. He would release them back to the four corners so they could resume their many and varied missions. He could no more snuff their candles than he could his own.
~~~

What to do? How to salvage my legacy? The world would know him not as the Great Enlightener, only as a petty and belligerent tyrant. But they would not *know* him.

Were the twins still alive? Was Daxton? No way to know. And he could no longer force anyone to tell him.

He reflected on his journey and quest for The Answer. It seemed both pointless and arbitrary in the harsh light of his failure to find it. Would mankind really have been better off if he had found it? . . . Absolutely. Would the lives of so many innocents have continued in quiet desperation if he'd never searched? Yes again.

It was definitely time for some cognac.

~~~

"Great," Camera-cop said when the elevator finally arrived. He didn't want to carry Ryder—and certainly wasn't going to carry Hanlon's guard—up two flights of stairs with only the help of two very shaky docs and a catatonic bubble-head.

The six of them boarded.

"Is it safe to ride in the elevator?" Gajra asked.

"Safer than what? You just came through a firefight without a scratch." Camera-cop slid along the guard's gurney and punched the button.

They rode to the fourth floor without speaking, but everyone's labored breathing and the off-and-on groaning of the injured men kept silence at bay.

"Which way?" Camera-cop asked.

Gajra led the way until she slammed into Elbow coming around a corner.

"You OK?" he asked.
~~~

"Yes."

"Where are you going?"

"Panic room," Camera-cop said.

"Think it'll hold?" Elbow asked.

"I don't know, but no time for the front door."

They were interrupted by thunder and the low rumbling of what seemed like the first significant earthquake in recorded Floridian history.

"Goddammit!" Elbow punched the wall.

"What was that?" Davies asked.

"Probably another blown up Wheelbarrow. Come on, let's keep going."

"Can't we go out the front now?" Davies asked. "Doesn't that mean the explosion is over?"

Elbow grabbed the guard's gurney and made double-time, encouraging Camera-cop to keep pace rolling Ryder. "No. It means the portal is gone."

~~~

Hanlon refilled the snifter and went back to stare out the window. He found the blackness of night beyond the perimeter lights to be soothing. Mankind would not make the transition from dark to light on this night.

A timid knock on the oak door.

"Come," Hanlon said.

"Excuse me, sir." The guard's head was barely in the room.

"What is it?"

"Some of the guests are wondering if they'll be leaving right away or spending the night here."

"Hood them all and take them to the bus."
~~~

"All together?"

"Yes."

"Please forgive me, Hanlon. But where can we take them safely?"

"You decide," Hanlon said. "It matters not to me. Take them to a public parking lot far away, and abandon the bus. Leave them some cash. They will find their own ways home."

He took another sip of cognac and turned back to the window. It ends tonight.

~~~

"Get him in there." Weitz hoped the brackish creek water wouldn't worsen Bandana's wounds.

Eagle grunted as he hoisted Bandana into the RHIB and laid him alongside the two other SWAT officers already prostrate against the far pontoon. Still chest-deep in water, he hollered up the hatch, "One more."

"Shut that door," Weitz said as the last of the team hurried into the hatch room. He realized that even with the addition of Leon and the two remaining team members, it wasn't nearly as cramped in this maintenance room as it should be. Not like it was three and a half hours ago when they were a baker's dozen strong.

"Robinson goes," Weitz said. They hoisted the next-most injured man and together they lowered him feet-first through the hatch to Eagle's ready arms.

~~~

"This thing won't fit." Elbow sized up the panic room. They needed to add six people in with Daxton's recliner, and Ryder was just going to have to lie on the floor next to his assailant.

Camera-cop and Elbow grabbed the sheet on either side and lifted Ryder off the gurney against his wishes. Gajra bent over Daxton and found a pulse, but it was weak. Davies put a blanket over Yvonne, who was curled up in a corner under pretense of staying out of the way.

Elbow gave the second gurney a stiff kick and it crashed into Daxton's expansive mahogany desk across the office. He slammed the vault-like door of the panic room and wrenched the lever 180 degrees from left to right. He could only hope the six one-inch, sixty-grade steel pins, each with a shear-strength of over forty-thousand pounds would be sufficient to withstand the expected blast.

Daxton wouldn't wake up. Ryder and the guard were happy to pass out. Yvonne whimpered. Gajra and Davies sat on the floor under the countertop, seeking any extra measure of protection.

"What now?" Camera-cop asked.

"We wait."

"For what?" Davies asked from under the counter.

"Salvation . . . or Armageddon."

~~~

"We must give lengthy deliberation to what has to be decided once and for all."

Hanlon read the words again. That it was written before Christ was relevant, and that it was said by a freed slave even more so. Hanlon had been forcibly freed from slavishly
~~~

searching for God or banishing Him as yet another outgrown myth.

He had started his quest for The Answer early in life, full of certainty and conviction. Now he would be convicted if they found him.

He sought The Answer to free all mankind from one last bond of ignorance. The strongest bond. The bond that held everyone back from *knowing*.

Hanlon realized now that he envied the masses he so wished to enlighten. Toiling in their workaday lives, raising their families and never giving serious thought to their purpose. The ant colony flourishes.

There were many questions about humanity he may never answer. Especially American humanity. Why are people so rarely without shelter so concerned with the weather? Why are people so worried about others' perception so perpetually petty and vindictive? Why are trivial pursuits pursued with such fervor?

There were precious few who have truly considered their lives and the meaning thereof. But they were noncohesive and scattered. Some were so focused on giving that they ultimately failed to help the needy find their own way. Others were driven beyond measure, but aimed at pointless goals like athletics, celebrity, or politics for personal aggrandizement.

He reserved his highest regard for those in the military and similar disciplines who would sacrifice life and limb to protect an ungrateful public.

Still, he wondered how often their dedication to purpose went beyond steadfast devotion to esoteric principles such as duty, honor, and country—without fully and completely grasping the true essence.

What was to become of Daxton? His nemesis should perish for obstruction.

"His was a noble quest, but not more noble than mine." Hanlon said it out loud to test whether words could be truer than thoughts.

The twins were another matter entirely. Their destinies were irrevocably intertwined with his from the moment their zygote became two. Hanlon was overwhelmed by the opportunity cost of Daxton's meddling and the twins' refusal to cooperate.

He read one last pearl of wisdom before reaching his conclusion. "A weak man has doubts before a decision; a strong man has them afterwards."

~~~

The blast sent a shock wave of disbelief through everyone from those who felt it first-hand in the panic room; to Leon and the SWAT team under the building; to those behind the barricades running from a glass shower; to those watching in their living rooms; to those watching on their cell phones in the subway; to those watching around the globe.

The fourth floor went first, sending a yard sale of splintered office furniture and equipment in all directions. It was accompanied by broken glass, drywall, and plaster raining down on the four men in the RHIB, even though they were already a hundred feet clear of the building.

Eagle did his best to spread his large body over the wounded men.

"Get back here!" Weitz said as the hatch thunked closed and he slid down the ladder into the water. Leon and the two remaining officers had started wading after the RHIB and
~~~

everyone did an about-face so they could take cover under the building.

Leon was first back and said, "We gotta get outta here."

"No good," Weitz said. "That was just the top floor. I bet the third goes next."

Eagle was back at the helm now, guiding the boat along the same stretch of river where McKinley had been felled by a sniper.

A few seconds later the third floor blew, doubling the flames above.

Weitz said with as much confidence as he could muster, "We ride it out here."

~~~

"Leo . . . Baby . . ." Sheila whimpered as the top half of the smoking and burning building began to yield. In the thirty-four seconds since the second blast, Sheila had run through every one of their shared experiences as both a couple and a family. It was all good, and now everything would be all different.

The building roared and shrieked mightily as it defiantly strained to remain standing. Smoke billowed straight up into the windless sky while the building came straight down into the stagnant swamp.

The third floor collapsed under the weight of the fourth; the second under the weight of the top two; and the first folded under the countless kips of the entirety.

Sheila knelt in the parking lot and hugged a sawhorse barricade. Without the mirrored building, the flashing light beams from all the emergency vehicles were no longer reflected. They were swallowed up by the rubble and flames and smoke.
~~~

She watched as the firefighters ran toward the demolished East Wing, eager to start work on saving the rest of the complex.

How can I save the rest of my life without my Leo?

~~~

"Not yet," Davies said.

"Why not?" Gajra asked.

"They need more time," Elbow said.

Camera-cop added, "I don't think the fire is out."

~~~

"I don't give a shit who you have to bribe, just get me some heavy equipment!" Kerwin said into the phone.

"They're still down there, man." Eagle stormed the command post.

Kerwin looked at the disorganized pile of rubble that was once an organized facility for research. He shook his head slowly and said, "No way."

"Fuck you, man," Eagle said. "I lost four brothers in there, and we don't know about those four."

Kerwin watched the paramedics transferring SWAT officers from the RHIB onto stretchers.

"The others have to be alive. Have to!"

"We have to face facts," Kerwin said.

"I'll tell you some facts." Eagle stepped into Kerwin's face. "Those pilings are reinforced concrete right down to the bedrock. The piling caps holding up the building are the strongest part of that whole structure, and the first floor slab can withstand a Cat-4, man."

Kerwin backed off. “We’re on it. We’re on it.”

“That’s where my boys were, and that’s where they still are.”

~~~

“I can wait no longer.” Gajra stepped over Ryder and the guard, then moved toward the latch.

“OK,” Elbow said, “I think the door is cool enough now.”

Elbow grabbed the lever and pulled it 180 degrees from right to left. He took a deep breath, and pushed the heavy vault door open a crack. Feeling no blast of hot air and seeing no flames, he felt it safe to swing the door wide open, but was glad he didn’t step out of the panic room.

The building was gone. Fifty feet below lay the crumbled and smoldering remains. Elbow looked down in amazement at the relatively unscathed column heading straight down into the rubble, but still supporting the panic room solidly. He and Gajra waved apprehensively to a news helicopter buzzing around the late-night sky.

Ryder stirred and slurred through his morphine haze and Gajra thought she heard, “Are we there yet?”

~~~

“We’re good!” Weitz yelled at the top of his lungs. His voice echoed rapid-fire in the still-sealed space between the chest-deep water and the overhead slab.

“Could use a few bananas in here.” Leon realized he missed dinner last night.

The four of them cheered when they heard the dozers and backhoes were almost through. They would be out by dawn.

Epilogue

One month later—Thanksgiving Day

"I'm dying Chrissy."

"You can't die, it'll ruin your image." She wiped away perspiration and the stray locks on his forehead.

"True. But even poor ol' Jack LaLanne had to give up the ghost."

She sat down on the stool next to his hospital bed. It seemed like she'd been spending all her time at Sarasota Memorial these days, bouncing from room to room and listening to the men whine.

"Any news from SETI?" he asked.

"Too soon. You know bureacracy takes time."

"Goddammit." He coughed. "We told them the coordinates, frequency, and wavelength."

"Oh, they're listening alright. Every available dish in the world is pointed at BiTerra. People are aiming their DirecTV dishes at it. You even have your own cult. It's just that—"

"What? They're still bitching about the band?"

"They still don't think it's narrow enough to have been artificially produced. At least not until someone picks up another transmission."

"Wow." He sighed.

"The media is calling it 'Wow-ii'."

"Fuckers. Hey, sit me up a bit."

Christine hit the button to raise the incline on his bed. Father and daughter were almost eye to eye.

"Chrissy, you need to listen good here."

"I figured this was coming after the morphine wore off," she said. "You want rebuild the East Wing and get Flight 4 rescheduled."

"No. I don't," Daxton said.

"No?" She looked straight at him.

"No. I want you to give it to NASA. The whole shebang."

"You're kidding."

"Not on this one," he said. "This is it. And get SETI some more funding for that KLT[6] thing Maccone wants. I don't care how, just do it."

"Why?"

Daxton sighed and slumped back against the bed. "Get me a cigar, will you?"

"No. Tell me what's gotten into you."

"A bullet. An infection. Pneumonia. Old age. You name it."

"So man up and get your program going again."

"I always liked your spirit. Your mother would have too."

"This isn't about me. You can't just quit."

"No choice, the body is shot . . . was shot." He tried to laugh but it hurt so he stopped. "You and Fly-Boy want to run the show?"

"Hell no. He's done and I never wanted to start."

"OK then. Get the lawyers to draft it up, and do it quick or you'll be doing it alone."

"Draft what up?" she asked.

"The donation."

"Everything?"

"Yes. The space station, the telescope, Allison, the *Golf Ball*, the antimatter lab, and all our research. They can have HQ too, if they want it and they agree to hire our best folks."

"Holy shit, Dad. You're serious."

"Serious as a heart attack. Get it done, but with conditions."

"Like what?"

"I want a permanent wing in the Air and Space Museum. And they have to build it on their dime, not yours."

"So you're going to give them your toys, then make them build a toy box?"

"No, goddammit." He lightly smacked the bed rail. "Make them restart the program, get Flight 4 launched, and build me a shrine."

"Are you sure that's—"

"And McKinley too. Make sure he's well represented. He would have hated the attention, but he earned it."

"I suppose they might take you up—"

"You'll make them do it. I know you will. And you need to do one more thing for me." He held out his hand.

She leaned forward and took his hand in hers.

He coughed, then took as deep a breath as he could and said, "Don't you dare marry that sonofabitch."

~~~

He drove along the magnificent Pacific Coast Highway through Big Sur. He was glad to be driving between the mountains and the ocean.

To his right were unexplored depths of a world still foreign to man. To his left were the glorious cliffs and bluffs carpeted in Chaparral.
~~~

Cone Peak loomed in the distance, providing a reminder of heights left unscaled, and the shining city upon a hill.

Top down, wind freely blowing, mind no longer swirling from the Battle at Dax. In the past month, Hanlon had seen much of America with new eyes, and much of it was to his liking. There is nothing more refreshing than an extended road-trip through the myriad possibilities of these United States. It is the biggest co-op party since Rome's heyday. Most everyone from elsewhere wishes to join the party, but curiously struggles to reform it in the image of whatever hole they fled.

Where else can you have such freedom yet be so dependent upon others? He had stopped at a McDonald's once, and allowed his mind to ponder the vast number of people involved in delivering that particular Big Mac to him at that particular table. Not just the direct employees, but everyone required for every aspect of that creation: advertising, lawyers, accountants, management, transportation, infrastructure, utilities, research, manufacturing, farming, supporting industries, supporting services, and a government established by the people and for the people.

Where else can there exist such radical dichotomies within individuals? Such as the young girl wearing a t-shirt proclaiming 'I loved my dog. He was much tastier than yours'. Or the ancient man's bumper sticker that read 'Honk if you love being cut off'.

He passed a man in a 1969 Camaro talking on a Bluetooth earpiece. The man was probably close to Hanlon in age. How odd that the man would avail himself of the latest in safer communication gear, yet forego features like shoulder belts, anti-lock brakes, and perhaps even an airbag or two. That man should go home and make a rotary dial call to the nearest new car dealer.

It was Thanksgiving Day. A day to give thanks. But give thanks to whom? To a scornful populace. To disdainful religious leaders. To a derisive scientific community. Was he to be forever relegated to the scrap-heap of crazed terrorists having fanatical motivations?

For what could he truly be thankful? His health. And his freedom. Small comforts when contrasted with what he could have accomplished. What he almost accomplished. What he should have accomplished.

~~~

One month later—Christmas Day

"Are you OK?" Christine asked.

Ryder snorted in the bathroom. "I'll live. Just blew my nose with a mouthful of Listerine and had an auto-masochistic waterboarding."

"Hurry up. They'll be here any minute."

"Oh goody. Christmas with the Bergers."

"You know you love the little wombats."

"Yeah, they're OK. Still too much like their old man."

Ryder shuffled out of the bathroom and Christine helped him back into the hospital bed. It was tough to get situated comfortably, and he was anxious to get started with fittings for a prosthetic left arm. "Can we tell them today?" he asked.

Christine paused to think about it again. "You're sure you're ready?"

"I'm Ready's calf." He winced and shifted his weight to the right. "How 'bout you?"

"I'm still bummed Dad can't walk me down the aisle. But I bet Leon will do it."
~~~

“Sheila will make him.”

“She’s one tough momma-bear.”

“I’m still glad I won’t have the Curmudgeon for a father-in-law. Poor ol’ Daxton.”

Christine started in for a chiding slap, but there were so few areas not still in various stages of healing. “We just buried him last week. That’s still not funny.”

“Always will be.”

“Last chance before we send the proposal to NASA,” she said. “You can still fly the *Golf Ball* right-handed.”

“Nope.” Ryder grunted and shifted. “I’m done. Time to settle down with my goodly Earth-Woman. Maybe you’ll buy me a nice suit and a Senate seat . . . I think Florida has one for sale.”

“You really think they can handle all our fancy toys?” she asked again.

“Better than we did.”

“You want to see the architect’s concept drawing?”

“Not really,” Ryder said. “Just make sure it’s big. They need lots of extra room in a museum for air and space.”

“Cute.”

“Uncle Ryder, Uncle Ryder!” Nathan and Felix squealed as they burst into the room.

“Hey, Little Bees!” Ryder leaned over as best he could and passed out one-armed hugs.

“How are you doing?” Sheila asked Ryder.

“Woke up on the right side of the dirt again, which is nice. How ‘bout Monkey-Boy?”

“Still hangin’, but not from the trees yet.” Leon plunked the gift bags on the small dresser in the cramped hospital room. Then he asked, “When is Mom coming?” as he hugged Christine.

"About an hour," she said.

"Hey, I came up with another business idea," Ryder said. "I'll start a web-site for old folks to broadcast all their aches, pains, and bowel movements. I'll call it 'Sputter'."

"Nice." Leon stood bedside and shook Ryder's hand.

The two men regarded each other for a brief moment. Both realized that with Leon's hair cut short and beard shaven, standing next to Ryder with his hair grown out; they could actually pass for twins.

"You ready to get back in the lab for some more link-tests?" Leon asked. "Gajra and Davies got some new ideas from his buddy in Egypt."

"Can I get my new arm first? Would anyone mind waiting for that?"

"The world wants to know what's up between you two," Sheila said.

"A brain surgeon, a priest, and an atheist walk into a bar—"

Nathan and Felix groaned in unison and said, "Heard it!"

~~~

This was the place of his choosing. Santa Barbara. A lovely old-world riviera on California's central coast. Still far enough removed from Los Angeles to have held a bulwark against the filth and effluence spreading there from.

Here the butterfly would become the chrysalis.

Hanlon set his bag on the bed in his room at the Inn of the Spanish Garden. He took a shower then sat down at the desk.

He could procrastinate no longer. He'd been imagining how a conversation with Peter might go, so he transcribed it to clear his mind.
~~~

PETER: Merry Christmas.

HANLON: It is not.

PETER: This is true. The FBI seized the estate.

HANLON: So I read. What of The Cluster?

PETER: You left them leaderless. Most were captured, many are in hiding.

HANLON: And Yelena?

PETER: No news. I suspect she has returned to her family.

HANLON: That would be unwise.

PETER: Indeed. But the assets are frozen and tithing cut off.

HANLON: I understand. My cash runs short.

PETER: You failed.

HANLON: I have another choice to make once and for all.

PETER: The twins are in Sarasota.

HANLON: What if they cannot reveal The Answer? What if humanity does not wish to know The Answer?

PETER: You must persist.

HANLON: I will not.

PETER: You will find The Answer. You will find It or we shall all burn in ignorance for eternity.

HANLON: I must atone for the havoc I have already wreaked.

PETER: Go back to Florida and find It! Mankind must know.

HANLON: I can no longer genuflect. The quest is open for another. I will not carry on.

PETER: You dare defy me?

HANLON: It now requires far less courage than even I possess.

PETER: You disappoint me.

HANLON: It has never been otherwise.

PETER: What has happened to you?

HANLON: I failed.

PETER: I will pray for you.

HANLON: That is not necessary.

Hanlon likened his predicament to that of Socrates, although he knew now that his name would never be spoken in the same context.

There was escape. He had escaped. No one, not even The Cluster knew his whereabouts. Long-term escape, however, must not stand. He must reinstate the long-forgotten axiom from one of his earliest teachers: 'Just because you can get away with it, doesn't make it right.'

What of the hemlock? He rejected it out of hand. He still had much to offer mankind, but knew that for them to receive it would require retribution for past transgressions. They may foist it upon him, being that Florida is one of the states still practicing capital punishment. However, he was not physically in Florida when the crimes were committed. Another item for the lawyers to wrangle.

Hanlon's newly embraced reasoning always led to the one satisfactory course of action: Atone for his sins as singularly sanctioned by the state. He would place his fate in the hands of the citizenry, just as Socrates had. He was not 'born again', but in the rebirth following his grand failure he had come to realize the importance of protecting and sanctifying the rule of law in this beloved country.

He left his room at the inn and walked in fading sunshine two blocks up Garden Street, then a half block down bustling Figueroa Street. He marched up the stairs and through the doors to the receptionist behind bullet-proof glass. He stood erect with head held high and announced, "Hello. My name is Hanlon. I wish to be incarcerated."

End

Author's Note: Thank you for reading Power Split! If you enjoyed this book (or not), please consider posting a review on your favorite site.

If you have any questions or comments specifically for me, please visit: www.WRonDrynan.com.

Bibliography

This list of reference sites is also available online at: www.WRonDrynan.com

[1] Jerry Ehman, "The Big Ear Wow! Signal (30th Anniversary Report)", *Big Ear Radio Observatory*, (Original Draft completed July 9, 2007). http://www.bigear.org/Wow30th/wow30th.htm

[2] Albert Einstein, *Relativity: The Special and the General Theory* (Reprint of 1920 translation by Robert W. Lawson ed.). (Routledge, 2001). ISBN 0415253845.

[3] Robert H. Fitts et al., "Prolonged space flight-induced alterations in the structure and function of human skeletal muscle fibres", *The Journal of Physiology*, 588, (September, 2010): 588, 3567–3592. http://jp.physoc.org/content/588/18/3567.abstract?ijkey=c008e4e51b4caad4742fddf16b32b535b2e98128&keytype2=tf_ipsecsha

[4] Austin Bradford Hill, "The Environment and Disease: Association or Causation?", *Proceedings of the Royal Society of Medicine*, Volume 58, (May, 1965): 295-300. http://www.edwardtufte.com/tufte/hill

[5] Richard B. Hoover, "Fossils of Cyanobacteria in CI1 Carbonaceous Meteorites", *Journal of Cosmology*, Volume 13, (March, 2011). http://journalofcosmology.com/Life100.html

[6] Claudio Maccone, "The KLT (Karhunen–Loève Transform) to extend SETI searches to broad-band and extremely feeble signals", *Acta Astronautica*, Volume 67, Issues 11-12 (December, 2010): 1427-1439. http://www.sciencedirect.com/science/article/B6V1N-509Y436-2/2/3c3232ae551aba1799a39df0a2fe9090

[7] Claudio Maccone, "Realistic targets at 1000 AU for interstellar precursor missions", *Acta Astronautica* Volume 67, Issues 5-6, (September-October, 2010): 526-538. http://www.sciencedirect.com/science/article/B6V1N-504CN9T-1/2/50a7902183ec1fe391b730049610f2a8

[8] Claudio Maccone, "SETI and SEH (Statistical Equation for Habitables)", *Acta Astronautica*, Volume 68, Issues 1-2 (January, 2011): 63-75. http://www.sciencedirect.com/science/article/B6V1N-50RFMPG-1/2/1c07a31030e4d219f378ca93b37975fc

[9] Claudio Maccone, *The Sun as a Gravitational Lens: Proposed Space Missions*, (United States: IPI Press, February, 1998). ISBN 1-880930-10-2.

[10] Tariq Malik, "Tool Bag Lost In Space Meets Fiery End", *Space.com*, (August 3, 2009). http://www.space.com/7088-tool-bag-lost-space-meets-fiery.html

[11] Matt McCormick, e-mail message to the author, December 4, 2010. http://atheismblog.blogspot.com/

[12] Pope Benedict XVI, "The Hope of Salvation for Infants Who Die Without Being Baptised", *International Theological Commission*, April 19, 2007. http://www.vatican.va/roman_curia/congregations/cfaith/cti_documents/rc_con_cfaith_doc_20070419_un-baptised-infants_en.html

[13] Pope John Paul II, "General Audience", August 4, 1999. http://www.vatican.va/holy_father/john_paul_ii/audiences/documents/hf_jp-ii_aud_04081999_en.html

[14] Robert D. Putnam and David E. Campbell, *American Grace: How Religion Divides and Unites Us*, (New York: Simon & Schuster, 2010). ISBN 978-1-4165-6671-7. http://americangrace.org/

[15] Marcus E. Raichle, "The Brain's Dark Energy," *Scientific American*, Volume 302 No. 3, (March, 2010): 44–49. http://www.scientificamerican.com/article.cfm?id=the-brains-dark-energy

[16] Marcus E. Raichle, e-mail message to the author, March 23, 2011. http://www.nil.wustl.edu/labs/raichle/

[17] Joe Richman of *Radio Diaries*, "'Identical Strangers' Explore Nature Vs. Nurture", for *NPR—All Things Considered*, October 25, 2007. http://www.npr.org/templates/story/story.php?storyId=15629096

[18] Bruce K. Siddle, "The Stress Paradox," *JEMS —Journal of Emergency Medical Services*, Volume 33, No. 10 (October, 2008): 28-31. http://www.jems.com/article/major-incidents/stress-paradox

[19] Susan Watanabe, "What's It Like Where Voyager Is?", *NASA Jet Propulsion Laboratory*, (May 24, 2005). http://www.nasa.gov/vision/universe/solarsystem/voyager-interstellar-terms.html

Note: The picture showing Voyagers 1 & 2 is in the public domain because it was created by NASA. NASA copyright policy states that "NASA material is not protected by copyright unless noted".

[20] Mail Foreign Service, "Shocking moment: dolphin desperate to escape captivity leaps out of its own tank during marine show", *Daily Mail Online*, (July 9, 2010). http://www.dailymail.co.uk/news/worldnews/article-1293379/Shocking-moment-dolphin-leaps-tank-marine-show.html

[21] Commercial Spaceflight Federation:
http://www.commercialspaceflight.org/

[22] NASA —National Aeronautics and Space Administration:
http://www.nasa.gov/

[23] New York City Blackout of 1977:
http://en.wikipedia.org/wiki/New_York_City_blackout_of_1977

[24] PlanetQuest —Exoplanet Exploration:
http://planetquest.jpl.nasa.gov/

[25] Relativity Calculator: http://www.1728.com/reltivty.htm

[26] CIRG —Critical Incident Response Group:
http://www.fbi.gov/about-us/cirg

[27] UNOOSA —United Nations Office for Outer Space Affairs:
http://www.oosa.unvienna.org/

[28] Ouray Ice Festival: http://ourayicefestival.com/

[29] White Nose Syndrome in Bats:
http://www.fws.gov/WhiteNoseSyndrome/

[30] The Giving Pledge: http://givingpledge.org

The most savage controversies are those about matters as to which there is no good evidence either way.

—Bertrand Russell, *Unpopular Essays*

Nice maneuver.

—Gorman Seedling, *Coneheads*

With a crippled command module and surviving by using the LEM's systems, there can be no easy maneuver.

—Jules Bergman, *Apollo 13 / ABC News (archive footage).*

Denial ain't just a river in Egypt.

—Mark Twain

I cannot escape death; am I not to escape the fear of it?

—Epictetus

We're all gonna die man!

—Hudson, *Aliens*

Hello, this is not an answering machine. It is a question machine. It is about to ask you the two most important questions of your entire existence . . . Who are you? . . . And what do you want?

—Paul Pearsall

We have too many high sounding words, and too few actions that correspond with them.

—Abigail Adams

You can't build a reputation on what you are going to do.

—Henry Ford

That's some bad hat, Harry.

—Chief Brody, *Jaws*.
—Also said on Bad Hat Harry Productions' vanity card for the TV show *House, M.D.*

[Quantum entanglement is] . . . spooky actions at a distance.

—Albert Einstein

Were I to invoke logic, however, logic clearly dictates that the needs of the many outweigh the needs of the few.

—Spock, *Star Trek II: The Wrath of Khan*

Glory built on selfish principles is shame and guilt.

—William Cowper

If one understands the term 'soul' as a continuum of individuality from moment to moment, from lifetime to lifetime, then one can say that Buddhism also accepts a concept of soul; there is a kind of continuum of consciousness.

—14th Dalai Lama

All phenomena are not Self; when this is seen with knowledge, one is freed from the illusion of affliction.

—Gautama Buddha

God, however, has not preserved the scientist from error and has not safeguarded science from shortcomings and faults.

—Alhazen (ibn al-Haytham)

Truth is sought for its own sake. And those who are engaged upon the quest for anything for its own sake are not interested in other things. Finding the truth is difficult, and the road to it is rough.

—Alhazen (ibn al-Haytham)

So perish every one that shall hereafter leap over my wall.

—Romulus

An extraordinary phenomenon such as this demands an extraordinary investigation.

—Budd Hopkins

Nothing emboldens sin so much as mercy.

—William Shakespeare, *Timon of Athens*

'Tis mightiest in the mightiest.

—William Shakespeare, *The Merchant of Venice*

Charity sees the need, not the cause.

—German Proverb

Never attribute to malice what can adequately be explained by stupidity.

—Robert J. Hanlon

Ay, there's the rub.

—William Shakespeare, *Hamlet*

Et tu Brute?

—William Shakespeare, *Julius Caesar*

All my possessions for a moment of time.

—Elizabeth I

Nothing is as far away as one minute ago.

—Jim Bishop

We must give lengthy deliberation to what has to be decided once and for all.

—Publilius Syrus

A weak man has doubts before a decision; a strong man has them afterwards.

—Karl Kraus

About the Author

W. Ron Drynan is a former systems analyst, project manager, and bank consultant turned voice-over guy, adventure tour guide, and author. He resides in beautiful Sarasota on Florida's Suncoast with his exquisite wife and three fantastic rescue dogs. When he's not making up stories, he's playing on the water or in the woods.

Visit the author on the web at: www.WRonDrynan.com

CPSIA information can be obtained at www.ICGtesting.com
Printed in the USA
LVOW060314051111

253372LV00004B/1/P

9 780983 503903